MW00509111

THE HEIR
ABERRANT

Book 3
Bell, Book and Claw

V C Sanford

THE HEIR ABERRANT

Published in the United States of America
By 341 Enterprise
Copyright 2020 by
ISBN: 978-1-7370688-39

For James Matthew
My own
Aberrant Heir

V C SANFORD

Three moon cycles earlier....

The faint sound of loose rock and gravel shifting under the weary gelding's hoofs startled Tyro from his doze just in time. Reacting on instinct; he somehow pulled his exhausted horse into an ungraceful slide, barely avoiding the sure death that waited just two strides beyond his ridged front hooves. Despite his wildly hammering heart, the weary merc held his composure. The bright glint in his eyes and the slow satisfied smile just peeking out from beneath his grizzled beard were the only outward signs of the adrenaline coursing through his straining veins.

His sides heaving, the exhausted steed dropped his head groundward, too tired to do more than stand and pant; each intake a sibilant whistle as the overworked horse struggled to breathe.

Slightly annoyed with himself over the entire situation, Tyro swung his leg across Onyx's lathered flank; losing his grin as he observed the warm salty foam soaking into his favorite pair of leather trousers. The coordinating hand tailored silk shirt had cost him three gold ryls, an exorbitant price, but well worth every coin. There was little hope that the brilliant emerald color wouldn't fade before he located a laundress capable of cleaning the expensive material. Considering the unorthodox manner in which he had vacated his most recent position, it could be a long time before he sought civilization again. Stepping around the gelding, he took three short steps forward before kneeling on the wide shelf of rock. From his position atop the rise, the exhausted traveler had an unencumbered view of the trading post nestled in the valley below. Not that the heavy black smoke rising from the rapidly burning building was difficult to miss. No, there was no way he could continue traveling toward Hyperion; not if he wanted to keep his head on his shoulders. Unconsciously, Tyro patted the small burlap sack tied at his waist, a souvenir of his short--- but profitable, stay at the small inn. For one moment, he thought of Keeyun and regretted the idea of never seeing the tempestuous young ranger again. Their brief friendship was something he rarely found, and the memories would remain for a long time. That was the only drawback to his ability, the memories. He wavered for a moment, wondering once again if he had made the wrong decision, but only for a moment. It was too late for second thoughts. He concentrated and shifted, matching his appearance to the pale-skinned easterner. Eyes shining brightly with unacknowledged tears, he removed the pale gray tunic from his backpack, then folded the bright green one before storing it in the pack. He had never visited Cabrell, but Keeyun had spoken highly regarding the city. There was sure to be someone there looking to hire a mercenary with his skills. Once again, he mounted Onyx, giving the faithful steed an apologetic pat before settling into a mile eating trot that guaranteed another night without sleep, and disappeared into the night.

***

"I told you we could not trust that stunted

whelp of a drunken camel," Brinn muttered. "I should've shoved my knife into his gut while I had the opening. But no... Keeyun had to give him one more chance. See where that chance got us." He leaned over and splashed a little more water on his face, then shrugged in disgust before dunking his entire head into the now dingy gray sluice; shaking his head like an animal to remove the excess wetness from his cropped blonde hair. The muscular hunter wore a long sleeveless tunic made from lizard skin, possibly wyvern, belted at his waist. The leather of his pants and boots, while of good quality, were well-worn and showed signs of multiple repairs.

Moth dropped the reins of his mare to the ground, before joining Brinn at the edge of the stream. The harsh tones of Brinn's voice caused the dark bay horse to shift her weight nervously. However, the mare had been trained too well to disobey the implied order to stay in place, ground tied, as he had taught her. Rabbit flinched once or twice as the wind blew a few stray embers in her direction, but the experienced mare settled on simply laying her ears back and rolling her eyes. The lingering smoke from the now extinguished fire irritated her eyes; however, the annoyance was not enough to risk Moth's erratic temper. Especially tonight.

"How were we supposed to know the blaggard was a backstabbing slaver," Moth replied, his voice soft for such a large man. He pushed his ivory moon-kissed hair back from his face with his free hand, allowing a slight grimace of distaste to cross his almost patrician features at the sight of his soot darkened fingers. "We've stopped at that trading post for as long as I've been in this territory. You did not know his side business, either." The pair locked gazes for a moment, and then Moth allowed a slight smile to cross his features, the movement softening the hard lines of his face in the moonlight.

"Almost cost too much this time," Brinn snorted. "If Jaxx could not get that earring out, we would have hauled ore from the mines for the rest of our days. It is bad enough that red-haired whore's son stole all our gold. Hels, I could deal with that; I can even understand it. But. No--- that drassted two-faced son of a mangy warg had to sell us. I will have to pay the priests a lot of ryls to remove the brand from my hand without leaving a scar. All we need is for someone to spot the brands and turn us in as runaway slaves. There are no clerics within two days' ride... and they are back the way we came."

The soft sound of horses' hoofs in the darkness caught his attention, and he turned to see Jaxx swinging his leg over the back of his steel gray gelding before sliding to the ground. Not that he had far to slide; the gangly young Duaar was taller than any in the group by at least a hand. At least Von was normal height. Moth was close to Jaxx in height; however, their weight was drastically different. The lanky young mage looked like he had never eaten a good meal. Brinn was almost portly in comparison. The pale mage's choice of attire further highlighted his emancipated appearance. The barbarians wove both the tunic and leggings of some unusual gray material that shifted color in the light and blended into most every shadow. They stained the leather of his boots and cloak a similar pale smoky color, which gave him even more of a spectral appearance. He had shaved his head entirely, leaving only a slender white topknot that dangled across one shoulder. Moth had woven small bits of bone and one or two metal beads into the braid, the only sign of vanity that his friends had ever seen him exhibit.

"You may forgive him..." Brinn grumbled, "... but me; I'm countin' on fate to offer me another opportunity to enfold our absent friend in my arms. Arms--- hands---, hell, just one hand would do. I'd crack his weasel neck like ol' Harpeth's cook snapped that stringy hen's neck for last night's stew. Just five ticks are all I'd need." Frustrated by Moth's less than enthusiastic encouragement, Raffiel lifted the back foot of a buckskin gelding, inspecting the horse's hoof before taking out his knife and removing a small stone from the frog. A stone could cripple a horse within a short distance and a man afoot was an easy target. Three feet later, Raffi was finally satisfied that the hooves were as clean as he could get them. He gathered the reins and swung his leg across the saddle of the now restless gelding. It was such a waste. He studied the shapeless heap of fire- blackened rubble. It was all that remained of what most considered the only decent stop-over for at least a hundred leagues. "Someone will remember what we look like. Might be wise for us to put some distance between us and whoever comes to investigate. Save us from too many questions we don't have any good answers for."

"I see no reason to remain, our opportunities for work just went up in smoke." Brinn sighed. Even with the heat radiating off the smoldering ruins, the mountain air was chilly. Greed had taken away their chance of a comfortable haven in which to wait out the possibly long period between contracts, and with winter coming on, the chance of them finding another was slim to none. It looked to be a hard winter, and it was a long ride to the homestead. Away from the heat, a slight dusting of snow covered the pines, a sure sign of worse weather soon to come. The five men rode east.

"Looks promising. Should we try the Keep on the hill?"

Moth had topped the rise first; pulling up sharply as the view of the stone walled city nestled in the valley below excited and surprised him out of his earlier misconceptions. Raffi, arriving astride his big buckskin just seconds behind him, let out a long, slow whistle of appreciation at the sight of the prosperous and completely unexpected farmstead located so far from the more commonly traveled roads and highways.

"Surely that is the home of a very rich man," Raffi agreed, as his eyes took in the high stone walls, neatly laid out streets and carefully manicured grounds surrounding the large manor built in the center of the highest grounds. "Must have cost a small fortune to have all that marble quarried, not to mention paying to have it installed. It had to be someone with more money than sense. There must be some way we can profit from that. Watch for a market. Someone has to be selling supplies."

"I certainly hope so. We will be down to eating the leather in our boots before long." Brinn examined the well maintained keep and the surrounding grounds a few minutes more before signally it was time to move on. Distances were deceptive in the mountains, and they had several candlemarks of travel ahead of them before they reached the gates of the nearest city. Even then, there was no guarantee the guard would admit them, much less that they could find work once inside. One man was all they could risk.

People did not build in secluded areas without reason. Whatever reason had brought the lord of the keep below, lack of funds had obviously not been one of them. And men with money usually brought their own security forces. Moth could see guards patrolling the walls below. From the outward appearance, this lord had prepared for almost any potential situation, choosing a highly defensive location, and then supplementing it with high stone walls topped with turrets. Even the keep entrances screamed security, with two double banded iron doors designed so that one would open only after the second one closed. Inside the walls, Moth could see a large inn, no less than twenty small businesses, one, possibly two public stables, and multiple private homes and outbuildings. The tiny village that supported the keep appeared clean and well maintained as well, unusual for such a rural area with a diverse population. Someone was maintaining a high level of control, which necessitated keeping a highly trained and well-armed force on hand, none of which boded well for their employment chances. Still, it was the only option available.

Raffi squinted out from under the floppy, wide-brimmed hat that now capped his unruly raven mop. He still sported the purplish brown remnants of the bruises gained after their undignified sea escape several nights before. Moth had asked Von to act as a kind of unofficial buffer, and he had obliged by keeping his horse between Raffiel's young stud and Rabbit. Since Rabbit was an ornery brute with a tendency to bite, Buck didn't complain about following behind the other horse. Moth laughed. It was extremely entertaining watching the procurer struggle to stay in the saddle every time the big black gelding's crow-hopped and twisted in its attempt to avoid Rabbits teeth. While it didn't make up for the hell they'd experienced, it made the time pass by a bit faster.

Raffi fixed his bloodshot eyes on the distant spires of the keep, doing a mental calculation of the distance in his mind... still several clicks away, at least half a day's ride, and it was all he could do to stay awake now. From habit, he reached inside his jerkin and checked once again for the small leather pouch nestled against his heart. At least he could afford a room when they arrived. No more mildewed hay lofts damp from leaking roofs. He might even invite Brinn to share. It wouldn't be the first time the two old friends had shared a bed. Keeyun had taken off after Tyro, ignoring their longstanding friendship. Kee should have let him go. That two-faced bastard could kiss his lily white behind and he would still lock the door in his face. Moth could have stopped him, and he didn't. As far as he was concerned, Moth could bunk with the two boys in the barn.

Raffi let his hand drop, running his fingers along the top of his left boot, gently caressing the ivory handle of his favorite dirk. He longed for the day to arrive when he could finally drive it into the breast of the bone-headed mage that had taken his place as Brinn's right-hand man. Just because he had made a few minor mistakes on the last campaign. It wasn't as if it had cost them anything. He was the one who spent three weeks languishing in that hellhole of a military prison. So, what; they asked them to leave town? They would not have settled down there, anyway. No, it was all Moth's fault. All he had to do was back him up, but no, the whore's son had just sat there guzzling beer and laughed as the city guard dragged him away. It was wicked Karma that they had sold him to the same group of slavers. He had laughed his ass off when Brinn and Moth were added to the chain. Not that he'd been unhappy when the boys pulled off the escape. They were a welcome addition to the small group. Surviving a life-or-death event built stronger bonds that any amount of coin ever could.

He shrugged and turned his horse toward the tiny village. A soft bed wasn't worth the risk. He'd buy a few supplies and they would manage until they reached a well-established town.

"Should we wait here for Keeyun to return?" Jaxx asked after Raffi rode away.

"Naw. It's not worth taking a chance. Let's head toward home. Keeyun can deal with Tyro. Then he will catch up when he can. Hopefully, he can find out where the scurrilous thief hid our money. If Raffi gets his hands on him, there won't be enough left to question. There will be other contracts after the weather breaks. Besides, Nyla is getting close to delivering the babe, and I'd like to be there when it is born." Brinn sighed. He didn't regret the last few years of his life, drifting from town to town, hiring out to whatever merc unit needed an extra hand or two. He could barely remember the last time he had stayed more than a fortnight in one spot. His life had been better since bonding with Nyla, even though she didn't enjoy being left at home alone. Still, his bed at home was soft, the supple female body lying next to him even softer, and he refused to consider the idea of another winter in the saddle. It had been a long stretch between contracts and even longer since he had enjoyed Nyla's willing embrace. His lips quirked as he remembered how he had met his wife. Over time, he had grown to ignore the pointed stares and snide remarks that accompanied their unusual group. It had taken him a while to adjust to being part of the quirky quartet. Moth, though handsome, was unusual enough, with that pale almost ghostly coloring; but put him alongside the lanky half-breed druid and the big Duaarien procurer and the four men were a combination sure set anyone's nerves on edge. Keeyun, his cousin, hadn't been blessed with Moths more attractive features, but that never seemed to inhibit his opportunities. Adding the two handsome young pups to the pack had taken the dangerous edge off. He had already noticed the difference in how people perceived the group.

Thinking about Raffi reminded him they would not need to wait much longer. Raffi had ridden into the village to pick up supplies. He was wearing a bandage on his hand that would prevent anyone from noticing the new brand. There was a slight risk, but highly unlikely anyone in the town had heard of the prison break. Raffi was the only one fluent in the common trade language spoken in this area.

Moth glimpsed movement at the edge of his vision. It looked like a bay horse heading away from the town.

He turned to Jaxx. "Is that Raffi?"

Jaxx nodded. If they started now, they would reach the road to the coast about the same time Raffi reached them. "He's riding easy, so everything must have gone as planned."

"You ready to ride?" Brin asked Moth.

The silent mage smiled and nodded. Von and Jaxx were already tightening the girths on their horses.

"Then let's go home." Brinn kicked Buck into a slow, easy trot. Without direction, the other horses moved to follow him, riding on a path that angled toward the man in the distance.

CHAPTER 2
Three moons later....

"I have to admit, I've seen nothing quite like this. What did you call it? Agar's Bane?" Keeyun blinked to adjust his vison to the light, then let his eyes scan the distant horizon. Nothing changed. It looked the same in every direction. Well, except the way they had come. The area directly outside the cave looked like an axe had sliced a giant rock in half and removed one side, leaving an almost flat face. The ledge they stood on held them, but he wasn't sure all that weight was a good idea. He stepped back into the cave, just in case. Besides, it was much cooler inside. Stepping from the cool cavern onto the ledge after the long trek underground had been like stepping into a fiery furnace. The rock face radiated heat. It did not burn the skin, but it was very close. At times like this, he almost missed the snow and ice at home.

Jaxx shook his head. "Azaar not Agar. I've seen the western border lands. There is no way to mistake this amount of desolation for anything else."

"Azaar's Bane?" Mekiva asked; a confused look upon her face as she gazed out at the desolate ground below. "What is that?"

"This land is Azaar's Bane. Well, this is the edges of it. The Red Zone ruins are much worse, but hopefully we won't need to go anywhere near the ruins. I was told they are so desolate; it makes this area look appealing. It's hard to believe this desert used to be one of the largest forests in Hyperion."

"At one time this was green?" Surprise showed on Mekiva's face. As far as she could see, it was sand, cracked clay, and rocks. The few plants that grew in the area were small and twisted. It was impossible for her to picture this dull brown sandpit as verdant farmland.

"I forget you were not raised in the city," Von said solemnly. "Every school-age child is told the story of the destruction of Avalon. Most can recite it by heart. It is not a happy tale, but it is one you should hear. But I am not good with stories. Perhaps one of you could tell the tale?"

"I will tell it," Gwen offered quietly. "That is, if no one else cares to?" She looked around at the others sitting close by. Seeing no one opposed, she began the story: "Once the shining star of Omission, Avalon was known far and wide as the jewel of our nation. Students and teachers from all the races gathered to share their experiences to benefit our planet. We, as a people, were not mechanically blind, but magic made many things obsolete. It was inefficient to move stones by hand when a spell could turn them into water or air...."

"And so on, and so on...." Raffi interrupted. "Gwen, if I had known you were going to recite the historical narrative, I would have stopped you before you ever began. Any of Castillo's hired goons that are still alive might still get across that chasm. We do not have time for the entire saga of Azaar."

"No offense, Gwen, but all I really wanted was to know who Azaar was," Mekiva said meekly. "And what a bane is?"

18

"Well, Mekiva," Raffi gave her a smug smirk. "It's like this... Azaar, a human mage, made a gem that magnified magic. He must have angered one of the Gods because it exploded and destroyed Avalon and everything for miles around. Nothing grows, nothing lives, it never rains. It is our planet's version of purgatory. All the wyvern signs point to us heading right into the middle of it. We might as well go fight a dragon for its hoard, there's not much difference in my book."

Keeyun laughed. "I've already faced my dragon. I'll take my chances in the wastelands. And since Raffi forgot to tell you, I think a bane is a type of curse."

"Too bad the humans went and blew it for everyone." Raffi said smugly. "Since the destruction, most of the races can't stand each other."

"Wait a minute... too bad the humans? Aren't Duaar human?" Once again, Mekiva looked puzzled.

Raffi laughed. "Nope. Close, but... notice that we are bigger and much stronger? Not to mention much better looking." Von punched him in the arm and Jaxx laughed. Jaxx was quite a bit bigger than Von, but he had never thought that much about it. Women considered both men attractive and were always propositioning one or the other. The scar across Vons's eye gave Jaxx a slight edge, however Jaxx never seemed that interested. He had been spending time with Gwen, and this surprised him. The shy healer hadn't responded to any of his brother's flirtations, but that could be because she was so young.

"Do you think that's where we will have to go? I'm exhausted." Gwen let her eyes move from

Von to Raffi to Jaxx as she spoke. Raffi and Keeyun might be old friends, but something about Kee made her uncomfortable. It wasn't because he was not the same race as her. She had realized Jaxx wasn't human when Gwen healed his wound after Von almost died. Raffi was a Duaar, too. Keeyun was different. He was tall, almost as tall as Raffi and Jaxx, but with that fish-belly skin and silvery white hair, it was clear he wasn't Duaar. Too thin. Besides, you couldn't see it for the hair, but both Jaxx and Raffi's ears were slightly pointed. Nothing like a Gynark's sharp point, but not round on top, either.

"Yes, but not today. We need supplies and horses. If we can locate someone to sell us any. There may be a few Gynark tribes, but they prefer to stay south of this area. The other nomads living in the borderlands are Zarni. Like Tula. They move around, following the water and grazing."

"The map says there's a small town called Nona a few days west of where I think we are. Since we no longer have the horses, we will have to walk to get there, but what's another week after the time we spent underground?"

"At least we know we will move in the right direction. Without supplies, there is zero chance we could try returning the way we came." Raffi had no intention of returning to the underground passage anytime soon. There was no temptation to go forward across the wasteland with limited food or water. The smart thing would be to keep heading west until they reached Nona, the only town listed on the map.

Von didn't want to hear it. "All this way, just to turn around and head back toward the coast. Why do I feel like we are going in circles?"

"It would be easier if it was a circle. It may take days to reach the edges of the Bane and longer to find the town once we reach the area. We will have to skirt the rock face and hope we find water somewhere. Until we do, what we are carrying will have to be rationed," Jaxx added.

Bored with listening to the two men argue, Mekiva interrupted the pair's diatribe to let them know they were ready to continue. "If you are all finished debating the obvious, we are ready to start down to the bottom. Once we reach the ground, with any luck we can find a freshwater spring. I'm sick of limey tasting cave water. And I want to get clean. I need a 'long soak until my skin wrinkles' bath."

Bored with listening to the two men berate themselves, Mekiva interrupted the pair's discussion to let them know they were ready to continue. "If you are all finished debating the obvious, I'm ready to start down to the bottom. With any luck we can find a freshwater spring. I'm sick of limey tasting cave water."

Von opened his pack and took out his extra tunic. It was in terrible shape, but it would have to do. At least his blade was sharp. It made cutting the material into strips much easier. He sliced the material into hand wide strips and passed them out to the other men, then Gwen, before walking over to where Mekiva sat against her pack.

"Tie the strip of cloth over your eyes; the twin sun's light is so intense you should have no trouble seeing through the cloth. It will reduce the red spots that dance across your vision and ease your headaches."

"Headache? I don't have a headache."

"You will. It's still early in the day. By high sun's the light will be so intense it blinds you." Only one of Omissions' twin suns was visible overhead. The second, larger sun remained hidden by the mountains they had just walked under. Most of the heat was being blocked by the stone. The girls had no idea how bad it was going to get. No one could move fast along the narrow switchback that wove its way down the face of the cliff. If they started now, they might reach the ground before the twin suns were both on this side of the range. Once that occurred, the rock face will be hot enough to burn skin. They needed to be on the ground by that time.

"Too bad we don't have wings like Twist. We could fly down in minutes."

"Speaking of the little pest, where is he?"

"He said something about mice and took off. I guess he's tired of lizards."

"You know, when you said it would be hot, I didn't expect it to be an oven." Mekiva poured a drop of water over her wrist and then watched as it evaporated almost instantly. "No, this is worse than an oven."

"How much farther do you think it is?" Gwen asked Von.

"I think we should be at the bottom soon," he said.

Gwen sighed. She had been born in the desert, but the land she grew in was nothing like the desolate area they would have to walk through. Even with the white headdress and loose-fitting desert clothes, the sun was drawing out every drop of moisture from her tender flesh. Cloth wrapped every inch of her body, including both hands. A few minutes earlier, she had slipped, pressing her palm flat against the rock face to catch her balance. Her hand had burned through the wrappings. She could only imagine how painful the rocks would feel to the others, with nothing to protect their arms and hands. She had convinced Mekiva to wear her extra tunic on her head, and all the men had copied her idea.

Von, Raffi and Jaxx had stopped shaving long ago, but their beards only covered part of their face; Gwen could see how the area near their eyes and forehead was raw and blistered. Keeyun's white skin was resistant to burning, unlike fair skinned humans. He did not have a beard, but his skin showed minimal pinking. She wondered if the same thing that protected his people from the ice and snow made it more resistant to the sun's rays. One day, she would ask him about it.

From above the desert land, the land near the base of the rock face was beautiful, a swath of rose and amber and purples against a backdrop of tans and browns, with an occasional touch of green to show that there had to be some rain. The light danced, faint shimmers that wavered as you watched it flicker and shine against the far horizon. But the closer they came to the desert floor, the more they realized how dangerous that beauty was. Mekiva learned to pray as she walked along, asking first for water, then perhaps a breeze, and finally for noise; any kind of sound to break up the monotonous silence. For there was always silence, a silence so oppressive it ate at your soul. It wasn't long before the girls were beseeching Rheaaz for darkness. Even the men muttered under their breath, just in case some benevolent deity was listening. Jaxx whistled just to make noise; any sound to break up the monotonous silence. Everything seemed the same, yet nothing was the same. Sand, color, wind, sound, ever changing but not changing; it could drive you insane. And Jaxx said it was worse near the center? Gwen shuddered.

"It's a peculiar sensation; feeling the heat suck the moisture directly from the air while your body slowly dehydrates." Mekiva somehow forced the words out. "My mouth is so dry my lips are cracking."

"Yeah, but at night it will be worse. The desert loses heat quickly on the suns go down." That's one thing that she was certain would be the same here as at home. With no vegetation overhead to trap the heat near the ground, it would dissipate much faster than the rocks had heated. It would be easier to travel once the land cooled. But the night brought its own dangers. Menaces, she was certain, indicated the bane lands and no other.

"A little cool air sounds great to me. It feels like we have been walking through this oven for days." She looked at Gwen for a moment and then looked away.

Von managed a little smile through his cracked lips but didn't answer. Still, Jaxx could hear his thoughts as clearly as if he had spoken out load. *It's only going to get worse if we don't find cover before nightfall. A fire would be a beacon in the desert, drawing any predator, two feet or four, within leagues in any direction.*

The travelers had come across the remains of a road about two candlemarks back that were going in the general direction that they had chosen. The possibility of civilization lifted their spirits. It wound throughout the barren countryside, and everyone hoped that whoever had built it had taken into consideration the need for water. Conserving what water they had, while dealing with the constant heat was difficult. The double red sun played tricks on them. The tired party trudged steadily toward what Raffi had assured them was the west, or at least it was toward the setting of one sun. The other seemed to track slightly north as it set. The land had gradually changed, growing less rocky and becoming more colorful the farther west they traveled with long stretches of sandy desert with scrub trees and a plant that resembled a yellowish colored cactus.

They had traveled farther than Raffi had estimated and still seen nothing that would even hint at water. Each traveler was allowed two sips of water after walking every league, but that was not enough to quench thirst. Now everyone was feeling the effects of the heat. The cloths that covered her eyes had eased the onset of headaches, but once they started, it did nothing to help with the throbbing bursts of pain.

Tempers flared, and conversation died to an occasional question and a snapped answer. Jaxx and Von blamed themselves for the girl's presence. The girls ignored them. The tension reminded Gwen of the time a dry storm had hung heavily upon the desert, sending clouds of blue, gray, and silver sand swirling aloft under the hot midday sun. I heavily charged the surrounding air with electricity; so much that the very action of walking causes enough static current that the hairs stand up along your arm and head. This felt the same way. Like something was waiting to happen. No one else seemed to sense the danger, so she kept walking in silence.

Keeyun enjoyed the peace when the playful Mir was off hunting, but when he spotted wings in the distance, he wasn't sure it was Twist returning. He stopped and pointed at the winged figure in the distance.

"Is that the pest or Gwen's creature?"

"I think it's Twist. It's too small to be the bird beast."

They watched as the Mir grew closer. It circled the group a few times, then landed on Mekiva's shoulder, chittering in her ear, *watergoodfish.*

Gwen's face broke into a wide grin. "Twist found water! He says there are fish. He's hungry so we better hurry or we will find a stuffed Mir-cat and muddy water when we get there." The Mir kept flying ahead and circling back to the exhausted friends, urging them onward. Despite his efforts, it was almost a candle mark before they arrived.

Von smelled the water long before they could see the tiny oasis of plants growing at the base of the bluff. The two girls' first instinct was to rush forward, but Von's outstretched arm prevented them from running to the spring. "Twist seems unconcerned about predators waiting for an easy target. Let Keeyun and I check out the area before you rush in." Raffi nodded his approval of Von's plan, silently agreeing he would stay behind with Jaxx and the girls; then the two men trotted off in the direction of the water hole. It seemed like forever before Von reappeared and waved them forward. "Everything looks good. You can all relax."

Raffi cautioned everyone to remain alert, but he wasted his efforts to preserve order. The girls turned away from the path and headed recklessly toward the fresh greenery growing near the water. They wasted no time in wading knee deep in the clear deep pool in their hurry to relieve their thirst. The time under the mountain had not been especially hard; but after being on the road for five long days with only brief stops to rest, everyone just wanted a chance to recuperate. The tiny oasis was just what everyone needed. The water was crystal clear and there were even a few trees that offered some shade from the scorching sun.

Jaxx groaned as he dropped his pack on the ground and slid to the ground beside it. "I say we make camp right here, and then start out early tomorrow morning. One bright side, we don't have to do without water tonight."

Gwen was curious about the tracks of a small animal in the sand nearby. She was also happy to see several waterfowl rise from the pool as they approached. Even now, they were settling back into the water nearby. Her thirst satisfied, she looked around for a long stick or a few rocks big enough to stun a bird long enough for her to catch it. Her brothers had not been fond of hunting, but they loved to eat. She hoped to make snares from the leather laces that held up her boots. With any luck at all, they would have a hot meal before too much longer. The wet robes were keeping her cool, and she figured they would not interfere with her aim too much. Once everyone else had bathed, she would slip away and enjoy the water.

Several carefully tossed rocks later, she had two good sized birds and was ready to return to the others. That's when she heard the pathetic cries of an injured animal.

She heard the beast before she saw it. Its low-pitched growls carried well in the silence that was only broken by its pitiful whine. Where it had come from, she did not know. The bush and bracken tangle were much too thick for her to notice it if it had remained silent. It crouched in a thicket of ferns, skirted by prickly briars below an undersized ledge near the small pool.

As she approached, it cried out, its mouth displaying two rows of bright white teeth.

It's got wings like Twist. The beasts' eyes followed her as she moved closer. She must have stepped over some invisible line because it hissed and extended six-inch long razor-sharp claws. The movement flexed his broken wing, and it cried out from the pain. Keeping a close watch on the strange animal, Gwen inched forward slowly, but she still looked around expectantly just in case others were hiding nearby. Hunters often used an injured animal as a lure and once the prey was within the trap, a miraculously healed beast could turn predator in seconds.

It was not huge, but the wings made it look bigger. The dark-colored feathers reflected the moonlight. Its body appeared to be covered in sand colored fur; except for clawed hands and its face, which was feathered with a curved beak that looked it could easily crack bones. She was certain it was a male. He was lean fleshed and toned; she could see the ripple of its muscles as it maneuvered to protect its injured wing. But the most amazing thing about it was its eyes, big and green, with black almond-shaped irises that ran from top to bottom instead of side to side. It looked like the result of some insane magicians transmogrify experiments, but this was no figment of anyone's imagination.

It turned to regard her like a cat would watch a mouse. Gwen froze, knowing those claws could easily tear her apart. *I wonder if it plays with its food like a cat?* For a breath or two, she imagined she could hear it laugh; that same mind instantly urged her to start running. But she collected her wits and stood as still as possible, knowing that movement could entice the animal to strike out of fear. The beast might attack regardless, but she did not want to do anything to encourage it.

She slowly removed her gloves and reached out to touch the injured wing. She winced and jerked back at the sharp pain. Something definitely hurt the wing, leaving at least two fractures and some muscle damage at the shoulder. Thick thorns blocked the beast's head, so she wasn't too worried about the beak, but she wasn't sure if the claws could reach her. She stretched her hand out again and touched the wing above the bone, concentrated, and prayed to her goddess. Almost immediately the warmth of Rheaaz's grace flowed through her, mending the fractures and healing the torn muscles. She smiled a little as the beast leaned into her hand, allowing her healing power to reach deeper into the damaged tissue. The agony in her arm and shoulder grew as she healed him, but she continued until she was certain he could move his wing without pain. Then she sat back on her heels and took a deep breath. Now, for the hard part. She had to pull the sharp thorns away from his body so he could rise from the bramble.

The creatures appeared to understand she was helping him. As soon as she had pulled the sharp thorns away, he stood and leaped up and outwards. With a sweep of his massive wings, he flew over her head and upward into the evening sky. Free! Before she reached dry land, he had vanished from sight.

It was a beautiful beast, whatever it was. Once she told the others about her experience, she was certain to hear about how stupid it had been for her to take such a chance with no one around to help her. Jaxx could be overprotective and felt no remorse when telling her about her fallacies.

She picked up the birds and looked upward, just in time to be slammed to the ground by the beast's plummeting body. The creature's landing jolted the breath from her lungs, leaving her gasping. She tried to toss it off, but it had wrapped its claws around her shoulder. But instead of tearing at her throat or gouging out her stomach with its clawed feet, it pinned her by her chest and shoulders and looked into her eyes. The beast's golden yellow beak was inches from her face. Gwen could smell its breath, heavy with the scent of fresh blood and raw meat. With a great effort, she resisted the urge to scream and struggle, somehow knowing that this would only anger the beast. For a couple of moments, they stared eye to eye, and then it huffed out a breath of air into her face and calmly flew away as though she no longer was of any concern. It returned long enough to grab a sip of water, throw one of the two dead birds she'd dropped over his shoulder, and then it launched itself upward again. Three flaps carried to the top of the ridge, where it circled once, puzzled to see Gwen still lying in the same position that it had left her. Once again, Gwen thought she heard laughter, and then it vanished over the ridge.

She lay there staring up at the sky....

"Gwen! Are you alright? I came as fast as I could." Jaxx's panicked voice seeped into her daze as he rolled her body back and forth, checking to make sure she was uninjured. Seconds later, Von joined them, followed closely by Raffi and Keeyun. Mekiva was standing nearby, watching the sky, as if she expected something to drop from the cloud cover at any moment.

"No, I am fine. Whatever it was, it did not hurt me. It seemed more amused than anything. But whatever it was, keep Twist away from it. It would enjoy a snack."

"Anything strong enough to survive here is something that none of us wants to anger. But now you can see why we said stay close to the campsite. It pinned you in seconds. That makes it one very dangerous animal."

"I do not think it was an animal. I think it was intelligent."

"Intelligent? Then you are indeed fortunate. There is only one intelligent race that fits the description and its carnivorous. Survivors say they enjoy the taste of human flesh." There were stories of rare species that survived the mage storm. Twisted mutations that would frighten the horrors living in most men's dreams. The rare survivor could not provide much of a description. Nothing to build an image. Wings. Claws. Not human, not animal, not bird. Dangerous. Did they lair nearby?

No one would not sleep easily that night.

CHAPTER 3

Jaxx stopped and held his hand up. "Quiet! Everyone remain still."

The small group froze, holding their breath as Jaxx and Raffi took aim at several scrawny rabbits lying asleep in the sun. The torpid hares were not a prize many warriors would brag about over a tankard of ale, but of far greater value to their shrunken stomachs. Two fell instantly, and Twist snatched another before it slipped into the warren beneath a heavy rock.

"We can camp here. There is enough dried brush nearby to make a fire and cook a stew with the last of the dried vegetables. A hot meal will be a welcome change." The second sun was moving toward the far horizon with little chance of finding a better campsite.

"Rheaaz be thanked," Gwen added as she accepted the stringy meat. Wuls had infested some of the outer flesh, and that meat had to be discarded, but they were too hungry to be picky. It had been a while since they had enough meat that they could look forward to a second meal.

The desert lost heat quickly with nothing to hold in the heat, so the small fire was a welcome addition. They built the fire against the big rock, enjoying how the heat was stored and reflected by the stone. The heat helped their aching muscles, and they were too tired to remain awake after the second sun went down.

Von leaned against his pack, holding Mekiva against his chest, enjoying the way she felt in his arms. Never a big woman, she had lost a lot of weight since beginning the quest. They all had. Lack of food was just one reality they were all facing. Foremost was the possibility that not everyone would make it out of the wastelands. It was only the hope of their future together that allowed him to fight his inner demons, closing his mind to all except the instinct to survive and the love of the woman beside him.

"How much farther do you think it is?" Mekiva asked Von as they bedded down once more for the night.

"No one knows. Raffi thinks we must be near the edge of the borderlands since we are seeing bits of green. The rabbits are also a good sign." Von knew the young mage was doubting both her decision to come with him and her decision to become a mage. Her tiny body could not handle this type of physical labor. He had taken to carrying her pack whenever he could convince her to allow it and knew how heavy the two books were.

Gradually, her interest in learning new spells had waned. The weight of the two larger books from the dead sorcerers' hidden cell had forced her to leave them at home; bringing only bring the smallest tome and the one she had created at school with her. Many of the spells in the ancient grimoire were beyond her ability. When they worked at all, they often reacted in unexpected ways.

Showing an early affinity for the elements, Mekiva had easily mastered fire and could now create enough water to fill a container once a day. She had not attempted many spells from the black tome. All she thought about was reaching safety.

Only Twist seemed impervious to their plight. He always located sufficient food to share with Mekiva, even though she was tired of lizard. The once tiny Mir cat had now grown too big for any in the group to easily pick up. Descended from magically created creatures, no one was sure what the capabilities of the winged cat were. By the size of the cat, when fully grown, he should weigh more than a good-sized human. No one was sure since he could somehow adjust his weight, becoming light enough to perch awkwardly on Mekiva's chest or shoulder or increasing it when he decided he wanted to pounce on Von or Jaxx. It bothered Von that Twist tolerated Raffi but would have nothing to do with Keeyun, despite the pale mercs' multiple attempts to make friends. The other animals were uncomfortable around him. He made it a point to keep one eye open at all times.

Mekiva nodded, but still she felt anxious. Even with the new spell, they were back to rationing water. Thirst was something they all understood. So was doubt. No one was unaffected by the uncertainty. Tempers frayed and everyone said words in anger. During the daylight, the group was on constant alert. Everyone kept a hand on their favorite weapon. Night was worse. Even with rotating guard duty, no one felt comfortable enough to get a good night's sleep. The best they could hope for was enough rest to keep going.

Jaxx refused to discuss it. That morning, he

had refused to eat, insisting that Gwen and Mekiva needed the food more than he did. He had sorted through the group's meager rations, calculating how long they could survive on the limited amount of food and water that remained. "Half rations it is, food and water and maybe we can stretch it out for three days."

For once, no one argued. The rabbits gave them hope. They needed it.

———

Keeyun flipped the bleached white skeleton and examined the teeth inside the skull; three rows of the smaller pointed teeth behind four oversized canines clearly designed to puncture and rip its prey. The jaw extended outward so that the four eye teeth rested outside the mouth. *Must run upright on its rear legs, the front legs were much smaller. Wonder what had killed it? The heat? It is too drassted hot.* He reached for his waterskin, then remembered he had emptied it earlier. Then he remembered Mekiva. *Maybe? It was worth trying.* She was sitting on her pack a few feet away, so he walked over and coughed.

Mekiva looked up.

"Go ahead, do your magic stuff." Keeyun wiggled his fingers, suggesting he was casting a spell.

"My magic stuff?" Mekiva did not know what he was insinuating.

"You know. Make some water. It's really hot and my flask is empty."

"Do you have any fish scales with you?" she asked, trying to keep her growing frustration under control.

"Fish scales? Why would you need fish scales?"

"Spell components. There's no way I can make water without them. I have two remaining. I am hanging on to them until we run completely out. That may be all we have to keep us alive."

"Then you need to make me some water, because my head hurts too much to see the path. My eyes are blurring."

Raffi passed him his almost empty water skin. "Make do. This is all we have. I will follow the trail. You can rest your eyes." Raffi kneeled on the hard packed ground and brushed the dried weeds away. "Tracks. A few days old, maybe less." The lone shoe print was enough to lift their spirits

Keeyun had located the game trail just after dawn. They were following as it wound between low, brush-covered foothills, through arroyos and gullies for most of the day. They had made slow progress. The narrow path often changed direction without warning. Keeyun lost the faint trail repeatedly among the broken rocks and had to backtrack, which added to the group's irritation. The terrain was gradually climbing upward, leaving the wastelands behind. They climbed into a region of shale benches, rough here, smooth there, with only an occasional scratch of an iron horseshoe to guide them. By high suns they faced a wide, natural gateway between great stone escarpments. Beyond this, they could look down on a valley of rolling land, partly desert, partly fertile, with long, dark lines of shallow streambeds winding away in the distance. And there, on the far horizon, was a great river.

"Fetch them." Edgar, chief butler to Lord

Baldric, remained stoic as the young page paled at his words. The boy nodded once and then took off in a dead run.

The remaining page, a slender blonde boy about eight with an angelic face, shifted his weight nervously from side to side, peering anxiously at the heavy double doors. Edgar muttered something about having to send to the farm to replace another one; then he sighed deeply and motioned to the trembling boy. Better to send the boy on an unnecessary task than risk damage to that face. He had the makings of a personal manservant in him, at least, if he could somehow prevent any serious damage to his appearance. He pulled a few ryls from his pocket and sent the boy to pick up a pair of shoes the cobbler was resoling.

Lord Baldric had just received another of the mysterious messengers that periodically appeared at the keep's back door. The shattered crystal was only the beginning of a gradual increase in anger that blood would only satisfy; first the unlucky page that delivered the missive, and then whomever came within reach. After burying several victims of Lord Baldric's displeasure, the established household servants had learned to contrive fictitious chores, requiring extended absences from the manor for their children anytime they appeared. It had become necessary to seek pages from distant villages, near the various farms owned by his Lordship. To avoid complete anarchy, Edgar had come up with a simple but elegant lottery system. He had sent the first page to fetch the "lucky winner" to clear away the debris from the masters' latest flare up. As usual, the winner was nowhere to be found.

The elderly manservant pulled the silken bell

cord multiple times, signaling for assistance, and received no response. Sound carried easily throughout the ancient building. Upon hearing the bell, any servant with seniority found an excuse to be busy. Others slipped silently away as soon as the shouting began. As usual, most of the panic-stricken servants had vanished before the first discordant crash of crystal goblets shattering against the back of the fireplace.

Hands shaking, he ran his fingers through his coarse white hair to smooth it into some sense of order. With a resigned sigh, he settled next to the closed door to wait. A tear ran down his cheek as he remembered that tomorrow was his youngest grandson's birthing day. From the volume of this latest tirade, the crystal would not be all that didn't survive the evening. He could hear most every word.

"You made me look like a fool. Over twenty of my men and a dozen mercenary fighters and they still got away? Tell me why I should not drive this dagger through your deceitful throat and still your lying tongue forever?"

"It's true that Gado failed me again," Izabal replied calmly, her sanguine voice smoothly drawing Lord Baldric's attention away from the source of his anger. "Although some of the blame must rest on your shoulders. By your description, the men should have easily slaughtered the entire party. You led me to believe that they were all adolescent fools, kids out on a lark. Instead, my men faced four experienced fighters and a powerful mage. They even have a Shii-lakka healer traveling with them."

"A mage? A first-year student... a student, I

might add, that has a long history of incompetency and failure. They dismissed her from her studies. Von has not reached his majority, and the Duaar can't be long out of his holdfast. And the other girl is a seamstress, a friend who tagged along for a lark. How can she be Shii-lakka? She's only a child---not even of age, to pledge her troth."

"Regardless of her age, she is Shii-lakka, and a powerful healer. I will accept the blame for Gado's failure; but little more. My investment is much more than a few gold coins."

He slammed his fist down on the table. "Enough! It's time for you to get involved and ensure nothing else goes wrong. Since your hired killer didn't stop them; you will. Whether it's blind luck or the favor of the Gods; they've stumbled upon Azaar's Bane. There's only one place they could be heading. It should be simple for you to set up an ambush before they arrive in Nona. Everything we have been working for depends on it."

"Your optimism is endearing," Izabal replied, "but foolish. Think about your words before the next time we converse. You may not like my response." She made a few quick hand gestures; uttered one sharply spoken command word, and then, with a bright flash of light, she vanished.

Lord Baldric finished his wine in one long swallow, picked up the bell on his desk, rang once, then waited. In a remarkably brief time, his call was answered; by Edgar..., instead of the usual half-grown imbecile, he'd shoved through the doorway.

"The witch thinks she controls me," he muttered. "Hah! No one controls me; I am Lord of this keep... about time she started earning some of the gold she throws around so easily." He sighed, then poured himself a second glass of wine and stared into the swirl of colors for a moment.

Edgar, certain that for the moment Lord Baldric did not expect an answer, continued to examine the ground before his feet as he waited.

"No one is to disturb me for the rest of the day. I am unavailable to all callers." He downed the second goblet of wine in one quaff; and then surprised the elderly servant by calmly placing it on a silver tray. Edger bowed once, retrieved the tray and left quickly his heart pounding. He secured the heavy door to the study before collapsing on the bench placed just outside; unsure exactly what had happened, but grateful for the opportunity to live to clean up after the recalcitrant noble another day.

Lord Baldric failed to notice Edgar's exit. Frustrated by the wine's inability to soothe his overwrought nerves; his mind returned to the contents of an elaborately carved marble box sitting atop the cabinet next to the window... and the small brass key that hung from a chain around his neck. Unable to control the trembling muscles, it took him three tries to get the key into the opening and release the cover. In his haste, his hand slipped, knocking the box to the floor, spilling the contents. Overcome by panic, he dropped to his knees, searching wildly for one of the small packets now scattered across the carpet. He tore open the pouch and thrust his face into the soft white powder inside, inhaling, then licking the rest up with his tongue like a cat. Seconds later, as his pulse and breathing returned to normal, he slid slowly to the carpeted floor, eyes wildly dilated and his head lolling around on his neck.

CHAPTER 4

"We may be walking into trouble." Von held his hand over his face to cut down the glare. His eyesight was better than most, yet he could make out little more than the shape of the shepherd's camp.

"Do we have a choice? It's the only path down. Even if we avoid the encampment, we do not know how far it will be to the next waterhole. Besides, I'm hungry and those goats look delicious. Our coin should be welcome." Raffi hated debating when there was no need. It was a given they would go forward. He did not intend to sit here until it grew too dark to be seen.

Mekiva was tired of being tired. She wanted to sleep without wondering if she'd wake up the next morning or be ripped apart by an unknown predator in the darkness. Von was too cautious and Keeyun was a jerk. She wanted someone to decide so they could move on.

"Why settle for a few coins when they can kill us and take it all?"

Raffi glared at Keeyun but didn't comment on his remark. It was always a possibility.

Jaxx was more pragmatic. "We may walk into another fight. But we can't afford to pass up the possibility of help. Tula said the people of the desert are noted for their hospitality. Though strangers, we have clearly faced dire times. Perhaps we will be received warmly." He was happy now that he had learned the traditional greetings Tula had taught him. She had taken a liking to him and treated him as she would her own child. Von always thought it was because his ears were pointed like hers and his were not. Her people were dark complexioned and Jaxx's were fair, but they could have been distantly related.

A horn sounded to the west as the tired travelers began descending the switchback. The alarm set men on horseback to shifting the animals, positioning them for quick movements if it became necessary.

At the foot of the hill, they entered a shallow stony valley where shepherds had set up a temporary encampment, surrounded by the scattered herd of sheep and goats.

This type of camp was not uncommon in the harsh desert borderlands. There were no stone houses as you would find in the mountains near Cabrell, but low tents woven of animal hair, large enough for several to share.

As the exhausted group approached the campsite, three horsemen trotted out to intercept us, heavy-browed sun worn men, armed and alert to the possibility of trouble.

Jaxx and Raffi held up their empty hands, signaling the traveler's peaceful intentions. The others remained standing nearby, hoping to assuage any misgiving the desert nomads might be feeling. Their leader, a magnificent young man in full desert dress, released the keffiyeh covering his face and tossed it back, trusting the agal to keep it in place. Like most who lived in the desert, he wore a knee-length tunic over loose trousers of combed wool bound by a camel's hair rope. Hanging from the rope around his waist was a sheathed sword and a short, recurved bow strapped to his back. A thick woolen cloak hung loosely from his shoulders. When the horse moved, they could see a quiver of black quilled arrows hung from his saddle.

The second figure was shorter, but more heavily built. He did not bother to remove his face covering and kept one hand on the pommel of his sword. The third rider, a smaller, possibly younger man, hung back, eyes constantly moving from face to face, ready to ride for help if anyone offered the smallest hint of danger.

"I am Hamza bin Mussa, and this is my father's camp. How may I assist you?" His eyes took in the odd assortment standing before him, a human male and a female, two Duaar, a Shiilakka healer. He did not know what race the tall, ghost pale male was, but there was something about him that brought his hairs on end. All looked trail worn and sun burned. On impulse, he removed the water skin from his saddle and passed it to the Shii girl.

Gwen thanked him and drank deeply before passing it to the slender, red-haired human girl. Then the men passed it among themselves. Hamza noticed the ghost kept it longer than the others, taking several drinks before passing it to the Duaar, awaiting his turn. Another mark against him.

Tula had taught Jaxx many of her tribe's traditional phrases and he decided he would thank him in his own tongue.

Hamza appeared surprised at his words, wondering how the young Duaar knew any of the flowery language. He shifted to Zarni and Jaxx did his best to keep up. He kept his answers short and finally waved both hands up in defeat.

Hamza laughed and slapped him on the back, impressed that he could answer any of the questions. He switched back to the common trade language they all spoke. "It saddens my heart to hear of the difficulties you have faced. Come, we will go to my father and seek the comforts of the camp." He turned to Mekiva. "May I offer you transport to the camp? My horse can easily carry two."

She glanced at Gwen, who was being helped onto a brown mare by a second rider. She nodded.

He helped her to mount, then took his horse by the bridle and, in one fluid motion, swung up behind her. Twist flew along behind them, snatching an occasional insect snack thrown up by the passing horse's hooves.

The third rider, which turned out to be a young woman, offered Jaxx a ride behind her, surprising Von and Raffi, who were the ones that usually caught most women's eyes. They shifted their packs and prepared for the walk to the encampment as the three horses cantered away.

It relieved all three when Hamza slowed by a group of herdsmen, raised a hand with three fingers. Within a few ticks, a rider with three additional horses began galloping their way.

Less than a candlemark later, they were approaching the camp. Four additional men fell in behind them as they traveled, curious about the newcomers. All eyes were upon them as they wove their way through the scattered tents toward the tribal chief house. It surprised Gwen to see so many horses wandering freely through the center of the camp. Hamza detoured around an area where men were working between four tall posts and a large firepit, before slowing to a stop beside a slightly larger tent near the center of the camp.

The armed escort dismounted and motioned for the five travelers to follow them. We hurried to comply, coming to a halt before an immense tent of with several colorful stripes. There was little to designate the tent we approached except for a single stripe of color and a black goat's hair roof covering. Before the tent, armed men lounged on overstuffed pillows of tanned animal skins. One rose and spoke briefly with Hamza, then nodded and went into the tent. He returned in minutes, opened the door flap, and waved us through the opening into the shadowy interior. A heavy odor of incense hung in the air, and the soft strumming of stringed instruments laid a muted pattern of sound behind the decoration curtains of gold and blue, silver, and green. At the far end of the room, with three other men, sat a middle-aged Zarr with blue-black hair and a clean-shaven chin. He popped a grape into his mouth as he studied the bedraggled group standing before him. He wiped his fingers negligently on a wisp of cloth, belched out loud and looked his unexpected visitors over. Finally, he spoke, "Welcome to my house. Would you not sit and rest?"

Jazz was surprised when Mussa greeted him with the decorum of a relative and motioned him to the place of honor on the carpet between the square hole in the ground that served as a hearth and the partition that separates the family's sleeping quarters from the main room.

As though some silent signal had been given, everything changed. The lee side of a desert tent is always open to the best breeze. If the wind shifts, the women take down the tent wall and set it up against another quarter, and in a moment their house has changed its outlook. This was also convenient when the chief honors a guest with a banquet. In moments, they had opened up an outside wall and scattered rugs and pillows around. As if awaiting the signal, guests appeared, each bringing their own offering to the meal to come. Some were as small as a handful of kafka seeds. Others brought baskets of fruits and loaves of fresh breads. Everyone gave as they could, and nothing was unappreciated.

"Deign to accept this humble offering," Mussa said as he passed around small seed cakes and cups of kafka, the bitter black drink brewed from the seeds of a poisonous plant. To the hardy desert people, the hot beverage was better than any nectar.

Jaxx bowed his head and accepted the first cup, sipping carefully, then passing it to Von, silently signaling he should sip and pass it along. He did, and no one spoke until the first cup had passed around the circle. It was empty and Jaxx had passed it back to the chieftain, with a murmured, "May you live long and be blessed!"

The servant with the carafe immediately refilled the cup with the return comment of "A double health."

To which Jaxx replied, "Upon your house and your heart!"

When the old chieftain smiled, he made a mental promise to buy a special gift for Tula before they returned home.

Once the cup had gone round and they had exchanged all necessary phrases of politeness, conversations broke out.

The young man who had brought them in was speaking to the chieftain about his new guests, explaining to his father and uncles how he had come across the exhausted travelers. "They came down from the passage in rags, their boot leathers dropping from their feet and wearing anything they could find to protect them from the suns. All were withered from lack of water; half-starved too, poor wretches."

Mussa nodded sagely at his son's words. "You must tell the story of you adventures. Many die from exposure, fatigue, or the unaccustomed climate; such is the burden of existence my people face during the summer's heats. But first, may I offer the use of my bath house? Perhaps the young women would enjoy the opportunity to remove the sand and salt of your trek from their skin and clothes. I am sure the honored Shii would enjoy a chance to feel the water against bare skin."

Mekiva's face lit up and there was a sparkle in Gwen's eyes.

———————

Mekiva sighed and rinsed the last of the soap from her hair before stepping away from the wooden basin. Someone still stretched Gwen out, enjoying the feel of the water on her bare skin. There were two new marks on her shoulder, permanent reminders of her recent brush with the flying creature. Most of the recent scars had faded, blending into a natural complexion, but Mekiva had seen her naked form often enough to know notice the recent additions. Gwen had a heart too big for her body. Always one who cared for those who could not care for themselves, she had come to the attention of her goddess at an early age, years before most caught the eye of Rheaaz. Not yet a novitiate, someone already blessed her with the ability to heal injuries beyond that of most senior clergy. But hints of her street life remained. Propped against the side of the tub, in easy reach, was a pair of daggers. Though she could throw a dagger with either hand, she could place the blade with deadly accuracy and surprising force with her left. Her heightened perception had saved her from danger many times before they had invited her to join the family of the seamstress, who had watched her activities from the door of her tiny shop.

The two girls had met in the market when the young Shii had tripped a city guardsman who was chasing one of the street rats who had stolen a piece of fruit. He had turned in time to see her leg slide back under the edge of the stall. Pulling her forcefully from the stall, he pulled his hand back to strike a blow that would remind the girl to never to get involved with patrol matters again.

Mekiva had recognized the look on his face. There was no way one blow would satisfy him. As the angry guardsman pulled back to strike her, Mekiva had muttered the words to a spell. Instantly his body was surrounded by a foul odor, the nauseant fumes concentrated around his body. A wave of retching struck him. Gwen slipped away, forgotten as the guard fought to take a breath without gagging. When it became obvious, he could not move away from the odor, he forgot Gwen completely and ran to the nearest temple, seeking to beseech a priest for help. That had been many turns ago, and the two girls were now closer than many sisters.

The scent of the sheep roasting was drawing growls and complaints from her empty stomach, so Mekiva urged Gwen to hurry so they could rejoin the others.

The guests inside the tent had grown during their absence. They made room for them in the circle round the hearth while the talk went on uninterrupted around them.

The girls were fascinated by how the tent had grown to encompass the new arrivals.

Zima, the young woman who had offered Jaxx a ride, understood the interest. "Our homes surprise many visitors. The tents are small and light, and yet so strongly anchored that the storms can do little to it; the tightly spun meshes of the goat's hair cloth swell and close together in the wet so that it needs continuous rain to dampen it, and the hair turns the sand grains away, preventing all but a very few from entering despite the strongest winds. And of course, the ease of relocation is clear. We can breakdown and have the camp ready to move within a candlemark."

The conversation was interrupted as four large men entered the tent. They were carrying an enormous metal platter of roasted meat, the juices still sizzling from the heat.

They set it down atop a low flat table. Other people carried great flat pots that smelled wonderful. They were thickset, broad-shouldered men, with features of marked irregularity, sloped foreheads and projecting teeth that differed from the aquiline features of their hosts. Instead of joining the gathering, they left without speaking.

"Gynarks," Von whispered to Mekiva. "I wonder what they are doing so far from their home?"

She shrugged. Her one and only experience had been during the attack at the bridge.

Mussa stood and clapped his hands. He gestured to the feast spread out before them. "Keewa. Eat."

Their hosts had prepared an excellent supper. In honor of their guests, the chieftain had ordered a sheep roasted. The succulent meat was served with steamed semolina wheat, heavily seasoned with black olives, raisins, and almonds. In the manner of the Zaar, instead of individual bowls, large pieces of flat bread were used to scoop the food from an enormous flat pot. Once everyone had eaten, they sent the remains out to be delivered to the men with the herds. It wasn't every day that they had such a feast. A hunk of bread, a few olives, a raw onion, and occasionally a bowl of cheese curd was their daily meal. The meal continued late into the evening as they talked. If Mussa was unhappy to see his carefully gathered store of firewood melt away and his kafka beans disappear by handfuls into the mortar, he never showed it. Gwen's experience with the winged creature particularly impressed them.

Hamza leaned forward. "There are certain places my people would never venture after dark—haunted wells to which thirsty men dared not approach, ruins such as the place where the young Shii healer had met her creature."

Mussa agreed. "The Gods indeed blessed you. No one approaches the Gundar Oasis. Only two turns ago, a family of Tabruk were murdered by the demons after stopping at the same oasis, as they traveled back from the eastern pasturages. My family has felt the scourge." He told them the tale of a distant cousin. A sandstorm had driven the third son of a well-regarded Zarrni chieftain off the main road and forced to stop in at the same oasis. "They sent the boy to fetch water while the men set up camp. He returned without the water, claiming a winged beast drove him away. Afterward, he ran back to his father's tents in fear. He swore he had seen a djinn, and that the flocks should not go down to water where it abode, lest they lose them all. The men laughed at him and called him names."

Von and Jaxx nodded. After years at sea, they were both familiar with the superstitions and of fears that clutch and squeeze the heart of men at night. The oceans were awash with stories of monsters climbing aboard in the dead of night, or beautiful sirens that entice a man into their arms in the water, only to be pulled down to the sea's eternal embrace.

Raffi and Keeyun maintained a respectful silence, allowing Jaxx to handle most of the delicate negotiations.

The evening was drawing to a close. It was easy to relax and enjoy the company well spent with new friends. The cook fire had long since died down. From time to time a draped head, with coal black elf locks curled round dusky cheeks under the striped Keffiyeh, bent forward towards the glow of the banked ashes to pick up a hot ember for the pipe bowl. The shrill scream of a terrified animal snapped Mekiva from her food induced stupor and she snapped upright, reaching for the dagger she carried at her belt as everyone ran toward the tents opening.

CHAPTER 5

The distraught animal's cry alerted the sentry on the hilltop. He gasped and fumbled with the horn hanging from his belt, then began sounding the alarm, the battered instrument releasing three sharp blasts, then a pause before repeating the signal once more. His partner scanned the sky, spotting an outstretched wing framed against the dim light of the waning moon. She raised her sword in time to block the blow intended for the horn player's neck, before a second Zivilyx drove sharp talons into her back, severing her spine. Warm blood sprayed the sentry, leaving splotches of gore upon his face and chest, but he continued to give warning, as the demon disappeared into the darkness with the paralyzed woman in its grasp.

Mad with fear, the animals bolted, scattering into smaller groups of two or three and making it harder for the men on horseback to shift them toward the camp. Occasionally, one of the Zivilyx swooped down and snatched an unsuspecting goat or sheep into the sky, only to be met with the blade of an angry nomad. Volleys of arrows whistled through the night's shadows as the camp defenders shot at the slightest hint of movement in the darkness.

"They are coming! Hurry." Zima and Hamza ran for their horses, racing toward the panicked herds to help move the animals toward the center of the camp. The older, more experienced animals had already begun racing that way, dodging the running horses as they wove their way between the tents.

"What's coming?" Jaxx asked as he released the leather ties that kept his axe strapped to his backpack.

"Zivilyx, demons!" one woman replied as she gathered her children around her.

"What should we do?" Von said as he ran.

"Pick a target. Kill it." The man turned and raced into the darkness.

Raffi had his sword out and was already following the main group toward the center of the encampment. He joined a group of men who were busy raising an enormous net of greased rope to the top of the four posts. Keeyun looked at what they were doing and then disappeared into the darkness, bow in hand. As soon as the net was raised, the women and children raced for cover and the men raised heavy lances with pointed metal tips. They used the poles to jab at any of the winged demons within reach. The frightened animals squeezed under when possible. Others ran into the tents, hoping the winged demons would go for the easier, visible targets.

A pair of the Zivilyx swooped low, slashing with long curved blades as they skimmed by less than a foot above the heads of three mounted men who were moving the bulk of the herd into the camp. One of the mounted men lost control of his horse and was thrown, landing on his back in the open. Almost before his body hit the ground, the winged beast was upon him. He scrabbled backward out of its reach, as his partner struggled to keep the other away, slashing wildly with his sword at anything within reach. One cut snagged the tender flesh of its wing pinion. Injured and unable to fly, the Zivilyx turned to run, only to feel the blade of the second horseman slide deep into its side. He jerked and screeched out a raw cry of agony before falling to its knees. The rider's second blow severed its neck as another man continued to battle the remaining assailants.

In minutes, the sky above the valley was teeming with the winged assailants. Most targeted lone sheep or goats that had strayed too far from the camp to reach the tentative safety. Others sought targets within the camp.

Mekiva watched as one of the winged demons sliced open a man's torso, then used its claws to rip his entrails from his belly. A second blow removed his screaming head, before the triumphant Zivilyx flew off with his prize. *Why was no one attacking them in the air? Were there no mages in the enclave*? She concentrated and muttered the words of a familiar spell, silently urging the air currents to obey. Sound howled throughout the valley as strong torrents of wind caught the wings of the Zivilyx and threw them to the ground. When the wings failed, it hit the ground where it was immediately swarmed by the furious tribesmen. Blades hacked away, adding bloody feathers and gore to the wind bursts.

Her attack surprised the demon, sending them high above the wind current where the air was calm. In seconds, the camp was clear, the winged demons vanishing as quickly as they appeared.

Mussa walked around the camp, assigning tasks as he identified them. The walking injured moved to an area where they could be helped by the uninjured. Many set to putting the camp back to rights, others rode out to round up the scattered sheep and goats and make an estimate of the losses.

Gwen offered to help with the injured and Mekiva joined her, even though all she could offer was a squeezed hand, a sip of water, or to listen to the wails and cries of bereavement as the identity of the missing were noted. She wondered what more she could have done to help prevent what had happened. The shepherds were returning from the fields, many leading horses with bodies draped downward across their saddles. As the solemn procession moved further into the firelight, Mekiva thought one horse looked familiar. Two men took the body from the animal and lay it on the ground before their chieftain's feet.

That's when Mussa fell to his knees, wrapped his hands in his hair and loosed an unearthly scream of anguish.

Von and Jaxx watched from a distance, feeling that they had no aid to give, knowing no words of solace would ease the pain. Raffi was standing near the girls, but they did not know where Keeyun was. One of the demons could have taken him away. No one had thought to search.

Gwen wasn't sure why no one was trying to help Hamza. She could see his hand move and there was fresh blood on this tunic. He was direly injured, but not dead. She took a deep breath and mustered up the courage to approach the grieving man.

Shock flared in the eyes of his father as she spoke. "He yet lives. May I have your permission to help him?"

"Do you think you can help heal this?" He lifted the torn edges of his son's tunic, showing the damage the Zivilyx claws had done. There were deep gouges from his ribs to his right thigh. At least two sections of his guts were severed, and vile fluids had leaked into the gaping cavity. Part of his liver was missing, and at least two ribs had broken through the skin. His breathing was labored. Shock was setting in. The chance of his surviving was extremely small... but—.

"I cannot promise he will not die beneath my hands, but I am certain he will die if I do not try."

Mussa looked into her eyes and saw hope. He nodded and the two men who had brought the body to his father lifted it and carried it into the tent.

"Mekiva, I will need your help. Ask someone to provide hot water and clean rags. I will need them to clean the wound. And find his mother, or another family member to bear witness." She turned and walked into the tent.

They had cleared the table, and the battered body was lying atop a white bedcover. Both men appeared uncomfortable to be alone in the tent with the Shii girl, but she did not have time to placate their sensibilities.

"You. Take a knife and cut away his clothing. Take care as you lift the material away from the wounds."

She turned to the other man. "Find me some

spirits. The stronger the better."

"Our people do not..."

"I have no time for your lies. Someone in camp has alcohol. Find it. Now."

She sighed and began scrubbing her hands.

Mekiva was puzzled. She had seen Gwen heal injuries that seemed much worse, so what was it about this one that made her unsure? It wasn't her goddess. Rheaaz had an intense hatred for demons. She finally asked and was surprised by Gwen's answer.

"It's simple. It's not simply healing what's there. It's the missing parts that worry me. I will need to repair as much of the damage as possible before I attempt to heal him. You know how it works. I can't take an injury that would knock me out. It would kill us both. Rheaaz would not allow it."

"So, what do we do first?"

"We have to clean as much of the poison from his body as possible. Then I will need to sew the innards back together. There's nothing I can do about the parts that are missing, but what's there is not bleeding as much as I was afraid it would be."

She looked up as the first man returned with rags and hot water. She would have preferred the strong spirits, but she would make do. There was still time for the second man to return before she closed the young heir's stomach.

A candlemark later, she was feeling better. Her hands were shaking, but some color had returned to Hamza's skin, and he appeared to be breathing better. She had resigned herself to the lack of spirits when the missing horseman ran back inside, a brown leather flask in hand.

He was grinning as he passed it to the tired young healer. The water had removed most of the solids, but she needed the alcohol to kill any hidden poisons left inside the body by the birds' filthy claws. Alcohol could prevent infections. The wound was large enough that she had been able to set the lower rib by herself. Once his wound was closed, she would need help to set the remaining broken bones, but other than being tired, she was feeling much better about his chances.

"I need you now," she said to his liegemen. "You must hold him down while I do this. It's going to hurt him. A lot." She looked around but saw nothing that might work, so she rolled one rag as tightly as possible and slipped it between the semi-conscious man's teeth. "Kiva, you need to stand behind his head and keep this in place, if you can."

She took a deep breath and poured the spirits.

Hamza sat upright, throwing both men across the floor, and jerked the roll from his mouth. A string of Zarni curses spewed from his mouth before he collapsed back to the table, unconscious.

"That went well," Gwen announced.

Mekiva rolled her eyes and passed her a clean rag to soak up the spirts that ran from his body and made ready to close the skin over the cavity.

CHAPTER 6

As the Wolfs-tail, the first gray forerunner of dawn's welcoming light, brushed away the stillness of the night, the grieving father placed the final shovel of sand upon the last grave.

Von looked around at the row of mounds hastily dug in the freshly turned sand. The flying demons surprise attack had been a slaughter; trapping the tribe like animals in a pen, just waiting for the butcher to arrive and cut their throats. He hung his head morosely, the weight of responsibility hanging heavy on his shoulders. "Any of those graves could contain one of us. They turned our celebration into a trap. And Izabal could still have men following us."

Raffi motioned for Keeyun to join them as they turned to walk back to the tents. When they left to help dig the graves, the girls were still sleeping. Whether from the attack or the healing afterward, they had passed out just before dawn and had not moved since.

Mussa waited outside the tent until the girls came out just before dawn. The two men who had assisted her throughout the night followed them. All four were shaking and pale. But they were all smiling.

"My son?" His voice cracked as he strained to retain the dignity of his position within the tribe.

"He's sleeping. He's had a long night, but I'm sure he will wake up in a few candlemarks and call for food. No meat today. Soup will be enough. Maybe some bread to soak in the broth. I want him to give his body as much rest as possible."

"He will be alright? He will be able to ride, and walk, and be as other men?"

"He should be able to continue his duties soon. He needs to rest and regain his strength."

"How can this be? I saw the damage." Mussa wasn't sure if he dared to believe the words the healer spoke. Was this some type of lucid dream from which he would awaken to stare at his son's grave?

Gwen sought empathy as she tried to explain his son's condition and what he would face over the next few ten-days. "It took a while. I had to reconnect some of the torn organs, and then Rheaaz took over. She put him back together. There were a few moments we were not sure we could hold him. He must have continued fighting the demons in his mind."

"But is he... um, will I be a grandfather?" Mussa blushed like a young girl the first time a boy whistled.

Gwen laughed. "I can't guarantee that, but there is nothing to keep him from trying to tame the eight-legged beast."

Mekiva winced as her heart sister reverted to the vulgar slang of the street urchins, a language bereft of dignity, spoken often in a gruff drawl with slow expressionless patterns. She sighed and shook her head. Hints of Gwen's early life in the slums returned at the strangest moments.

Once they found some privacy, she intended to discuss the need to be more diplomatic when telling Mussa that Hamza may have to try a little harder, since one of his jewels had been severely damaged. Rheaaz had restored it, but it would need a few years of growth before it matched the other side. Not that anyone that mattered would notice it.

Gwen had already assured Hamza of his ability to sire the next generation, and the fortunate young warrior had promised to name his first daughter after her.

"Rheaaz has healed my son!" the jubilant tribal chieftain screamed at the top of his voice.

Upon hearing Mussa's ecstatic words, the excited tribe members began celebrating, dancing, and shouting themselves hoarse as they praised Rheaaz. Jubilant nomads ran through the camp, declaring her name exalted and calling down blessings on Gwen and all Shi'i Lakka healers. Elated by Gwen's success, young men raced through the camp at a wild gallop, standing in their stirrups, swords held high above their heads. They swept down upon the exhausted healer with wild cries of lah-lah-lah-lah-lah. Hamza's friends slapped each other on the back while calling out a ringing shout of triumph. All the tumultuous behavior raised clouds of loose sand and dust while waking any stragglers that hoped to steal a few extra moments of sleep.

While Mussa was ordering the preparation of breakfast, Jaxx explained the rules of hospitality to the others. "Tradition is extremely important to the people of the borderlands. All uphold the rules of guests' rights. Tula always said that visitors were like fresh fish... Welcome the first day, accepted the second, but they stank by the third. We are on our second day."

"That means we need to start figuring out where we go from here."

"Does anyone have any idea how far we are from the nearest town?" Von shrugged and turned to Raffi. "Jaxx mentioned the possibility of purchasing horses for the leg of their journey. Have you noticed the way they treat their horses? They wander around loose and think nothing of walking into a tent to get out of the sun. I'm not so sure they will sell any of them."

Von's instinct turned out to be correct. While Mussa was thankful for everything the girls had done to help his son, he would sell none of the horses. He did, however, agree to provide them with transportation to Nona, the town closest to the edge of the borderlands.

"One of my nephews will ride with you and ensure you arrive safely. I can also suggest you consider obtaining the services of an aide acquainted with preparation of our foods and care of the animals. I can suggest Sayed bin Moammar. He is brusk, but he speaks common well and has experience in both the borderlands and the highly populated lands beyond. I think you will find him an excellent addition to your company."

We engaged Sayed on the spot, a big shambling man with a hawklike profile and appealing, deep brown eyes that looked forth unblinking, like the eyes of the family dog. Nothing about him lined up. His nose was crooked after being broken left unset. A narrow scar along one side pulled his mouth out of line, and a smart person would never gamble about the straight setting of his eyes. Yet his manner was gentle and obliging, his conversation more intelligent than any we had met along the way, and he was full of good counsel and even better resources.

Gwen, who was usually hesitant around strangers, took to him immediately. She looked right through the rough exterior into the desert man's heart. Whatever she found there was enough to win her over. That was enough for Mekiva.

Raffi wasn't certain he would be worth the trouble. "He might be an excellent cook, but he had one fatal drawback, he's incurably lazy."

Mekiva thought his argument hilarious. "He's no more a rogue than you are. He will clearly fit in with the rest of the men."

Sayed spent a candlemark with them, finding out what they expected of him and asking his questions. Finally, they hammered out a plan between them.

To our cook and new guide, Sayed, fell the genial task of getting everyone caught up on the latest gossip. Over the last two months, a lot happened. He told us of the war that had broken out between the Elderfae and the city of Hyperion. The only pass through the mountains was now closed, and any freight had to be delivered by ship. The route Jaxx and Vin had planned on developing depended on that mountain pass, so they hoped the war ended soon.

Word of our imminent departure was spreading quickly. Members of the tribe would drop by the staging area and leave a token of respect, often a favorite food packed for travel or an item of clothing.

Within a candlemark of suns up, we were ready to tell Mussa and Hamza goodbye. We gathered at the front of the tent and exchanged our last farewells.

Hamza strode out through the front opening of his tent, halting for a moment to let his gaze sweep over the lines of camel-hair tents that surrounded him. His eyes rested on the white-robed figures that stood talking to his father. It was amazing how much the six strangers that had changed his life in such a short time. If they had not been visiting his father's tent, he would most likely be nothing more than a fond memory of the surviving tribesmen. Walking with him was a young man, barely into his teens that he introduced as Majed, his cousin.

Majed was excited to be included in the trip to Nona. This was to be his first opportunity to travel outside the tribe's usual migration route.

"My father has entrusted me to ensure the great healer arrives safely at her destination. I am honored to be chosen for this." He realized they would require him to do most of the chores his uncle Sayed hated doing, but it was still his first opportunity to travel beyond the nomadic tribe's normal route.

Gwen felt like it was not much of an honor, but she could see the happiness reflected in his eyes at the opportunity the trip presented. She had felt the same anticipation when Mekiva asked her to go with her to find Von's boyhood home so many months before. So much had happened since they took that '*three day*' trip.

Mussa had provided each with one of his sleek desert horses. Sayed was also in charge of the mule that carried supplies. It had surprised Von to see a mule, since donkeys were not a common sight in the desert.

"My desert flower was not born near the border-lands. I once traveled to Edonn. Unfortunately, the citizens of that fair city were not as happy to see me as I was to reach my destination. After a brief visit, I discovered my horse was no longer healthy enough for the long trip back. There were not a lot of replace-ments available to choose from. Finding her was a blessing." He tried to keep the smile off his face as he told the story. There was still a reward posted for his head, though they cared little if it was on his shoul-ders or not. He had slipped through their fingers five years before, using a trick that would be difficult to pull off second time in the same place. The prize had been carefully packed in a metal box and placed in the care of his brother Mussa, where it would remain until his return. Shortly after his departure, the ruler of that province had died of a mysterious and linger-ing illness—poison was suspected and his name had been whispered, but there had been no proof.

Raffi had a feeling there was more to the story than Sayed was saying. Edonn was a large trading port with several busy animal markets. It should have been easy to buy a replacement. He decided to keep an eye on the newest member of the group. His new shadow might make that difficult, but there would be many opportunities.

Majed was not as vivacious in his responses, pre-ferring short, simple answers to questions. He asked questions, but they were more in line with what any-one on their first trip away from home would ask. Somehow the boy had decided Raffi was the one he wanted to emulate, and he was spending as much time as possible studying his every move.

After walking for the last two months, traveling on horseback quickly grew unpleasant. Gwen didn't want to complain about the awkward walking pace the old gelding had. Her rearend had gone numb miles ago. She glanced over at Mekiva, who rode just to her side, with Twist perched on the back of her saddle pad.

Kiva's mare had an easy swaying gait that made the long ride bearable, however; she wasn't happy about the Mir cat's presence. She was constantly fighting the reins, twisting her torso and crow hopping, hoping to dislodge the winged feline. Gwen knew the inside of her heart sister's thighs would be chapped and raw for days.

When Raffi finally decided they could stop for the night and set up camp, she was too tired to celebrate. As she slipped from the lathered mare's back, her legs trembled, and her muscles cramped. Jaxx supported her as she stumbled over to a nearby rock. Once she was settled, he went back to help Gwen dismount.

They pitched tents and picketed the horses, while Sayed gathered dried branches of the prickly hedge. Once he had what looked like an enormous amount, he lighted a cookfire of the briars and dead scrub. The night was dry and hot; there was rain in the hills just west of us, but none fell near our campsite.

Majid explained that rain was considered a blessing from the Gods. "To receive more than a brief shower is unheard of, to have more than an inch falling on the desert could be a disaster."

"Why? It seems like that would be a blessing

for everyone."

"Flash floods could wipeout a tent enclave before anyone realized the danger."

Mekiva sighed. "It was doubtful they would be lucky enough to enjoy the experience."

So far, he had avoided detection, but Keeyun knew his streak of good luck was bound to end sometime. Dealing with Raffi alone had been bad enough. Now, with the addition of Moth and Brinn, he was sure to be unmasked as a fraud the first time any serious combat occurred. He could mimic Keeyun's ability to manipulate nature around anyone that was not familiar with it, but it would not help in an actual fight. He'd stayed out of sight during the Xyvelix attack. In an actual battle, that lack of ability could result in at least one of the group being severely hurt, or possibly killed. This group was too big to take on headfirst. It would be safer to find another way, or at least find a more defensible position, to explain his absence. He sighed and jabbed his blade into his thigh, allowing the blood to flow freely.

CHAPTER 7

Gwen's words returned to haunt her two mornings later as they reached the last stretch of rough terrain before the town of Nona. The views to the south across the green plain were enchanting; to the north the hills rose in unbroken slopes, to the east was a small village. They were all too tired to get excited.

Only Raffi broke out with a full faced grin. *Well, I'll be a Gynark's milk brother... A strange sensation of Déjà vu struck him. Nona! That's why the name sounded familiar.*

As they wound their way down the switchback toward town, a brief but intense shower surprised them. The rain lasted a very few minutes, but the results were miraculous. The hard mud of the trail quickly assumed the consistency of honey while the slopes became as slippery as glass. The horse's feet sunk up the fetlocks in the mire on the level sections. Instead of the smoothly packed soil, they faced a slippery morass of mud. Most of the drop-offs were less than a tall man's height, but the mud made the sides so precipitous that they had to dismount and proceed with the utmost of care. Even on foot, it was almost impossible to remain upright. Before long, mud coated every available surface, adding to their discomfort.

Upon reaching the foot of the northern slopes of the western hills, the tired travelers entered a great rolling plain like the one they had crossed on the road back to Cabrell after their brief stint in prison. The scent of fresh water sent the tired animals into a quick footed dance as they neared the clear, flowing stream. Along the riverbank there was real greenery growing. The ground was carpeted with young grass and fast-growing weeds like yellow dandelions since the animals ate anything they could reach while grazing, but it was still green. As they watered the thirsty animals, a young boy looked up from baiting his hook, decided there was nothing in the group that concerned him, and threw the line far out into the river. Beyond the river they could see olive orchards and cultivated fields, the serene landscape broken here and there with the now familiar shepherd and their flocks of sheep and goats. Like most towns that skirted the wastelands, they built Nona on a hill. Shepherds took the flocks down into the plain to graze the thick grass that grew along the banks of the river. In the summer, when the smaller streams dry up, they moved the flocks to share the uncultivated slopes near the city with the horses and cattle.

Along the far side of the river, the land rose from the rich bottomland near the water, on terrace after terrace, until the upper stretches of its orchards showed clear against the evening sky. A fortified tower guarding the town stood within a few hundred feet of the main business district. Most of the town's inhabitants lived in a roughly built mud block homes around the town's edges and sent their animals out into the fields to forage.

As they rode, they passed the ruined remains of low walls built of rough-hewn stones laid without mortar, and three ancient rock-cut cisterns. Originally, the cisterns had been intended to hold water. With the river being dammed downstream, they no longer needed to store water, and the old cisterns had been repurposed to hold the dried corn for the animals. Something about the corn cisterns was nagging at Raffi. He turned to ask Keeyun if he noticed anything, but the druid was no longer riding with the rest of the group.

"Anyone know where Keeyun went?"

Jaxx pointed to a group of men that were sitting on horses about a half a league away.

Raffi could see a bay horse riding toward a trio of men on horseback. The three horsemen trotted out to intercept him as he drew closer. Like most of the horsemen that they had met, these three were swarthy, black-browed, armed to the teeth, and menacing of aspect. He wished Keeyun had discussed it with him before taking it upon himself to approach the local horsemen. This was the second time he had done something out of character. There was going to be a discussion as soon as they settled in for the night.

As they approached the town, they noticed other people traveling along the road they intended to follow. The dirt track along the river was the shortest route to the sacred city of Hatra. As part of their year of service, the church required religious students and novitiate clergy to make the yearly pilgrimage. Locals knew to dress for the hotter weather. It was easy to spot unprepared travelers on every road, trudging patiently under the hot sun or through the brief bursts of rain, often clothed in the heavy cloaks or furs of their own country, and bearing in their hands a staff cut from a young sapling along the way.

As the weary group rode along the edge of the river embankment, they talked of the potential advantages that the land might reap from proper irrigation.

Sayed was convinced too much water was a bad thing. "It makes men weak when there are no obstacles to survival."

Nona seemed to survive and prosper. The main section of town was on a knoll, and composed of little more than a general store, a tavern that let rooms for the night, and a livery stable with a resident blacksmith. Here and there were signs of growth, a scattering of stuccoed block houses, many painted white to lighten the red mud bricks. The citizens of Nona went about their daily business, recognizing that there were few opportunities to better their existence, but were unprepared to consider moving away.

There was also a small temple. The clerics went among the people, offering hopes and dreams for a small donation. At the end of life, most people were too tired to care about what might happen after their years of labor ended. The church made enough to remain open, but little remained to benefit the city's inhabitants.

The horses perked up as they cantered across a stone bridge and down slopes grazed short, though they yielded forage enough for the resident's sheep and goats and entered the business district. It surprised them to find a typical rustic village built around a square, like many of the larger towns.

Gwen spotted a small fire burning, the first one that she remembered seeing outside of a tiny brazier, or the welcome bonfire Mussa had built. Fuel was too expensive. Several women were gathered around a huge vat of boiling water that was suspended over the roaring fire. She watched as a woman bending over a zinc tub scrubbed laundry on a washboard. A second woman would wring out each piece of clothing to remove the soap; then put them into the vat of boiling water. The third woman moved the clean clothes from the hot vat to barrels of cool water. She used the same wooden paddle to stir the clothes until they were rinsed clear of the soap. Then she would check each piece; either returning it back to the soap vat for further washing or placing it into a basket to be wrung out and hung on a nearby line to air dry.

An older man was toiling over a pile of cut logs, cutting the larger sections into stove sized pieces. Despite its small size, this must be a prosperous city as wood for burning would need to be brought in by wagon. A younger boy was stacking the cut wood into neat cords according to their size and type. The simplicity of their perfect village life charmed the women but did not impress the men.

"Not a lot of choices," Raffi said. The sleepy little town had grown in the five years since the last time he'd visited. New construction was everywhere, the sign of an emergent prosperity. Even the older buildings were reflecting the prosperity. Fresh paint glistened on stucco walls, and the smell of fresh thatch was everywhere. It had never crossed his mind that Nona could be the four buildings near Brinn's homestead.

He stopped his horse before the general store. "I will be right back. I need to check something out."

Von and the girls we happy to remain where they were, but Jaxx decided he might be needed if Raffi could not understand the local dialect.

The variations of accent struck the men as they attempted to convey their needs. Finally, one clerk went and brought back an older man who spoke fluid common. Raffi immediately confirmed his guess.

"We seek the home of Brinn bin Ahmet. Could you please direct us to his homestead?"

"You are friends of Brinn?"

"Friends and family. It has been five full turns since we last traveled these roads. A lot has changed in our absence."

His eyes widened as Keeyun entered. "That one... I have no trouble seeing the family likeness. Moth will be pleased to know a relative has arrived. Alas, you must forgive me as I see no similar family traits among the other members of your group."

Raffi nodded. "I would be surprised if you had. I was adopted. The others are all friends."

"Then you must be Raffiel. Brinn speaks of you during our weekly card gathering."

Raffi nodded. "Among friends, it is Raffi."

"Then I hope that one day you might consider me a friend as Brinn does."

Raffi thanked him for his time and headed back to the waiting travelers. He was whistling a jaunty tune, one that the small band often sang when out on the road.

Hearing the whistling, Von and Jaxx broke into broad grins and joined in, remembering their time in prison and on the road home.

Keeyun ignored the tune. "We ready to ride?" He swung back into the saddle without a word.

Raffi continued to whistle as he mounted the borrowed horse. "I got the name of a horse breeder not far out of town. We should be able to get anything we need from him. We can set up camp near his place. The rest can wait until tomorrow." It surprised him that Keeyun had not recognized the area.

"Then I guess I will catch you tomorrow. I need a drink. That tavern is calling my name." Without waiting to hear his reply, Keeyun urged the gelding toward the small tavern.

Keeyun's lack of interest left Raffi feeling as if someone had slugged him in the gut. He took a breath, steadying himself before responding with words he might later come to regret. They would need to have a talk with him, but that discussion could wait until after he talked to Moth and confirmed his fears. Something was up with his friend. He realized it had been a while since the young hunter had been in the area, but he should have recognized the surrounding area. He was a trained tracker, one of the best Raffi had ever met. And he was usually excited to see his cousin. Keeyun's reclusive attitude was getting on his nerves. Something had happened while they were stuck inside the prison. Maybe Moth could get him to talk about what happened.

The homestead was about a league outside of town, and the horses were already tired. With luck, they should arrive well before suns down, in time for supper. Trail food was sustaining, but little more. For now, he wanted to reach the compound and relax. Enjoy a good meal. Maybe sleep for a day or two. A hot bath followed by a good night's sleep would work wonders. He urged his horse on.

CHAPTER 8

As the tired travelers grew nearer to the compound, he could see smoke. It was growing
late in the afternoon, when smoke meant supper,
and they were all hungry after a long time on the
road. It was common for hospitality to be offered
to travelers, but no one expected the horse trader
to invite them to stay for a meal with the town
nearby.

It surprised Raffi to see how much the
homestead had grown over the past five years.
The original block and stucco building had been
expanded. It was now a large rambling home
surrounding an interior patio garden area. Walls
of the same material surrounded the main house
and several additional buildings built along the
perimeter. Brinn had built irrigation channels
on the rolling land surrounding the homestead,
with narrow arched bridges over the channels.
He looked and spotted the white stallion and
steel gray mare belonging to Moth amongst
about twenty other mares. On the opposite side
of the compound there was a similar setup, except that stallion was the color of fire, a deep
chestnut red coat that gleamed in the light if reflecting the twin suns. It was too far to make out
details of the animals beyond the compound, but

logic said that's where Brinn kept most of his riding and work stock.

"Nice place. Horses must pay well." Jaxx wiped a drip of sweat from his forehead, standing up in the stirrups to get a better view. Beside the olive trees he expected to see scattered around the pastures, there were also expansive groves of fruit and a large vineyard. Along the edges of the waterways grew tall stalks of seed corn. A month in the fierce heat of the twin suns saw the plants through bud and bloom to stalk ripened ears.

Raffi looked around, trying to take it all in. "Lots of coin. That plus hard work," he answered. Like Moth, Raffi had invested in the homestead. He was pleased to see how his investment had grown.

Look at those orchards. It has all paid off. The almond, kiwi, and apricot trees showed nothing but bare boughs. They would not flower until the weather stabilized. However, the vineyards were already heavy with fruit. Raffi was pleased to see how large the fig bushes they had planted had grown since he last visited. He had carried the cuttings from Mu, with the roots wrapped in wet paper.

The fields were full of sheep and goats, many with young frolicking at their heels. It seemed as if his retirement investment had paid off. He was whistling as they walked along the road toward the compound.

The horses perked up when they realized they were approaching the entrance of the compound. Thick walls surrounded the main part of the house, easily twice the height of most men. The only way in was through a heavy metal gate that opened from the inside.

Von wondered if they would be allowed in. The group was tired and dirty, not exactly the type of visitor someone who lived in a home like this would host. He might be polite and sell a few animals to strangers, but it was doubtful he would offer any more than that.

Raffi slid from his horse and headed straight for the iron bound portal, opened the gate wide enough to slip through, and went inside, walking directly to a man standing near the gatehouse. They spoke for a moment, and then the man signaled to someone. The gate opened.

The man headed for the house, and Raffi returned to his horse. "That went well," he said. He didn't bother remounting, instead he led the tired gelding through the gate. Everyone else followed.

The man must have alerted the household to the visitors, because a young woman appeared at the house's main entrance. She offered a friendly wave and a smile of greeting as she approached. Like the others, she was covered from head to toe in the long flowing robes worn by the women of the desert tribes. The narrow, dark blue attire drew attention to her bare ankles as she walked. A dark blue cotton veil covered most of her face, and a snowy white headdress fell down her back, almost to the ground. Henna designs decorated her slender hands, delicate patterns of flowers and birds. It must have taken candlemarks to apply the tint to her skin.

"Raffiel! It is wonderful to see you again. Brinn did not mention you were coming. I would have ensured everything was ready before you arrived."

"It's great to see you again, Nyla. Brinn didn't mention it because I did not know I was coming here until I reached Nona and recognized the town."

"Where is Keeyun? Moth misses his cousin. He often regrets not continuing to Cabrell with you and Raffi. From Brinn's description, I can guess that this is Von and Jaxx. But my husband did not mention there were woman in the party." Her eyes darted from person to person, as if waiting for an explanation.

Raffi seemed to understand what needed to be said. "Another thing Brinn would not have known. The addition happened later, under unusual circumstances. I hope it is not too much of an inconvenience?"

"No. No. Of course not. Brinn will be excited to see you all. I am afraid becoming a father again has caused him more than the usual stress. He took one look into his daughter's eyes, and she stole his heart. The boys are rough and tumble terrors. They are into everything. Nyiela is a bit fussy, so he took advantage of the need to visit a nearby farm to enjoy a day away. I think Brinn worries the boys will turn her into a female version of them as soon as she can toddle along behind them."

Sayed did not look happy to find they would stay there instead of returning to town. He was a difficult person to fathom. Just when you felt you were getting an idea of the man, his personality would change. She was more interested in learning more about her new hostess.

Nyla looked to be only a few years older than Mekiva; however, there was something about her eyes that gave her the sense of quiet experience. She was quite impressive. They were about the same height; however, unlike Kiva, this woman appeared slender, almost delicate, through the enshrouding material. She stared at the unexpected visitors with big green eyes that shone in the evening sunlight. Then she lowered the hood of her burnoose, and they saw the tips of pointy ears peeking through titian hair; a brilliant gold-tinged auburn with a hint of red. Short spiky lengths framed her face and grew gracefully back until it formed a fiery mane flowing down her back. She wondered if Brinn was also of fae blood. The Duaar were very open about their bloodlines, but other Fae races were wary of giving out personal information.

Nyla smiled, startling Mekiva. *Could she hear her thoughts?*

"Brinn and Moth have ridden over to look at a young bull owned by a neighboring farmer. I will send one boy to tell him of our unexpected guests. Meanwhile, let me see you to your rooms. You can rest and get comfortable. The bath houses are available. I will ensure they are stocked."

"They?" Raffiel asked.

"We have found it easier to have two. My preferences do not always align with my husbands." She turned to the girls. "Emil will see to the men's comfort."

The men passed the reins to a stableboy, who immediately left to take care of the tired horses. Sayed went with him to help. The others followed Emil, stopping just inside the door to remove their boots. Raffi was chatting with Emil as they walked inside. Von swung the pack across one shoulder. Carrying his boots in one hand and his sword in the other, he followed

Jaxx into the house.

Mekiva didn't attempt to hide her pleasure as she trailed behind Nyla. She would have fought her way through a horde of Gynarks to reach a hot bath. Her thighs felt as if someone was jabbing hit needles into the muscles. She tried to walk normally, but a hobbling shuffle was all she could manage. The sight of the swimming pool sized tub almost brought tears to her eyes. Even Gwen perked up.

"My husband is away quite often. I had the two baths installed when the doctor mentioned the heat would help me relax during my labor. It surprised Brinn when he returned, but after a few days soaking in his tub, he forgot about the cost."

"If I had to be married, that's the kind of husband I would want." Grinning, Kiva stripped off her boots, then slipped the brown leggings down her legs, frowning at how loose they had become. More gangly than shapely, she had lost even more weight over the last two months. She was almost as lean as a man now. If not for her firm breasts and the slight curve of her hips, she could easily pretend to be one. Her tattered tunic joined the road worn cape and keffiyeh. The voluminous desert clothing did little to accent what curves remained after the meager trail meals. The burn on her leg was now a pink scar that would fade. She felt guilty for wishing it away, considering what Gwen had to live with as a cleric of Rheaaz.

Nyla noticed the scar, and her eyes went to Gwen. She looked like she wanted to ask questions but respected the rules of hospitality. "The pitchers are full of rainwater. There is plenty available, so do not feel you need to skimp." She pointed at several handled urns sitting on a table set beside a metal grate.

"Shall I pour for you?" Gwen asked. She would wait until Nyla left before joining her in the steaming water.

Mekiva nodded. The cool water drew a shiver but felt wonderful on her skin. Once Gwen had removed the surface dust, Mekiva slid into the soaking pool with a heartfelt sigh.

Gwen stood silently and watched her friend relax.

As if sensing the young Shi'i Lakka's hesitation, Nyla spoke. "Please forgive me. I need to check on my other guests and discuss the food being prepared for the evening meal." Mekiva cracked her eyes long enough to notice she took her dirty clothing with her.

Shortly after she left, Mekiva heard the sound of water being poured over Gwen's head and body. Then her heart sister slipped into the pool. She was must have dozed off, wakening when she heard a woman's scream, followed by a slamming door and string of shouted invectives in a language she could barely understand. The three words she was certain of were roast, cat, and kill. *Twist! Drasst. Nyla had taken her clothes!*

Somehow, Nyla had returned without either girl noticing. Even better, she had left a stack of toweling cloths, and two changes of clothing. Since one outfit was long-sleeved, it was obvious they meant the other for her use.

Gwen was still giggling as they toweled off and slipped on the soft trousers, using the rope ties to adjust them to their waists. Next was the long shirt and over tunic. Nyla had not replaced the keffiyehs. But she had left Gwen's extra veils.

There were cloth slippers to wear inside the house, but Mekiva didn't want to get them dirty, so she ran barefoot toward the kitchen.

Raffi and Von were trying to placate the irate cook over the loss of a string of sausage she'd intended for stuffing into the roast hen. Nyla was translating, and everyone was certain she was toning down some of the cook's language at the same time.

"I am so sorry," Mekiva exclaimed as she ran up. "I was so excited by the idea of soaking in a hot bath, I forgot about Twist. He looks dangerous, but he's still a big kid. I should have realized how hungry he was. I remembered to tell him to leave the animals alone. I didn't think about a string of sausage."

Gwen joined them and added her apologies to Mekiva's. She remembered the last time Twist had raided the butcher's stall and taken the string of sausages.

Nyla soothed the irate cook and promised to keep the Mir-cat out of her kitchen. Then everyone returned to the salon to talk.

It was after dark before Brinn, and Moth returned to discover the new arrivals. The boy that his wife had dispatched to locate him had lingered along the way with two friends. Surprised by the imminent darkness and alarmed by the lateness of the candlemark, he had returned home without fulfilling his mission. They had found him asleep in the hay in the last stall of the barn. Brinn laid a finger on his lips and then he covered the boy with a thick blanket used on the horses. He would talk to the boy in the morning and explain how his actions could have endangered the homestead.

———————

Izabal wasn't convinced Lord Baldric's plan had been examined from all angles. "What if your nephew awakens out of his sound sleep? He might observe the motion of the door. Will he be more suspicious if the door opened in a single continuous motion; or if it slowly opened, little by little? Which would signal danger and put him on alert?"

"Alright. I admit it would be best to slip in while he is asleep. But why can't your man port into the bedchamber? You have no trouble popping in here whenever you choose to appear."

"He can't teleport blind. He could end up inside a wall or half on one floor, half on the other. That can be very messy, especially if he lives long enough to divulge information about why he was there." Her body shivered, the tiniest hint of how bad it could be. She did not want to risk her man, but Torrin insisted no one else had a chance of getting close enough. Mages that could teleport were plentiful. But no one could replace her assassin.

Lord Baldric's gaze fell on her hand. His eyes betrayed his sudden interest. "New ring?" he asked. The jeweler had crafted it of heavy gold with two unusual stones forming the eyes of the leering gargoyle. It surprised him how much he wanted it. Izabal was wearing the ring on her left hand, the middle finger. The ring was much too large for her to wear comfortably. They designed it for a man, a big one. He needed to be careful. One wrong word and things could quickly spin out of control. He needed Izabal much more than he needed the ring.

Izabal wanted to see how much it was worth to him. She intended him to have the ring, anyway. That is why she wore it. It was much too large for her. She could cast the same spell if the need for a stone skin arose. But she wanted to tease him, just to see how long she could make him suffer.

"My agent could not send enough data for me to pinpoint the exact location of the homestead. However, I can join him at his location, and we can make our plans there. No one will recognize me, and the agent will still be able to continue to monitor your nephew."

"And after the job is done?"

"Our assassin will find he needs all his skills to survive undetected until the treasure is in his hands."

CHAPTER 9

The arrow flew straight before finding the target less than a finger's length away from the previous two. So far, he had shot five arrows, and all five had hit the black circle. Three shots almost dead center. Raffi frowned and held his hand out, dropping a gold coin in the palm of

Jaxx's hand. They may not see eye to eye on many things, but he had to admit the surly southerner certainly could shoot. Looking back over the past thirty years, he could not recall meeting a single person who could out-shoot Keeyun. Whether he was bagging a sly old stag or stalking an assailant shadowed against the skyline, the pale man's aim was uncannily true. In a region of born marksmen, his skill stood forth supreme. Until now.

Key had arrived at the compound early the following morning after his decision to spend the night in town. Raffi was certain he had a *'friend'* he was visiting. One he didn't think Moth would approve of. There had to more than a thirst for strong ale and a card game. He could have both at home. His sharp eyes had noticed several inconsistencies in his usual behavior, but moments later he would say something that was so typical of Keeyun it eased any doubts. His gut was telling him something wasn't right, but his eyes saw his friend, albeit a surlier version of the happy-go-lucky young man he knew. So, he had held his tongue and waited to see how Moth would react.

So far Moth had noticed nothing, or if he had, he was not letting anyone know.

Gwen used the match as an opportunity to ask a few questions that had been needling her for a fortnight. After meeting Moth, her curiosity had swollen to where she could contain herself no longer. "So how you meet? You are such a diverse group; I can't see where your paths would intersect."

Brinn laughed aloud, something he was not prone to do.

"That's a long story. I met Moth when he was trying to kill me. He almost succeeded, too. I still bear the scar to prove it."

"He tried to kill you. I'm not sure I could become friends with someone under those circumstances."

Moth laughed. "As usual, Raffi was at the center of the conflict."

Brinn's grin grew broader as he looked back at his memories, remembering a few things he preferred Nyla never discovered. "Raffi was playing cards with a man that owed me money. The arrogant Duaar was trimming away at the small pile of coins lying on the table before Leoni. I could see my money disappearing before my eyes. I easily recognized the skill in his hands. It takes an extremely dexterous player to move the cards the way he did. His hands didn't get that nimble doing normal work. An expert had trained him. I watched instead of confronting Leoni about the coin he owed. Pretty soon, the game was over, and the old man was broke. That's when

Leoni noticed me sitting behind him. Thought the old man was going to give up the ghost right there. He started coughing and choking like he couldn't breathe. I passed him a shot of rotgut, and he tossed it down like water. Then he took up his pack and beat it, saying nothing and looking sick. That's when Raffi got this funny look on his face and lunged across the table at me. I blocked his axe with the back of arm. Then I rolled backward and pulled my sword in time to use it instead of my left forearm. We swung back and forth for about a candlemark before we realized we would be there the next morning exchanging blows with no better results."

"Yeah," Raffi said. "It was entertaining to fleece Leoni of so many coins before killing Brinn. Except, he's nothing like the decrepit old man I was expecting. I finally said the Hells with it and called for a pitcher of beer. It was only after I called for the beer that I realized Moth was behind me with a sword in his hand, ready to take me out if Brinn got injured. We sat and talked."

Brinn nodded. "After talking to Raffi, I realized I had a problem I needed to take care of in Hyperion. Raffi wanted to discuss the misrepresented details of contract with the man who hired him. Before I knew it, I had a new partner. It was just the three of us for many years. Then Moth's cousin Keeyun showed up and Moth took him under his wing. The four of us covered a lot of territory for many years. Then we met Von and Jaxx. But that's another story."

Ali, the head of Brinn's small security force, interrupted them. Word had spread that a healer was staying at the homestead. A woman has arrived at the gate and requested the Shi'i Lakka healer.

Brinn turned to Gwen. "It is your choice. You do not have to speak with her."

"She must be desperate to walk all the way to the compound alone. I cannot let her leave without at least hearing why she felt she had to come." She stood and followed Ali to where the woman waited.

When Gwen appeared, the distraught woman fell to her knees and implored her to heal her husband.

Gwen glanced over at Brinn, and he shrugged. He had seen the woman carrying water from the well. He knew her husband was a shepherd. That was the extent of his knowledge. "What ails your husband?" he asked.

"A Zivilyx attacked him while defending the flocks."

Brinn stepped forward. "When did this happen? I have received no notice of a demon attack." The winged demons rarely traveled this direction when hunting, preferring the highly populated eastern edge of the borderlands. Sheep were one of their favorite meats. If they were expanding along the western border, it could quickly devastate his flocks. He would need to add additional sentries whenever the shepherds went to the far pastures.

"My pardon, but the honored magistrate had not yet returned from his business trip." She continued to kneel in the dirt, keeping her eyes lowered.

Not returned? He had been back almost two moons. Had the men been ill all this time? "Was there no healer available?"

"No one but old Maryam, and she is little more

than a midwife. She knows how to brew a ti-
sane to break a fever or what plants to bring on
a mother's milk, but not a lot about caring for a
man's wounds."

Gwen looked at her and Mekiva knew the
Shi'i had already decided. She sighed. She might
as well tag along and make sure an injury too
dire for her to handle did not overwhelm her impetuous friend.

Nyla provided a small carriage to carry them
instead of their horses, since the woman had
come afoot. They passed through the main section of town before turning on a narrow strip
of land that followed the hillside until it dipped
down into a vale. At the base of the hill was a
collection of windowless, one room, mud-brick
houses. The sour odor of infection assaulted
them before they pushed aside the door drap-
ing's and entered the house.

The injured man was lying on a thin pallet
in a dark corner of the windowless room. Someone had wrapped his face, but the bandages were
now stained with blood and a pus-filled discharge. That was the sour odor they smelled.

Once the dirty bandages were removed, a
horrible wound was revealed. The demon's claws
had sliced a gash that had passed through the
cheek and shattered the jaw. It would have been
difficult to heal it if Gwen had addressed it before
the infection set in. Now it could be beyond her
meager skills.

Mekiva saw the doubt reflected in her
friends' eyes. She could argue the danger, but
Gwen would never walk away and do nothing.
To her, that was condemning the injured man to

death, something she could never do.

Gwen cleaned the wound and applied a natural antiseptic before imploring Rheaaz to heal the wound. She carefully scraped as much of the dead flesh as possible away from the infected gash. Then she used clean rags to hold the gash closed. He squirmed and twisted his body but made no complaints as she worked. Finally, once she was certain she had done everything she could do, she fell to her knees and begged the Goddess to heal the man. Almost instantly, she felt the familiar heat in her hands. The red glow spread across the swollen flesh to the gash. She could feel the heat increasing as Rheaaz burned away the infection. Then the glow turned white, and a cooling sensation washed over the man's face. As the glow spread, it quickly reduced the wound to a pink scar. The relief that swept across the suffering man's face was all the thanks she needed.

"Rheaaz has blessed him with her touch. The scar will fade in time. In the meantime, it will remain a reminder of her grace."

The woman fell to her knees, crying out her thanks to the goddess, promising to honor her and tell her children of her blessing in the future.

Gwen swayed and sat down in an empty chair nearby. Mekiva would bring the cart around. But before she left, she wanted the woman to understand she would not be there the next time the demons attacked. "If anyone is hurt by the winged demons again, remember that you must keep the wound extremely clean. After they are washed, boil the dressings before allowing them to dry. It is imperative that you keep the wrappings clean. Above all, not to let him the patient become depressed. Measure carefully, some medicines can hurt as well as heal."

The woman promised she would make sure everyone in town understood her words. She was still crying and praising Rheaaz as they disappeared into the distance.

Jaxx had been drinking steadily since dinner, so climbing the steps to his room was not as simple as it sounded. He had waited until he was certain the girls were back in the compound before thanking his hosts and making his way to the awaiting bed. The idea of crisp linen and a real mattress was more tempting than another candlemark of cards, so he staggered his way down the hall to his assigned bedchamber.

Sporadic muttering and the sounds of movement in the room at the end of the hall alerted Jaxx to the possibility that his room was not empty. He felt the hairs on his arm rise on end, and the back of his neck itched. Both signs he had learned meant something was tickling his intuition. He tried the handle to the door, and finding it locked securely. He had unlocked it when he went downstairs. His axe was inside the room. He had three knives on him; they would have to do for now. He stepped back and kicked the door, causing it to burst into small wooden projectiles that peppered the unprepared occupants. Jaxx threw a knife at the rapidly gesturing sorcerer, missing him and striking a man who was loading a crossbow. The sorcerer finished his spell with a muttered command word.

"Don't forget to bring the gate key," he snapped and then stepped forward through a shimmering doorway that disappeared as quickly as it had appeared. Noticing that the bowman had finished his preparations to fire, Jaxx dove forward, rolling up against the base of a table. Realizing he left himself exposed, he turned it on its side as a shield against the deadly bolts heading his way. He cursed briefly as one bolt drove through the heavy wood and then through his leather armor. The force lodged the bolt in his shoulder, sending searing pain into the muscle and a wave of agony to run down the nerves of his arm.

"Gods drasst it all! That hurts." It was becoming difficult to grip the handle of his knife, so he threw it, wincing as the blade did minor damage. He sighed and shifted his weight to the other side. Then he drew another knife from his boot with his off hand. He hesitated, knowing how slim the probability was of taking out the assailant with another knife. The steady drip of blood from the gash in the side of the archer's neck didn't seem to slow him. He would have to strike an area that would disable him on the next throw, or his new friend would get off a shot. The chance of him becoming disabled or dead was much higher. He needed to get close and that meant he needed a distraction… but what. His eyes darted around, checking everything within reach. Too bad Brinn's housekeeper was so good at her job. His mouth quirked as he spotted one possibility. It was a long shot; but it wasn't as if he had a wide assortment of options.

He grabbed and threw all in one motion. It flew through the air and landed exactly where he hoped, high on the face of the man aiming the crossbow his way.

He winced at the loud snap but wasted no time rolling back outside the door. The distraction only lasted moments. However, Jaxx was willing to bet the man's nose began swelling immediately. Someone must have greased the mousetrap recently because it slammed home and refused to release its prey. Jaxx's last blade followed immediately, burying itself up to the hilt in the softer tissue of the man's stomach. He looked up, the trap dangling from his swollen nose, an expression of surprised disbelief on his face. As he fell to the floor, his finger tightened on the trigger of the crossbow. Released by the pressure, the bolt flew across the room, missing Moth by inches as it buried itself in the jamb of the busted door. By the time he got himself situated, it was over.

The dead assassin lay in a pool of his own blood less than two feet from a similar pool where Jaxx kneeled, the haft of his ax holding him upright. Once he saw his friends coming through the door, he slumped against the wall, unconscious.

———

Gwen wiped her hands on a clean cloth and sighed. Jaxx had a new scar to match the eight others he had garnered since she had met him a little over a year ago. She had no idea why the young Duaar that seemed to attract sharp objects, but he had been injured as often as all the others combined.

"Did they say anything at all?" Moth asked.

"Don't forget the key? And something about a treasure. I wasn't paying a lot of attention. My memory is a little woozy on the details."

Despite the apparent safety of their surroundings, all three knew the danger had not passed. That was not a random attack. That strike had been carefully planned and executed. That meant someone paid a lot of coin.

Jaxx had never considered the possibility of being attached inside the walled compound. "Walls mean very little if you can teleport. The burning question is, how did they find us? And who is trying to kill us?"

Gwen shrugged.

Mekiva wasn't so sure. This made three attempts, and she was now certain there was more to it than an arbitrary attack on four young adventurers. "Maybe we have been thinking about this the wrong way. Maybe it's not us they are trying to kill? All the attacks have centered on one person, Jaxx."

Von's bewildered face said it all. "Why would anyone want to kill Jaxx?"

CHAPTER 10

"This is a waste of time. I can't think of anything the skinny rats ever said that was worth the effort to ride out here." Keeyun made a spitting sound before he realized the wind would blow it back at him.

Moth let his horse drift away from his cousin. "You could be right. It could also provide the clue we need. It's worth our time and a keg of beer." He wasn't sure what had happened to drastically change his cousin's demeanor. Less than three months had passed since the group had split up, with Raffi and Keeyun going with Von and Jaxx to Cabrell, while he had returned to the homestead with Brinn. It worried him that his cousin had not trusted him enough to reveal what was going on in his mind. He couldn't help if he did not know what had happened.

Raffi didn't care what had happened. One day Keeyun had been fine, the next he had become sullen and reclusive. He figured it involved a romantic liaison of some type. Perhaps he had discovered his love had replaced him with another. That could trigger a temporary personality change. Key had been drinking more than he usually drank. Once or twice, he'd found empty vials of poppy powder on the floor of their room.

He'd mentioned his find to Brinn and Moth, but neither was sure if they should bring it up.

When Brinn mentioned riding over to the Gynark enclave to talk to Gar, Keeyun had surprised them by declaring he intended on joining them. Raffi had a hunch there was more to his sudden interest than a desire for their company.

Von was riding next to Mekiva, holding a conversation about the various races and how they had changed since Adon's magical mishap destroyed one of Omissions' largest cities and killed everyone and everything within the blast radius. Jaxx and Gwen had remained behind. Jaxx because he sneezed whenever he got around Gynarks and didn't want to visit enclave. Gwen was still recovering from her healing efforts the previous day.

"Since when have the Gynarks allowed visitors to their enclave? I thought they wanted to wipe out humanity." Keeyun asked as he moved his horse to the front.

"Most of the non-humanoid species reached a pact of peace. This was thousands of years before man developed the capacity to reason. The rogue Gynarks are not part of the greater Gynark nation. They consider the treaty void after the congress of nations was broken."

"What caused it to fall apart?" Von asked.

"Magic. The mages were more concerned with gaining power than peace. To them, the mage's actions were further proof that humans should be avoided. The mage war that had destroyed so much of the planet had only supported their theory---that humanity was simply a pest, like a vole or a rat, to be eradicated."

"I guess that's why they attack and kill anyone that crosses into their territory."

"They wish they could kill us all. The nonhumanoid races produced much faster, but their lives were much shorter. It's too bad their memory isn't just as short. Theres a lot we could teach each other."

"Is that why Brinn is going to the enclave today?"

"No. We are going to the weekly story session. Gar is speaking. It's always informative when he talks. Today he promises a story of the Bane."

"How does he know that would interest us?"

Raffi shrugged his shoulders. They were approaching the edge of the enclave. It was better to remain silent for now.

"Welcome. Garyannotis awaits your presence," a loud but friendly voice called out as we approached the edge of the Gynarks' village. Standing at the edge of the tree line was an elderly Gynark in a dark blue robe. He was carrying several enormous books.

Mekiva wondered what subjects they covered.

Soon everyone had gathered in a circle around one of the oldest Gynarks Von had ever seen. Even the aged healer seemed like a spring lamb next to this grizzled old soldier. His form was familiar, with the same slightly pointed chin and ears that Moth had. But there the resemblance ended. Unlike the ethereal mage, this cagey old warrior was grounded and definitely wolfish, from the fuzz tipped pointy ears that were constantly moving; to the lackluster gray fur that crowned his grizzled head before blending into a shaggy ruff about his shoulders. Although touches of hoar frost tipped his granite-colored pelt, he was not a warrior to be taken lightly. Like the healer, he was perched in a place of honor atop one of the scattered tree stumps that surrounded the bonfire set in the center of the village. Everyone else was clustered around him, some on logs, but most everyone had brought warm rugs and blankets for comfort. As he spoke, everyone leaned forward to better hear him tell his tale. He spoke a language the girls weren't familiar with, but once the speaker understood her problem, he translated the words for her, somehow relaying them directly to their minds.

"Come closer to the fire and hear my story. Know ye, the old divinities, the Gods whose names have faded from the minds of the common people, still hold sway under changed names. Do not think that they no longer have a hand in the daily affairs of hard-working people. They watch and laugh as the new upstarts spread stories of their own power and wait until they fail, knowing it's easy to sweep up the dregs and add them to their own followers. There was a time when I was one of the doubtful, not believing any of the old stories. Now I know...."

He stopped and made sure everyone was listening before he began speaking. "... *Listen well, as I tell my story. It is one of pain and woe; one I am certain you can all appreciate. My name*---he paused dramatically - *is unimportant. But you may call me Gar. I am, or I guess I should say, I was, a warrior of the Red Moon tribe of the land now known as Azaar's Bane. Our ancestral home is adjacent to the old stronghold of Blue Storm; close, but not too close, you understand, since nothing remains to sustain life in the land between the rivers. I have come back to the grotto to tell my story for the last time,"* he grinned, showing long teeth yellowed from age. *"It is here, I chose, for my old bones to rest until that time as I would return to the soil of Omission."* Gar stopped talking long enough to take a drink from the water-skin a young Gynark had brought, and then he winked at the travelers before continuing his story.

"It is only by chance that I still live to tell my tale. Times were lean five cycles ago, and that winter many cubs cried from the gnawing pain of empty stomachs. Like many of my tribe, I spent most of my time hunting deep into the lands bordering the red sands. I found myself far from my usual territory, as there was no game to be found nearby. High upon the mountain, above the slowly recovering terrain, there is a forest, thick with young growth. I chanced upon a buck, an old and noble beast; much like myself. The deer ran left, then right, changing direction randomly to throw me off its scent. But I was determined that my tribe would have meat. Like an impetuous youth, I sprung aloft for the kill, my impatience causing me to underestimate the deer's speed. Thus, my landing was off. Instead of enjoying my fill of meat, I found my body impaled upon a broken branch, hanging several feet above the ground. What was worse, I was seriously injured; rapidly losing blood, and unable to free myself. I resigned myself to death, and even turned to Diauna, Our Lady of the Forest, in hopes that she would release me from the pain and take me into her arms."

Gar sighed melodramatically, took a long drink from his carafe and then continued his story--- after he was certain everyone listening was once again, hanging onto every word he spoke. *"But my lady ignored my pleas; choosing instead to leave me to my tribulations. She wasn't yet ready for my wayward son to take my place on the hunter's path. Thankfully, we Gynarks are a hardy folk, and difficult to kill. Instead of hunting in the fields and forest of Diauna, after a few days of inept writhing, the weight of my body broke the branch away from the tree. I crawled away, still impaled, but mobile now; looking for a safe spot to heal. The lady must have guided me, for I stumbled upon an overgrown game trail. Half blinded by pain and fever, I followed it until it opened up into a red valley where the ruins of a burnt-out temple stood; one lone tower standing untouched. At one time it must have been beautiful; keeping watch over the scattered remains of the bones nearby. But it was a refuge for me, a place where I could die in peace. I lay inside for over a week, my body healing just enough to prevent the death I so desired."* Gar seemed pensive, like he was remembering something he wasn't ready to share. He shifted a bit, and then he continued with his story.

"In time my faith failed me--- and I came to curse my Lady Diauna, not understanding why she would ignore my pleas. I begged for release from my suffering. However, the fates had woven a different web for me. As I lay upon my deathbed, an Aarakocra appeared. The noble warrior cared for me, removing the stick that prevented me from fully healing. He gave me food and water and in time we became friends. He told me about his family, his life, and travels. He also showed me something that

I will never forget. It was an unusually carved stone--- he called it shuet-ka. When it was time for us to leave the hidden valley, he left the stone behind hidden somewhere in the ancient temple, in a location known only to him. I never saw him again."

Satisfied that his tale had evoked the proper response from the young people gathered around his feet, Gar stretched again, wiggling his body a little closer to the warm fire. *"I now believe Malaam, not Diauna, was the hand guiding me to the valley. And it is his will that guided me here, to tell you, my story."*

There was a soft round of applause and many murmurs of appreciation before many of the listeners wandered off into the darkness.

Brinn sat and talked with the old Gynark for a while before rejoining us. Then the old Gynark wandered off toward his tent and we headed back to the compound.

CHAPTER 11

Mekiva was grinning. "Well, that was interesting. It's nothing like I expected, but I'm glad I could hear him speak."

"There are many unusual customs among the desert, both good and bad, but the good outnumber the many. Take blood feuds, for example." Brinn was happy to have something to talk about on the ride home. Moth had something earlier that was eating at his conscious, and he was glad to have anything to take his mind off his comment.

"You mean keep fighting until one is dead?"

"That's the normal chain of events. But not always in the desert. Say the maiden daughter sees a young man who does not know her father and has no reason to approach him. She might have her father declare a blood feud because the son embarrassed the maiden before her friends. The father of the young man who injured the young maiden knows his son has done nothing to bring on a blood feud. So, he gives notice that he wishes to bring the blood feud to an end."

The women were enjoying the story, but none of the men seemed to care about anything Brinn was talking about. Not that Brinn cared either way. It was a true story, and one of the few that had not involved Raffi and Keeyun. He hated riding in silence because his mind went places, he didn't like when he had time to think. He was going to finish his story and they could ignore him if they liked. "They set a time for the father and son to come together in the maiden's tent who had been offended. That's when the crazy starts. First the maiden walks through the room and ignores the young man in front of witnesses, restoring her honor. After she leaves the room, the boy's father bares his sword and, after turning to all four directions, he draws a circle on the sandy floor, calling upon Mesbah and Rheaaz to bear witness."

Brinn finally got the attention of the four men. He wasn't certain if it was the Gods or the sword, but something drew them back to the story.

"The ceremony is still not complete. The girl's father takes his knife and cuts a shred of cloth from the of side of the tent, then rubs a handful of ashes from the hearth into the materiel and throws it into the circle in the sand. Then he takes his sword in hand and walks around the circle, striking the line seven times along the way with his naked sword. When the father completes the circle, the young man leaps into the circle, and cries aloud: *I take the dishonor upon me!*"

"So does the father curse the young man or call a demon to carry him away?"

"Mekiva thinks magic is the answer to every problem."

"Not every problem, but it tends to scare off a lot of future ones," she replied. "That looks like rain. And it's heading this way."

Brinn studied the clouds. They were very close and growing closer by the minute. It was a pleasant surprise. The upper wind currents rarely pushed anything in this direction. At the rate it was moving, it would catch them about a half mile from home. "Looks like we might get wet. Should we hurry and try to beat it or enjoy the cool rain?"

No one wanted to hurry. The unexpected shower offered a little relief from the oppressive days of summer heat. Brinn hoped it might signal a change in the weather patterns, a chance that the late summer drought might relinquish its hold on the sunbaked wasteland. There was no shortage of water now, but people who lived their lives in the arid country knew how fast that could change. The sky cleared quickly, with occasional puffs of cottony white, however the distant rumblings in the west offered the welcome possibility of more relief several candlemarks into the future.

They were all still damp when they reached the compound, but no one was complaining.

Nala had outdone herself for dinner that evening. The cook had prepared a native dish of roasted game hens stuffed with wild rice, dates, and roasted cashew nuts. There were also baked squash and kava beams, and a sweet brown bread made from the fruit of a local tree. The men ate a spread of roasted locusts and goat cheese on the bread, but Mekiva and Gwen passed on the traditional desert treat.

Nala had asked two of the young men that lived in the compound to play a few songs while they ate dinner. In between the loud thumping of a darbouka drum and the plaintive twanging of an oddly shaped, stringed instrument, there was little opportunity to talk. Mekiva enjoyed the wooden flute the third man played and would have been happy to do without the other two instruments.

After dinner they moved out to the patio where the men played cards with their host, drinking cups of the strong kafka and smoking their pipes while the woman enjoyed tiny tea cakes drizzled with honey and fruit juice.

Nala allowed them a candlemark to enjoy their game before she reminded him that were other visitors in the house.

Brinn apologized and asked what the women might enjoy.

"I don't know about the rest, but I would like to hear the end of the story." Gwen hated the way men would drop one thing and start another without warning. She was curious about how the romance ended.

Brinn called for wine, and Nyla rushed to bring glasses for everyone. She also ordered cheese, figs and grapes, and a tray of tiny tarts still warm from the ovens. Once everyone had a glass in hand, Brinn went back to his story.

"And then there is peace." Brinn raised his glass in a salute and then drained about half, before leaning back against one of the oversized pillows.

"Wait a minute. That's it. That's the way the blood feud ended. No curse, no one dies? Nothing?"

Nyla laughed. "There's always more to the story. Though usually in the background, the women have much power in the tribes. We watch the unmarried maidens and keep them away from eligible young men. For if a maiden says before witnesses: 'I would have such a man as Sayed for my husband,' Sayed must bond with her lest she be shamed before the members of the tribe. That didn't happen with Amir. During the ceremony, Amir took the dishonor upon himself. Now it was up to him to figure out a way to win his bride."

Jaxx was skeptical. "Seems like a crazy way to get a woman's attention. First ignore her and then when she gets upset, he has to turn around and figure out a way to get her to accept him."

Von was glad Mekiva didn't expect him to behave in that manner. He winced when she replied, "That's because the only women you spend any time with are the coin girls at the local tavern."

"Yeah, and I don't have to talk to them," Jaxx added. "I just flash a few coins and they drag me toward the back rooms."

Gwen turned to Brinn and said, "I'm still not sure why you had to be involved. There was nothing to judge."

"That comes later in the story. First, the young man has to get his intended to declare she wants him. That's not always easy to do. She may prefer to find a different man. Now that he has made her availability public, she could have a bigger pool to choose from."

"That explains why only the bonded men attend the feasts. Too many single women."

Nyla laughed again. "It doesn't matter if the man is bonded. If he has less than four wives, it is good that he takes another. If he has four, then he should divorce one that has not produced sons, or is too old to bear, and bond with the maiden who has chosen him, as she will bear him many children."

All the men turned to look at Brinn.

"Don't look at me that way. Nyla is all the wife I need. One family is all I can handle."

I bet. Raffi was pleased to see that Nyla had recovered her pre-pregnancy figure and was once again the mischievous young thief he remembered. She was enjoying playing the shy, devoted wife and mother. He didn't have the heart to ruin her fun.

"So how did he finally catch her attention?" Jaxx asked.

"He waited until dark and stole all the man's camels."

"What in the seven Hels does that have to do with wooing a woman?" Von wondered if Brinn was making the story up as he spoke.

"I used to wonder about that myself, thinking there was no way to enforce my authority over unruly tribes that refuse to release the old ways. Plus, they continue to travel from oasis to oasis, making it almost impossible to find them if a complaint it brought. Then I got this case, and it became clear."

They all looked at him, clearly unsure how he could see an obvious answer to the convoluted story.

"I have to be missing something. They just steal a camel and that means what?"

Gwen giggled at the confused look on Mekiva's face.

"Do they expect you to travel through the borderlands and look for them?"

Brinn laughed. "I still do not know the answer to that question. They eventually turn up and I make my decision."

Brinn continued his story. "Once the blood feud is settled, it's still not over. You would think they would understand stealing a man's camels is illegal. But it always happens the same way. Then the owner of the camels comes to my gate and asks to be heard. I listen to his complaint, and then I ride out alone or with Moth through the desert until I locate the camp of the camel thief. It's usually easy to locate his tent, as he keeps the new camels close by, in plain view. We make as much noise as possible as we dismount and approach the tent. As though he expected me, the father throws open the door and bids me to enter. Then what does the lord of the tent do? He makes kafka and treats me as an honored guest. But when we have drunk the coffee, I have to place money by the hearth, saying, 'Take this coin.'"

"So, you literally pay for anything you eat or drink?" This surprised Jaxx, as he could not imagine Mussa accepting payment for his hospitality.

"Ceremony is very important to these people. Everything has to happen in the correct manner. Or it could insult one or the other party. Then we depart, leaving orders that the son must appear at the homestead in half a moon cycle with the camels. The robber gathers together the camels he has taken and brings them back, all except one. As Judge, I have to ask the owner if all of his camels are there. He says no, there should be nine, but there are only eight. I then ask him, what is the value of the missing camel?"

"Three silvers."

"I say to the thief, *Pay him three silvers*. He

pays him, and they hug. Then they both leave as friends to plan the wedding. I can't understand it, but it's been how they have handled it for hundreds of cycles."

Jaxx found a spot on the wall he could stare at and avoid being pulled into the conversation. He had heard the story years ago being told by a different man, but it was essentially the same tale. He turned to Von, "You sure you don't want to be involved in the planning?"

Von shook his head and lay back on the divan.

Jaxx shrugged and walked over to Brinn. "We need to make some decisions about the search. You mentioned you had a map?" He wanted a chance to study the route. There were things they needed to discuss. They also needed to go into town and order supplies. Brinn had plenty of horses, so that would not be a problem. They needed to purchase a couple of pack animals, also saddles and other tack.

Von had mentioned he wanted to buy some new clothes and a new pair of boots. The leather on his was so thin he could feel every stone. He said nothing for a while, content to listen to the others argue back and forth.

Von stretched out on the divan and closed his eyes. Jaxx could handle it. There was nothing that required his input. Lately, when he said or did things on impulse, it made matter worse. He would rather take a nap.

He was sound asleep when the Nyla returned with the map a few minutes later.

Brinn's map collection would be the envy

of many librarians. Mekiva couldn't hear what they were discussing, but it was clear from the wild gestures and various facial expressions there was some disagreement involved. The men were standing around the table, on which they had stretched a large map of the area. Every so often, one of them would point at a location on the map, make a comment, and the others would either nod silently or the crazy arguing would start up again.

"Should we interrupt?" Mekiva wasn't sure she wanted to get involved, but she was not good at waiting patiently to be invited to join a conversation.

"Nothing they are talking about matters. It will matter even less in few minutes." She pointed and Mekiva's face lit up. It was hard to tell with Gwen. Only her eyes showed, and they had narrowed into the contented cat slits she favored.

The three women ignored their deliberation, contenting themselves with the contents of two crystal decanters filled with golden amber liquid of the dozen or so arrayed upon the top of a carved wooden buffet. The brandy was excellent. By the time they finished the first decanter, the men had become unimportant. By halfway through the second, they were nonexistent.

CHAPTER 12

Von pulled the gelding back into line behind Jaxx with a sign. Mekiva was still not talking to him. He did not know what he had done to make her slap him. The purple and tan bruise on his face was proof that it must have angered her quite a bit. He must have deserved it, since no one was teasing him about getting slapped. It had surprised him to see the discoloration when he woke that morning, however the women had made it crystal clear he'd stepped over a line, one that he was going to regret crossing for some time.

Mekiva had stood there staring at him for several moments when he entered the dining area that morning, before turning and walking away without saying a word. Gwen's eyes never left him as he filled his plate. The others did their best to avoid making eye contact. He hid his discomfort behind a sardonic expression as he finished his breakfast. Once he cleared his plate, he poured himself another cup of Kafka, added a liberal amount of thick cream and honey, and waited. Whatever he had done, it had complicated things in a way he wasn't sure he could fix. Especially, since he had no idea what the Hel he had done.

Market day in every town was insane, with farmers hawking farm fresh milk, eggs and produce, butchers claiming they have the choicest, most tender meats, and artisans displaying their wares in every conceivable manner. The raucous clamor was all to get the attention of the hundreds of browsers making their way up and down each aisle. Street vendors proffered freshly cooked delicacies alongside open aired eateries operated by neighborhood first-wife's hoping to supplement the family income with a home cooked specialty. The air was full of amazing odors. Some, like fresh bread baking she could easily identify, others made her realize how hungry she was.

Mekiva sighed. They had rushed breakfast that morning. Her empty stomach released another irritated groan in response to the fragrant aroma of chokeberry hand pies frying in hot grease. It was becoming difficult to ignore its noisy hints. Perhaps it was time to eat the mid-day meal? She reminded the others it had been several candlemarks since they had eaten breakfast.

Hearing a rustling near her foot, she glanced down, spotting a skinny gray rat foraging for his dinner. The sight of the hungry rodent searching among the rubbish was oddly comforting. Rats were the same everywhere, it seemed. She tried to force her lips into a pleasant neutrality, but the expression she managed was a more sardonic smirk.

How does one prepare for a journey to the doorway of Ligazra's Nine Realms? Everyone had their own list of necessities. The men were concentrating on food and other supplies. They would not sell the things she needed in a regular store. Spell components for battles could be difficult to get. Most likely, they would have to fight their way across the borderlands. The memory of the winged demons was forefront in everyone's mind. If they survived to reach the Red Zone, they would walk in blind. No one had a clear idea what they would face when they arrived. With only a few hints as to where they needed to go, they would have to prepare for the worst and hope it never happened.

She had her own list of supplies to locate, and there was only one store intown. It was doubtful they would carry many of the things she needed.

At least the storefront was in a large block building instead of the more common tent. Inside of the shop was neat and organized. Once inside, they followed a clearly defined path that threaded a maze of narrow aisles between boxes and piles set on colorful blankets. Along one side of the building were piles of harness, saddle blankets and other animals care supplies. Crates of nails, stacks of canvas, and coils of rope lined another wall. Study wood tables were piled with woven wool blankets, knitted hats and gloves, pots and pans, and an assortment of riding gear. Besides the traditional dry goods, the owner specialized in food designed to survive a long journey, smoked and salted meats and fish, wheels of cheese, fresh and dried fruits and vegetables, and sacks of cornmeal and brown flour.

Two clerks were busy with a customer, one hastily scribbling note in a ledger and the second pulling and packing the purchase for delivery. Both looked up and nodded as they entered, but neither seemed surprised when Brinn walked directly to the rear of the store. They inspected the various goods inside the building, selecting not only the few suggested by Sayed but many chosen by Brinn. The last purchase was the most important, saddles to replace the ones left behind.

"Saddles are no problem. A mule, alas, is not available. However, I have a pair of Oryx and several camels." He smiled. "You might consider goats. They can carry a load and provide a meal if needed."

"We would like to see what you have available."

He nodded. "Colo," he called out, and a tall, blond-bearded man opened a flap in the store's back wall. Unlike the bandy legs common to the desert, this man walked with the spring of someone long familiar with extended trails afoot. The colorful headwear of the desert tribes prevented Von from seeing if the hair on his head was as light as his beard, but the skin around the pale blue eyes had showed the weathered wrinkles brought on by the blistering sun.

He stopped behind Sayed and did not speak, waiting instead for instructions.

Considering how different his appearance was from the other men, the subtle nameless distrust of strangers surprised Von. His dislike was as clear as the almost colorless lightness of the eyes that fixated upon him.

"They will need five saddles. The magistrate is providing the horses. And something to carry their purchases."

Colo accepted this with an almost imperceptible nod. Shadowed eyes searched and probed each face for latent threats hidden behind smiles. It was the keen intelligence of a man who educated by life, not an implied distrust in the young mean at present. "I will bring the string." Then he turned his back and walked away.

Sayed picked out five of the larger goats and the only available camels. It surprised the storekeeper when Brinn also purchased the Oryx. Many were uncomfortable around the omnivorous pack animals, preferring something that was happy with a diet of fresh plants and did not snap up anything small enough for a meal that crossed their path. The oversized birds had wide splayed feet that enabled them to cross the loose sand without sinking. They were as fast and sometimes faster than a horse and could carry more weight.

While Brinn discussed their needs with the owner, everyone else scattered throughout the store. Jaxx and Raffi wanted boots. They were perched atop wooden boxes, trying on the new and used stock, hoping to find something big enough to fit their feet. There was also an assortment of used leathers and mail. Not a big choice, but anything was better than none.

The girls were more interested in replacing their worn-out clothing. He had a decent supply, but they designed most to be worn by men. That was fine with the girls. They preferred to dress similarly. However, there were certain items a man did not need, and he did not carry.

Mekiva finally asked if there was anyone in town that supplied mage reagents. The clerk appeared surprised but had a ready answer, directing her to a tent area just west of the town. "Ask for Hossein. Most know his tent. You can purchase your spell components there."

After informing Brinn of their destination,

the girls hurried away to find Hossein. They had no trouble locating the vale behind the livery stable. Finding Hossein was going to be harder. The clerk ha mentioned Hossein's tent had faded to a dull brown with a blue striped awning outside. From where they were standing, almost all the tents fit that description. Farther down the primary thoroughfare were brightly colored tents that appeared to be much larger than most of the faded brown ones.

Gathered before the largest tent were several horses, all standing free, with bridles thrown over their heads so the reins trailed on the ground. Lounging on overstuffed cushions just inside the open front were a trio of lanky desert men. Some wore leather pants, but most wore the traditional loose woven tunics and trousers seen so often in the desert. Around their waists all wore thick leather belts with sharp curved blades hanging in ornate silver decorated scabbards.

The two women walked through the horses, noticing that none had bits to prevent them from enjoying the hay they were eating. Mekiva waited until one man looked their way, then asked which tent belonged to Hossein.

His eyes went from her to Gwen, identifying her as a Shii healer, and back to her face before addressing Mekiva. He spit a brown stream of tobacco into a brass cuspidor and grinned, displaying stained yet good teeth. "Hossein's tent is the third one on the right after you pass the goat traders. He should everything you will need. He might even have a few items to tempt the honored healer. It's been a few days since we've seen a mage heading that way, so he should have a well-stocked cabinet. I saw Magda making a delivery this morning."

The two women stood at the entrance of the tent and waited to be invited inside. The main room of the tent was open. Near the back was a short-legged table around which several men leaned on against desert saddles: playing cards. A wizened old man struggled to his feet and took a few steps closer to the strangers. His long face had a roguish cast, but his smile was welcoming. The rather plain face was heavily lined, not with age, but with the weathered look found on so many of the desert inhabitants. His eyes were of the same golden-brown hue yet burning with little fiery flecks in their depths. He appeared short of stature because of a curvature of the spine, but as he straightened up, it was clear he would have been tall before old age twisted the bones out of line.

Several of the loungers left as Mekiva engaged the old man in conversation, introducing herself, and explaining her needs. Hossein invited them into the back room, where he kept most of his special trade goods. They inspected the various items, selecting not only the usual spell components, but quite a few suggested by Hossein. Gwen surprised her with several of her suggestions. She had never considered the combinations the quiet Shii-Lakka healer suggested, but they all made sense. Within minutes, they had secured everything Mekiva wanted, and all the items Gwen had suggested, and still had coin left over. Mekiva even purchased a special belt made with multiple small compartments and pouches attached to hold the various components. The belt would allow her to carry more of the spell components with her at all times, ensuring they would be ready at hand in an emergency.

They were almost back at the edge of the tent town when Gwen spotted twin kids gamboling around their mother. The tiny goats couldn't have been more than a week or two old. Both girls dropped to their knees to cuddle the tiny goats. Finally, Mekiva rose with a sigh and gestured for Gwen to do the same. "Let's hurry back before they get worried and come looking for us. I wouldn't want anyone to get hurt because we stopped to play with some baby goats."

In less than a candlemark, the men had secured their supplies. Most fit inside the wagon and Sayed headed for the compound, the Oryx pair plodded along, satisfied to be moving to a different location as long as there was sufficient water nearby. They had surprised the storekeeper when Raffi hitched up the Oryx. He had worked around the omnivorous pack animals in the past and knew their habits. The oversized birds were not his first choice, but he could see why Brinn had bought them. Sayed had the team well in hand and Colo would deliver the remaining animals to the compound.

They watched as the wagon passed out of sight, then decided they could all use a hot meal.

That's when Von noticed the girls were not back. "Should we look for them?"

"No. They should be back soon. They probably stopped and asked Nyla's father for directions. Even if they didn't, he would know who they were and make sure no one bothered them."

Moth nodded. "I can see them now. They just passed the livery stable. They seem to be in a good mood. They must have found everything they needed."

"Let's head down toward the tavern. If we start walking that way, we should arrive about the same time. I don't know about you, but I could use a drink."

Lilliana could see the group clearly as they approached the tavern. It was the only one in town and the last place she expected to see them. She could not afford to be recognized. Von and Jaxx would never believe she just 'happened to appear' in this no name village after working in the trading post where they were forced into slavery. Moth and Brinn would wonder why she showed up in towns so far apart, especially wearing the same outfit. If she were spotted, she would have to scrap this identity. This was aggravating after she had spent so much time and effort establishing it. They must have been shopping because several carried packages. Drasst.

Other than Brinn, all the men were now dressed in studded leather and odds and end of armor. Nothing matched, but that was to be expected when buying used. Two of them wore pale, hooded cloaks. Mercenaries liked them because they cover the body from chest to ankle and were heavy enough to keep thorns away when walking. The packages they carried would include the tunic and pants they had been wearing, as well as any new purchases. She sat back and evaluated them as a stranger might.

Von now carried a bow. The black leather armor accented his trim build, showing off his muscular build. Her view was blocked by an evergreen and when he stepped into sight on the other side, he had tossed back his hood. Someone had trimmed that wavy brown hair. The fresh cut drew attention to his exceptionally handsome face. That scar might discourage a few admirers, but that was balanced by the roguish appearance added by the leather patch that covered one eye.

Jaxx was of average height for a Duaar, which meant he was taller than everyone except Raffi. He was stockier and more heavily muscled. Unlike Von, his muscular build could not easily be hidden, even by the cloak he was wearing. He smiled as he walked along and seemed to be interested in everything in the stores they passed by. That easy going manner was deceptive. He was harder to get a grasp on than either of the other men.

Two women joined them, but it was clear they were not the usual type of doxies seen plying their trade in seedy taverns. The young mage scared her. That was difficult to admit since she could not recall a woman affecting her before. She radiated power. If she survived long enough to learn how to control it, there would not be many stronger mages, male or female. The young Shi'i-lakka was a mystery, but nothing she needed to concern herself with.

She wondered where the others were. Perhaps inside the tavern, waiting. Another reason she needed to cut her foray short and head for home. She shifted her weight to move back away from the edge, then winced as a chunk of broken tile slid off the roof.

The tile falling from the top of the building crashed to the ground before she could grab it, barely missing the burly Duaar, who stepped to the side just in time. The others watched and laughed.

As nimble as a cat, she leaned forward, trying to get a better look at him.

Raffiel looked up as the tile hit and noticed her for the first time. He cocked his head and allowed the tiniest lift of his lips. As if on cue, the rest of them looked up directly at Lilliana. When Raffi moved, it was liquid, flowing effortlessly into action. In less than a heartbeat, he was on the roof and had her by the throat and pinned to the rocky wall.

"What do we have here?" he crowed. An angel? Or what he figured an angel would look like if one dared get close enough to where he could make out their features. Of course, with his luck, it was more likely she was a demon. Or a djinn. When he threw back her veil, he could see she was a stranger. Dusky skin as soft as the down on an eider duck, narrow braided dreadlocks to her waist, mesmerizing eyes with just a hint of a tilt, lush red lips and a tongue that could flay the skin off a man faster than a sandstorm. He could not resist stealing a kiss.

Lilliana shoved him away and shifted her scarf so that her face was hidden. Then she vanished into the shadows. Laughter followed her until they had moved toward the tavern nearby.

It had been close... too close. One slipup like that and it would be over. Moth would recognize her if he got a glimpse of her face. He would tell Brinn she was in town, and it would all be over. They would start hunting and not stop until they cornered their prey. She needed to get out-of-town now. It was going to be close, but it wasn't the first time. There was a blurring, and then a large grey wolf trotted into the darkness, leaving a pile of discarded clothing lying in the shadows. Once it reached the outskirts of town, it broke into a run, cutting across the fields as it loped across the distant farmland.

Moth listened to Raffi explain about the exotic woman and the kiss he'd stolen. There was something about the way he described her that sounded familiar. Brinn was leaning against the bar, talking to the barkeep, and not really paying much attention to Raffi's story. Moth couldn't let the idea go. Had he ever run into her before? He made a mental note to ask Keeyun about her when he got home. Once again, he wished Key had come with them. His cousin had the best memory of faces he'd ever known. If they had ever crossed paths, Keeyun would remember where and when it was.

The woman slipped from his mind as a servant began placing multiple platters of food on the table. A second servant placed bowls of steaming water and small hand towels before each person. He could see two more waiting to unload their trays. The fresh hummus was seasoned perfectly, and accompanied by triangles of thin flatbread, cheese, and olives. There was a large platter stacked with wooden skewers of meat, seasoned and grilled with fresh root vegetables and mushrooms. A smaller platter held steamed pork dumplings. The last bowl was his favorite, an old-style country stew.

Jaxx and Von were already eating. Bashful yet flirtatious; the attractive young women flitted by Von and Jaxx with downcast eyes and a shy smile, but no words. She ignored the girls. Von pondered over Brinn's words about claiming husbands while he ate, wondering if it pertained to women who worked in taverns, too? Was it worth the risk?

Despite the way the boys were digging in, the two girls hesitated. The last time Jaxx had been this excited over food, they had ended up with some type of pickled lizard in a sour cream sauce.

"Go on," Jaxx said. "Try it. You will like it." He tore off a chunk of the warm bread and used it to scoop up a small portion from the steaming bowl.

Gwen tasted it tentatively, then ate with relish. He was right. The lightly spiced stew of chicken and vegetables was delicious. The rich multi grain bread had just come from the oven. She did not know what kind of meat was on the skewers, but it was tender, and they cooked the vegetables to perfection. Even the beer was good, bold but nutty, with a hint of something fruity. Maybe orange? Whatever it was, it was definitely not a sour lizard.

After their meal, they sat sipping their beers and talking while Moth and Brinn played darts and Raffi flirted with one of the serving maids.

Von had noticed an unfamiliar man sitting in the main section of the tavern with his back to a wall, at a table perfectly positioned to observe anyone entering or leaving the building. His eyes were constantly shifting, never resting on one spot for more than a moment. He glanced up anytime someone entered the restaurant, then he quickly shifted his attention away to keep from drawing their attention. If Brinn or Moth were worried about him, neither man showed it. It was hard to tell if Raffi noticed him. He would show no interest in the man until he put a blade to his throat.

The first sun was setting as they began the short ride back to the compound. Most everyone rode in silence, but Von had indulged in enough beer to loosen his tongue. Jaxx tried to warn him he was venturing into dangerous territory.

"Unless you want your right eye to mirror your left, I suggest you watch your words around Mekiva."

Von was not in the mood to listen. Jaxx decided he deserved what he got and rode up to ride beside Moth and Brinn. Mekiva's face was taut, and her voice has risen to a shrill pitch. Gwen allowed her mare to drop back behind them. If Mekiva began casting spells, she wanted to be outside the range... just in case.

Von had decided Mekiva could learn more about a woman's place in life from the tribeswomen. He seemed oblivious to her growing anger.

"I don't see the comparison," she replied.

Von paused, thinking about how he should say what he was thinking. "It is unusual to find a woman of so many words; but you must learn to carefully choose the words you speak. Words carry weight."

"Interesting that you should see it that way."

"That's what I meant. You don't realize what you are saying."

"And you want me to behave more like you?"

"No. Perhaps you should talk to Nyla. I am sure she would be happy to advise you."

"Perhaps." Mekiva replied. Nyla would likely advise her to kick him in the testicles or, if angered, cut them off and shove them in his mouth.

Von's eyes hardened. "It is to be expected, you not having parents around to advise you on the streets of Cabrell."

Mekiva didn't reply. Not for the first time, she

realized Von had selective memory. She had ever explained that the waif he had played with was anything more than an indigent farm girl. She could easily imagine the look on her father's face when she introduced them. He was such a prick about social responsibility. She sighed, remembering their last conversation...

Mekiva slammed the heavy oaken door behind her as she entered her father's study for the fourth time that morning; wincing from the sound of glass striking stone as the wind from the door's movement blew a delicate figurine off a nearby table. Her father, a portly man of middle years, reacted with a sigh and a slight frown; but only for a moment--- before he once again displayed a determined, stony facade. Much as he loved his daughter, enough was enough. He had made up his mind; no argument she presented, however logical, would sway his decision. Now all he had to do was survive long enough to tell her about it.

"I refuse to discuss the matter any longer", he announced before she had a chance to offer yet another of her seemingly unlimited arguments. "You will obey me. I have a reputation to uphold. Rumors of my only daughter being spotted in some of the most disreputable dives in the city cannot continue. I will no longer tolerate your irresponsible behavior. The arrangements have been made. Your trunks have been packed and loaded onto the carriage. Raven Hurst Academy has an excellent reputation; and I have the chancellors guarantee you will return to me a cultured, elegant young woman with manners more suited to your position as

my daughter." Duke Hullthorne couldn't help feeling a brief twinge of guilt as he noticed his beloved daughter struggle to keep the tears from escaping her now brimming eyes. And she had such lovely green eyes. How someone could be so beautiful on the outside and so full of anger on the inside, he would never understand. While he had hoped for a son, he had never regretted his precious daughter, even when her dear mother succumbed to the wasting disease so soon after her birth. Maybe it was his fault? He had refused to remarry despite the advice of so many of his councilors. Mekiva could have used the influence of a female hand in her upbringing. She was a fighter, headstrong, and determined to experience life to its fullest, much as he had been at her age, maybe too much like he had been. Women of her social standing were expected to be decorative, marry well, and produce as many heirs as possible for her husband. But what man would want a hellion for a wife? That Mekiva was possibly the most intelligent young person of his acquaintance; well, that was probably more a detriment than a benefit. She was always looking for answers, many of which led her into situations she would have been better served staying far away from. She was also secretive, something he had discovered accidentally when he had stumbled into one of her training sessions down at the stable. That she had hired a weapons master without his knowledge was humiliating enough, that she had been taking lessons for several years without him knowing, was beyond belief. Oh Well, she would forgive him eventually. Sighing deeply, he grasped Mekiva by the arm and determination glaring in his eyes, began walking toward the manor's main doors, dragging his loudly protesting daughter with him. Upon arriving at the exit, he motioned for the doorman to maintain a safe distance as he pulled the kicking and screaming young duchess toward the open carriage door. "I realize you believe you hate me right now, but after you have thought about it for a while, you will understand I am doing this for your own good. Now get into the carriage!" He thrust the desperately struggling girl inside and slammed the door shut behind her. "Don't stop until you reach Raven Hurst", he shouted as the reins master whipped the horses into an immediate trot. The pale faced driver saluted with a wave of his whip before returning once more to the job before him. The lady Mekiva had ways of making people suffer when she felt betrayed; and she would consider this the ultimate betrayal. It would be several candlemarks before he could take a break, and he wanted to deliver his package and be on the way back home by nightfall. And as far away from the rampaging noblewoman as possible...

The memory made Mekiva grin. One day soon, she needed to have a serious discussion with Von about a few tiny misunderstandings. Soon, but not today.

CHAPTER 13

"Will that be enough water to take us there and back?" Von counted the waterskins and barrels. It did not appear to be enough for three men, much less the entire party. Sayed might be the acknowledged expert on desert travel, but his brief experience in the bane lands had burnt a permanent reminder into his conscious mind.

Sayed nodded. "We will travel from oasis to oasis as much as possible. We may not make as many leagues as we would walking a straight line, but we will not die of thirst along the way."

Brinn tied the last bag of grain to the lead goat. Every animal carried several packs of food and at least one bola of water. He would never have thought about using his future dinner to carry necessities; however, Sayed had explained that it was common practice among his people. Spreading the water out among several animals was also a good idea. If they lost one, they could continue to the next oasis or well.

"What if we arrive and the owners will not allow us to fill our skins?" Mekiva asked.

"To welcome a traveler as a guest is the unwritten law of the desert. No desert tribe would refuse you or your animal a drink if it meant endangering your life. But they would allow no one to enter their tribal land by force to take their water or try to supplant them and risk their families or their stock. Why, even the Gynarks respect desert law! All but Alegi!"

"Alegi?" Von vaguely remembered hearing someone mention that name when they stayed in the tent city of Sayed's tribe.

"An outlaw, a thief. A castoff, not even the Gynarks wanted. Alegi's men steal the blood of our life—water—our oasis. God's gift to the desert! Someone must wipe out the scourge to my people."

"Who is this Alegi? If he's that bad, why haven't the men of your tribe killed him?"

Brinn turned away from the goats and answered Von's question. "When he was a young Gynark chieftain, I heard stories of how he was driven from his mother's band after she took up with another male. With no father, he would not be welcome once he started eyeing the unmated females. Word is, he struck out on his own and started raiding travelers' camps, gathered a few outlaws. Now he has a powerful band of his own. His band of young bucks has been causing a lot of problems in the area. Most are younger sons of the various tribes, cast out to prevent fighting inside the camps."

"Gynarks cast out younger sons?"

"To preserve the safety of the tribe, yes. No one wants the possibility of a split over who should lead the tribe after the old chieftain dies."

"But what about him is so different?"

"Most Gynarks are thieves, but Alegi is worse than most. He surrounded himself with the worst he could find. They travel the bane lands and the border country, moving constantly to prevent anyone from locating their encampment. Under the cover of the darkness, they search for targets, then they are in and out before anyone realizes they are there. It's difficult to admit the possibility that the little vermin have been here in our midst, and we didn't realize they were around. There's no telling how often they slipped in and out without us noticing them."

"I thought there was a treaty. I haven't heard of any problems with the Gynark tribes in several years."

"The treaty is the problem. The young pups are grown now and bored. There is no way for them to establish themselves as adults. No war to fight and gain honor. Unless they are the oldest son of a wealthy chieftain, there is little prospect to gain the prestige and wealth needed to attract wives. It was only a matter of time before they rebelled and went back to the old ways. Alegi is smart and educated, a dangerous combination. He had no help to win them over. His band has grown from a handful of castoffs into a large and powerful organization. Now he is consolidating his power by eliminating the smaller tribal chiefs. He is also trying to claim traditional tribal lands, and the water rights for Gynarks only."

"Do you think the group we saw was part of Alegi's rogue band of young males?"

"Most likely they are part of Alegi's band. He would consider us a tempting target."

"So, there's nothing we can do about it?"

"We can kill him. That will usually stop the theft." His gaze grew fixed, steely, certain. "The band steals a few goats, kills a sheep or a cow here and there. But most of the tribesmen are more upset about the oasis. With no way to stop the theft, it's difficult for the tribe to spend any length of time in one spot. Yet the fear that there will be no oasis remaining, just a dry pool when they return, keeps the tribe nearby. They can't follow the trade routes, so money is tight. They often gave the old and sickly to the desert."

"You mean..."

"Yes. They leave them to die alone. It's a harsh life. Nomads have to be alert at all times, not only for the winged demons, but they also have to watch for Alegi's Gynark raiders."

"Well... at least we have a few days before we need to start setting picket lines and guard. There are two tribes camping along the route we are taking. Enjoy it while it lasts."

CHAPTER 14

The devastated land called by natives, the Gates of Hel, stretched in roughly a square between a mountain range on the eastern edge and the border-lands that followed the other three sides. On most maps of the area, the mapmakers commonly labeled it the Red Zone. It got its name from the reddish tint of the sand, a remnant of the magic misfire that destroyed the area. It was approximately fifty square leagues of barren, waterless land, unmercifully scorched and burned by a pair of merciless suns.

Slowly, over the years, life had moved back into the borderlands, especially near the sparsely scattered waterholes and natural wells. It was only in the last decade that they had found life inside the apex of destruction. He did not know why all the signs pointed to the ruins in the center of the destruction as the location of his family treasure. The odds were against him or anyone else finding anything worth the expense of the caravan. Yet here they were, the day's ride from Brinn's home and three times that much to cover.

Sayed was confident they would have enough water to make it to the center of the bane lands. "There is a well near to the edge of the zone," Sayed said. "It's deep and has always provided water. There are no plants living nearby, but we should be able to secure water to refill the containers before entering the worst of the Bane."

"Is it marked? I looked on the map and nothing shows." He unfolded the map and Sayed pointed out where they were and several other landmarks that did not show on Brinn's map.

Von had little he could add to the conversation, so he sharpened his sword instead. It was something he should have done before leaving Brinn's homestead. One day, he hoped to have a place of his own. Maybe even a few children. Walking up in bed next to Mekiva didn't sound half bad.

It surprised him by how much he missed the bed in his room back at Brinn's place. He had never been a fan of Inn's, but the farm was different. Homey. It had been a long time since he felt that way. The sand made a decent bed. Von had rolled up his extra clothes in a wool blanket and strapped it tightly to the back of the saddle. Along with the cloak and the desert robes, he would need the thick blanket to stay warm. It cooled off quickly in the desert. They all wore basic leather armor. It was some protection, but not what he would choose to wear into battle. The surviving leather was loose. No one was as heavy after seven cycles underground without enough food. Like children with toys, they had dug through the trade-ins and bought anything that came close to fitting from the trader. Even with the additional coverage the armor offered, a top-notch archer could take him out easily. Even a rank-and-file bowman could get lucky. There was still plenty of open skin to target.

He used a little of his water to moisten a

strip of cloth to clean the sand from the horses' eyes and mouth before giving them a few sips of the warm water.

"If it's this hot here, I wonder what the Red Zone will be like." Von licked his dry lips and wished he had some grease he could rub on them to prevent further cracking.

"I suspect that's the reason it's called the Gates of Hel. All we know about it is stories we have heard. We are lucky to know anyone that has actually been inside the zone. Sayed is our only genuine source of information, though why he wanted to travel back into this Gods forsaken place I will never understand. It is obvious he was it a cook, even though most of his concoctions are pretty good."

Von tried to hide a smile. "I guess we will never know. He could be one of those men that were always looking for the next tidbit of knowledge. Too bad he never found a recipe book."

"It's not like Brinn to take a chance on someone like that. He's still antsy after what happened at the trading post. At least we were strangers. Can you imagine how he feels, thinking the man was a friend all these cycles, only to discover he was a drasted slaver?"

"Life was like that. Just when you think you have a winning hand, someone draws a queen's court. There was no possibility you would win if you don't play."

"What in Ligazra's Nine Hels does that have to do with it?"

"Nothing. But my grandfather always said it and it sounded good."

Von rolled his eyes and fell into line behind

Moth, ignoring Jaxx's laughter.

The funny thing about being in the desert, you never know what to expect. We rode steadily toward what Raffi had assured us was the east, or at least it was toward the setting of one sun. The second sun seemed to go slightly south as it passed overhead.

The land had gradually changed, becoming more arid the farther we traveled away from Brinn's homestead. They were now riding through long stretches of sandy desert filled with scrub trees and a spiny plant that resembled a yellowish-brown porcupine. The mountains in the distance had proved to be more like a string of large buttes, some of which stretched leagues in either direction. The first few days had been exactly as he'd expected. Sayed had led them from water hole to water hole, following his tribe's usual route, though they had passed this area over a moon earlier, heading in the opposite direction. They had come across the remains of a road about two days back that was going in the general direction that Sayed had chosen. Brinn had suggested following it as it wound throughout the barren county side, hoping that whoever had built the road had taken into consideration the need for water.

Jaxx used the side of his headdress to mop the dribbles of sweat from around his eyes. The double red sun played tricks on him as he rode. After a while, he had squinted from the glare, slightly closing his eyes to help ease the burning from the heat and the sand; then closing them entirely for stretches at a time, hoping to relieve the red spots that danced across his vision. Even with the light-colored headdress and loose-fitting clothing, the sun was burning his tender flesh as it drew out every drop of moisture from his skin. It made time spent working in his parents' mines a lot more attractive.

Late in the afternoon, once the first of the two suns had passed beyond the mountains, the desert land was beautiful, a sea of rose and amber and purples against a backdrop of tans and browns lit by the fading red sun. The air danced, faint shimmers that wavered as you watched them against the far horizon. A furnace could not be hotter. It was a peculiar sensation, the experience of having your body slowly dehydrate as the heat sucks the moisture directly from the air. Your mouth becomes dry and you your lips crack until you fight to keep from drinking all the water the waterskin held. Jaxx could not imagine what magic could turn fertile farmland into this. Or what God would allow it.

Gwen would often pray as she rode, asking for Rheaaz for water, then perhaps a breeze, and finally for noise; any kind of sound to break up the monotonous silence. For there is always silence, a silence so oppressive it eats at your soul. Everything is the same, but nothing is the same. Sand, color, wind, sound, ever changing but not changing; it could drive you insane. The caves were dark, but there were shadows, and it was never completely quiet. The rocks amplified the slightest breath.

Every day a storm hung heavily upon the desert, clouds of blue and gray and silver, swirling with the hot midday sand. It charged the air with electricity; so much that the very action of walking caused enough static current that the hairs stand up along your arm and head.

At night, it was worse. The desert lost heat quickly with nothing to hold in the heat. Within minutes, it would grow cool. Then cold as your body lost its ability to produce enough heat to keep itself warm. Then your blood grows cold, causing tremors and chills throughout your muscles that no amount of clothing could block completely. Fire helped, but only enough to survive, never enough for genuine comfort. Even the bravest of souls has failed in the face of the forgotten lands. The urge from our consciousness to turn tail and run just to stay alive is a constant reminder of the mortality of both man and were. Only the two Duaars seemed unaffected. Of course, fear is something a Duaar had trouble understanding at all. But thirst was something we all appreciated and as the days passed by, we were all worrying.

They would have missed the hidden well completely if Brinn had not been curious about what was drawing the attention of the circling Vuls. The sand-colored scavengers had detoured long enough to check it out. Long before anyone could make out the actual body, they spotted scattered pools of blood and occasional bits of bodies. There had been a fight, and at least one combatant was dead. From the number of flies hovering over the mess that had once been a living being, the body had been lying there for several days.

Raffi used the back of his sword to shoo the flies away from the dead Xvvelix's face, hoping to get a better idea of what it was. Unlike the one that almost killed him, it was male, and he was not a young demon. Strands of gray tipped the ends of his feathers. This contrasted sharply with its muscular, well-developed physiques. The acrid stink of urine and sulfur rose from his filthy gore encrusted plumage and dried blood pooled underneath his body. There was no way to know how long he had been dead, but it had been long enough for the maggots to hatch.

One leg and most of the internal organs were missing. Something had savaged the second leg, tearing great chunks of meat away from the calf and thighs. The first impression was the arrow had killed it. But that didn't explain what had savaged the body. The mouth that had done that damage was nothing like the tears of a hungry Vul's beak. And there were tracks on the ground. Humanoid, but at least twice the size of Jaxx's enormous feet.

Brinn removed the waterskin and picked up a knife lying near the winged demon's outstretched hand. The knife had dried blood on the blade. The waterskin was full.

"He must have filled this right before it killed him. Look around, maybe we can find where the water came from."

"Good idea. But keep an eye open. My nervous bump is itching." Jaxx was certain someone had watched them approach the area beneath the circling vuls.

It was only a few minutes before Keeyun found the well near a cluster of rocks. Instead of an open pool, there was a long wooden pole that pumped the water up to the surface. It surprised them to see how much grass was growing near the pump. Sayed was also surprised he had never realized the well was there. He had always traveled two additional days to reach the oasis on his tribe's route.

"I wonder if this is one of the primary sources of water for the Gynark tribes? It has to be in constant use for so much grass to grow nearby. That would explain the arrow." The horses were happy to take a break and let the travelers satisfy their curiosity. It gave them a chance to enjoy the sparse grass growing near the well.

"Maybe not. Look at this." Raffi had pulled one clump of grass up, exposing the roots. As he expected, the roots had grown extremely long to reach the water table. Another adaptation was the storage bulb along the length of the root. He squeezed one and water flowed out freely. "This explains how the plants are spreading with no obvious source of water."

"Much as I hate to say it, I don't think we should camp here. The well is the only source of water in the area, and that makes anyone nearby a target. As soon as everyone fills their skins and the animals have drunk their fill, we need to put some distance between us and the well. If we travel all night, we could reach the oasis late tomorrow afternoon. We can stay an extra day and rest up there.

There were no arguments.

Not long after they left the well; Keeyun had spotted something large and gray paralleling their trail. He kept his horse walking as if nothing had changed and called out to Raffi, "Don't look around, but we have company."

"Don't tell me. More demons. Or one of those weird creatures they keep as pets?"

"We can't be that lucky. Whatever this is, it's bigger than a Spine Bender. Smart, too. It's staying back far enough that most could not see it. It's nothing more than luck that I was relieving a full bladder and spotted it shifting position."

"So, what do we do?"

"We keep moving. Maybe it will tire of following and turn back to the well. The first sun is about to come up. By second sun rise it will be hot. It might seek shelter since there's no sign of it carrying water."

CHAPTER 15

SFor the last league of so, they had been travel-ing through the ruins of a major population center. None of the buildings were whole, but they had found several with enough walls stand-ing to provide limited shade. The first sun had risen by the time Brinn decided they were not likely to find a better location to make a brief rest stop.

Sayed disagreed. "The oasis is not much farther. Maybe a league. It is best we continue." There were several mumbled complaints, but they continued.

First the two camels, then Von's horse smelled the water long before he could see the tiny oasis of plants growing in a clearing near the center of the ruins. The mare fought me for the first time, pulling against the leather reins as he fought to keep control. But his efforts were wast-ed as she turned away from the path and trotted deliberately in the greenery's direction. Jaxx and Raffi quickly scouted the perimeter and then de-clared the tiny oasis safe.

Sayed allowed the goats to run free. The camels fought until he let them run behind the goats.

Von's mare wasted no time on drinking, wading knee deep in the tiny pool in her hurry to relieve her thirst, followed shortly by Jaxx's gelding and the pack mule. He swung off the mare and turned her loose, knowing that she would not wander far from the water and the stringy grass growing along its bank. They had not ridden hard, but they had been on the road for five long days with only brief stops to rest. Now we all had a chance to recuperate. Brinn quickly took care of the other three horses. The water was clear and pure and there were even a few trees that offered some shade from the hot sun.

There were tracks of some type of small animal in the sand nearby and several waterfowl had risen from the pool as we approached. Even now, they were settling back into the water nearby. Satisfied that the horses were settled in for an evening of grazing; Keeyun wanted to pick off a few of the birds. Sayed would ensure we would enjoy a hot meal before long, but fresh roasted duck sounded great. It's funny what hunger will do to your mindset. Things that you felt previously were impossible suddenly became a matter of finding a solution that would fit. Keeyun's solution was simple; keep shooting until he hit the bird. With that resolved, it was only a matter of time before we were all enjoying a dinner of roast fowl. Even Twist behaved long enough for them to bag enough of the birds to satisfy his burgeoning appetite.

Mekiva wiped her forehead with a wet cloth, removing a layer of sweat and salt. "You know, when you said it would be hot, I did not expect it to be this hot."

Von managed a little smile through his cracked lips before answering. "If you changed your mind, now is the time to say so. We can turn back. No one will hold it against you."

Mekiva raised her head and glared at Von, her narrowed eyes a clear sign he had insulted her by suggesting she could not continue on their quest.

"In the future if anything changes, you will be the first to know." Without waiting for a response, Mekiva picked up her pack and moved off to the tent. Moments later, Von could hear her moving things around as she prepared for bed.

Jaxx shook his head. Von could be so dense at time. He could tell from the stiff way Mekiva was carrying herself that Von had done it again. The sad part was he crossed into unfamiliar territory without understanding what he had said to upset her. This was the third time had offended her deeply. Mekiva was not the type to give up. The determination to finish what she started must be from her time at the mage school. Von needed to set things right.

Raffi surprised him when he pulled him to the side to talk. "Stop being such an ass. Give her time to calm herself before you try to discover what you said this time. You upset her. I realize you have trouble understanding women, but this becoming a problem. Mekiva has a good heart and does not hold to anger for long. By morning, I am sure she will have forgiven you." He dropped his saddle and bedroll next to a section of a wall that provided some shade.

Von shrugged. "I just want her safe. We have been through so much and barely survived. We should have left them with Nyla."

"Nyla? The only reason she is not here is the new baby."

"Brinn would have said no."

"And she would have come regardless of what he said. Let Mekiva make her own decisions. She knows the dangers we face. It's her choice."

Sayed looked up at Von and nodded. "Mekiva understands the dangers involved. You may not think we notice, but everyone here knows how you feel about Mekiva. You only see the woman you care for and the danger to her. She is a strong Elementalist and will only grow stronger. The mage school tried to form her into a tool for others to use. She is not the type to accept another's control. Do not seek to take her free will from her, it will only rebound on you. That choice is hers to make. She's here. Accept it."

Von wondered if he could.

Jaxx decided the best thing he could do was to stay out of the argument. Von would figure it out, or Mekiva would set him straight. Besides, unless he hurried, someone would stake out all the best sleeping spots before he claimed his. He walked along the wall a few feet and dropped his pack. Then he rolled out his bedroll beside it.

After judging that the late afternoon haze would veil any smoke, Sayed built a pocket-size fire. Once he had completed the awkward and messy business of skinning them, he stripped and seared rather than roasted the plump rodents Twist had delivered just after they made camp. The hungry travelers tore into the meat from the delicate bones, alternating with pan bread and greedy mouthfuls of warm water.

Von looked up from his breakfast. Leaning

against the archway that led into the gray-stone building was Gwen. The slender young woman had her arms crossed and a distinctive frown on her face.

Apparently, Von had screwed up again. He wondered what he had done this time.

Gwen's smile looked more like a smirk. "Did you forget something?"

"Oh, you know me, m'lady. There's always something I forgot in my rush to complete a different task."

"My lady? Hardly. There's not a drop of noble blood flowing through these veins. However, you... are an ass."

"Ass? Wait! What did I do to deserve this?"

"Hush. You know very well what's today is."

"What do you mean?" Von asked, completely confused by her remarks.

"I told you a before we left the homestead that today is Mekiva's name day. Please tell me you remembered."

Von looked like he was about to lose his breakfast.

Gwen rolled her eyes. *Of course, he forgot.* She pulled a delicate bracelet from her pocket and passed it to Von. "You owe me big time for this one. Now I have to find her something else or make another gift."

"Thank you. She's hinted about it several times. I can't believe I forgot it."

"I hope Jaxx remembered. I'm out of gifts."

Jaxx removed his axe from the sling on his back and sat down on the rock. Holding his whetstone in one hand and the unruly weapon in the other, he began making slow but steady strokes along the edge of the blade. Slowly, steadily, he ran the hone along its length, focusing his attention on keeping an even pressure on the edge. One by one, the whet stone removed the inevitable nicks. Once he was satisfied with how the edge looked, he flipped the axe over and began sharpening the opposite side. Only the sound of his name being said in such an annoyed manner jolted his attention back to his surroundings. He was curious what Von had done to upset Gwen this time.

"Remembered what?" Jaxx asked as he walked up.

The tiny Shi'a lakka maiden seemed to grow larger in stature as she glowered at Jaxx. "Why the Gods made men the dominant sex, I will never understand."

Both men shifted uncomfortably at the stinging words; particularly when they realized she wasn't through chastising them. As though sensing her mood, Twist padded over, softly crooning encouragement. Von went in search of Mekiva. He rubbed up against Gwen in a soothing manner a few times, gave a quick lick, and followed Von.

CHAPTER 16

Moth lay his cards down and looked around, but nothing unusual caught his eye. He stood and stretched, using the movement as an excuse to take a better look.

"What's up?" Brinn asked.

"The horse's sense something. Look at Mischa's ears. And the camels are up on their feet."

"Think it's the same thing you spotted near the well?"

"I hope not. From the size of its print, it's not gonna care if I hit it with an arrow."

"At least everyone is together."

Moth looked around the clearing. Keeyun was sleeping and Raffi was playing cards with Jaxx and Gwen. "Drasst it. Von and Mekiva went walking. I'm certain from the way they were looking at each other, neither one will be watching for an ambush."

"Do you mind looking? It might be best if someone stays with the horses."

"Will do it now." He glanced back at the tent, noticing Keeyun still was stretched out on his bedroll, sound asleep. "Something must be bothering him. He's usually senses something wrong with the area long before the animals react."

Von had chosen his destination and hidden the bracelet behind a rock in the rubble. Then he spread the blanket he used under his saddle on the sand.

I had pleased Mekiva when he asked her if she wanted to take a stroll and talk. She had smiled when he led her to the sheltered alcove, recognizing the blanket as the one he often used as a pillow. When he pulled her down beside him, she had smiled and blushed. That smile had turned into a grin when Von pulled the bracelet from its hiding spot.

Moving closer to Mekiva, he gave her a slightly devilish smile that melted her insides before snapping the clasp around her wrist. Without a word, Von put his lips over her mouth, cutting off whatever she had intended to say. Once she finished talking, he pulled her into a second, deeper kiss. Maybe the day would not be a total disaster. His hands circled her hips. She was close enough there was no mistaking his intentions.

Apparently, Mekiva was not interested in celebrating in the same manner as him. She stood and brushed the sand away from her clothing. "Thank you for my gift. I'm going to go show Gwen my bracelet."

Von reached for her arm, but she was already moving back toward the others. He thought about going after her. Stopped and thought about it. That could cause friction within the group. Not a great idea. Instead, he reached for the Mir-cat, who had followed them to the secluded building. Twist could be a pain, but there was nothing more comforting than the feisty winged cat when things did not go his way. It was strange. Von had not wanted the unusual creature along when they started the trip, but now, when he watched Mekiva's chimera side-kick at play, it reminded him more and more of the ship's cat he had befriended. Necessity had forced him to leave her on board the Sirens Breath, as the crew could little afford the loss of its ships-cat. Good mousers were more valuable than deck hands any day. Twist's hairless, scaled tail was more like the tail of the pouched rodents his uncle raised to feed his draft lizards, and the bat wings felt strange at first, but now he loved cuddling up with him. Especially when his plans did not go as he hoped.

Mekiva felt no remorse as she walked away from Von's impromptu bower. She knew she had spoiled Von's plans but figured he would get over it. Today was her name day, not his. Besides, he had forgotten all about it. She knew that as soon as she saw the bracelet. Gwen had noticed her admiring it in the market weeks before Von and Jaxx returned from their prison adventure. Since the seller had not set up on market day since they had seen it, it was clear Gwen had bought it for her. Her friend was always thinking ahead.

She would thank her for the gift later. For now, she was enjoying torturing Von too much. The look on his face when she said she was going to show the bracelet to Gwen was priceless. He did not know what to say. She would let him mope a little longer and then go back.

She wished she had thought to bring water. It was so hot. The red sand reflected the heat upward, making it difficult to find a cool spot. Vons little love nest was in a perfect location, private with lots of shade. She had squeezed her eyes into narrow slits when she stepped back into the sun after sitting in the shadowed alcove. The sudden brightness had hurt her eyes. Several minutes passed before her vision returned to normal. Just as her vison cleared, and she took a step, a glancing blow from the behemoth's clawed hand sent her flying back against a large rock, knocking her wind from her. She gasped for air as then screamed as the beast lumbered toward her, intent on finishing what his initial blow had begun.

As the Troll reached for the terrified young woman, she reacted on instinct, throwing her hands out in front of her. A powerful gust of wind struck the troll in the chest, knocking it back against a pile of rubble. Somehow, she convinced her legs to move and ran, knowing it would be back on its feet in seconds. The stiletto she carried strapped to her leg would not even anger the troll. It would heal any damage she did as soon as she removed the blade. Knowing there was little Von could do on his own against a troll, she ran toward camp, hoping the monster would follow her.

Gwen's scream echoed across the rubble filled landscape. Brinn decided the horses would be fine and began running toward the sound. Moth was already heading that way. Hopefully, he would arrive in time to prevent either teen from being killed.

Mekiva had no idea what kind of fighter Brinn was, but it thrilled her to see him running that way. She did not know where Von was or even if he was still alive. She had realized she had wandered away from the path they had taken to reach his special spot and was surprised how quickly Brinn had found her. He had his sword in hand as he ran toward the enormous sand colored beast troll. At least she thought it was a troll. It was skinnier than the darker, rock-colored giants that harassed her father's herds. Brinn hit him a few times, but he ignored the sword, intent on reaching Mekiva and getting away with his prize before anyone else arrived.

The others were probably heading that direction. It confirmed her guess when Von rounded a boulder and a blade flew past her head, landing with a thunk in the right eye of the troll. The irritated troll stopped running toward the girl and turned his attention to the tall man standing behind her. His face broke into a smirk as he popped the damaged eye out with the dagger and tossed them over his shoulder.

Then he charged at Von.

Von had his belt knife in hand when he caught up with Mekiva. He did not know how he was going to stop a troll. Brinn was slicing at any part that came within reach, but the magical beast was regenerating faster than he could cut parts away. Von was determined to try if for no other reason than giving Mekiva a chance to focus on a spell. The troll was unfazed by the loss of his eye. Nor did he appear to be concerned by the boot knife Von was holding.

"Fire!" he screamed as he swung at the troll's back. "That's all that will stop it. Try a fireball."

Fire. He would say fire. Fire was her weakest spell. Some choice. Try to cast a fire spell or stand there doing nothing and watch them die. *She had started a cook fire. You can do this.* Mekiva took a deep breath and began inching toward the fight. The possibility of dying before she completed the spell didn't help her concentration. After she saw how it shook off Jaxx's blow, Mekiva realized there little she could do to hurt it, but she would be damned if she was going to stand there and watch as it took the men of the group down. As the troll started towards her, she concentrated like they had been trying to get her to do all year in school. She knew the possibility of dying increased with every step the troll took. She wasn't sure how she felt about being a target. Once she was close enough to hit the troll and not Von, she threw her braid over her shoulder, loosened her shoulders and gestured, concentrating on fire the same as when she lit the logs the night before. There was small poof of flame that was instantly quenched by the falling rain. *Water. She tries for fire in the desert and gets water.* In the distance, thunder rolled, and the sky was lit by a bright white light.

The rain falling from the sky was the first warning the others had that Brinn was going to need help. There was only one person in the party that could call up a storm in the middle of the desert. If Mekiva was tossing spells around, it was something more than Brinn and Von could handle.

Jaxx shouldered his ax and ran. Raffi was nowhere to be seen.

Moth shrugged. He did not know if Jaxx was heading in the right direction. At least Keeyun was awake now. "Help Gwen watch the animals. It could be a distraction. I'll follow Jaxx."

For once Keeyun didn't argue. He motioned for Gwen to stay near him, then pulled his sword. Moth was right, it could be a diversion, and the horses were the likeliest target.

Jaxx arrived in time to see the troll toss Brinn toward the same rock Mekiva had crashed into. As its attention locked on Von, he shifted his grip on his axe and allowed instinct to take over. As soon as he moved into position and raised his weapon, the battle scene sprang into sharp focus. Time slowed, allowing him to think before acting. His father enjoyed hunting trolls for sport. Trolls may be shaped like humans, but they were little smarter than the average dog. You could easily fool a young one, but the one they were facing was an old troll, smarter than normal, with the body of an enormous beast, strong and almost invulnerable. To kill one, you had to stop its regeneration. You could slow it down by cutting off a limb and forcing it to regrow, instead of quickly healing an injury. But that wouldn't kill it. He'd seen one pick up its head from the ground and set it back in place. Only burning the wound will prevent it from healing. And there was nothing to burn in the area. He brought the axe point up and caught it underneath the hand, catching the taloned fingers as they pulled away. The trolls forward movement ended quickly, as he lopped off the talons on one hand. He screamed in agony—a sound Jaxx had heard before, but only when surrounded by his companions as they finished one off.

Brinn was out of the fight. He had hit that rock hard. He was back on his feet, but he was swaying. Von's arm was bleeding from the thing's claws. He was losing too much blood. Somehow, he needed to slow it down until Mekiva got a fire going.

The troll was looking at Brinn, knowing he had hurt him. Jaxx took advantage of the distraction and moved closer. Before the troll registered his presence, he raised the ax overhead and brought it down across the troll's forearm.

The razor-sharp blade sliced through the muscles behind the hand, sending it flying toward the same rock. The trolls forward movement ended quickly. He grasped his injured wrist and screamed defiance.

Jaxx wanted to make sure this troll would remember this fight. Swinging his ax like a scythe, he could remove the talons as fast as the regrew. He caught it stepping forward, and one foot followed the talons. Without a foot, one leg was longer than the other, making it difficult for the beast to stand upright. There were already bulbs of flesh growing on its wrists, and he could see the beginnings of a fleshy growth on the bone above what he'd left of its ankle.

Von could see the troll's leg was not resting on the ground. Taking advantage of the troll's temporary disability, he rushed at it from behind, throwing his body at the injured leg. His weight caused the beast's knees to buckle, and it fell, landing most of its weight on Von. It immediately struck his trapped body with the stub of his arm. He swung his knife and sliced off the remaining two talons on its hand. The ugly gray behemoth snatched its wounded paw back against its chest. It glared at him like he'd offended it for a long moment. Before he rolled away, the beast leaned forward, trying to crush his head with one gigantic paw, while the other paw did its best to eviscerate him.

Jaxx knew he had to hurry before the Troll crushed Von's skull. He ran forward, chopping at the arm like he split a log. The bone shattered, but the arm remained attached. The troll forgot Von as it lunged toward Jaxx, crawling on his knees as it struggled to get back to his feet.

Swinging an ax at anything within reach was not

the best tactic to use when fighting a troll, but Jaxx was desperate. As the smelly behemoths regrown fingers spread out, he did what the dull-witted creature least expected him to do—he charged forward as the blade fell, wincing as the ax head buried itself deep into the brute's body. Usually, when he did a maneuver like that, he met with some type of resistance. No matter how sharp the blade is, when you cleave a body, it hits bone and muscle, and your arm jerks. Unless the weapon is magic or blessed by a God, it will not slice cleanly thru any part of the muscular body. Knowing this, he ignored what the blacksmith tried to tell him and put all his strength into driving the edge of his ax through the troll's body.

His ax passed through the limbs of this troll like a hot knife thru butter. The ax wasn't magic. The last time he was inside a temple, the priests were too busy trying to kill him to consider a blessing. He was already cursed. He was too busy to dwell on the question, but he intended to find an answer if he survived.

While Jaxx attacked the troll, Von scrambled away. Blood dripped from several deep gashes, and the back of his neck burned. He was seriously hurt. In between bouts of intense pain and nausea, he noticed Moth heading that way. Moth usually carried a few healing potions with him, even if he did not have a healing spell handy. He needed to avoid the troll until his friends could help him.

Mekiva saw Von fall and tried to get around the troll to go to him. This only drew the troll's attention. He began lumbering her way, moving faster than something that big should be able to move.

Moth saw the troll change direction and knew Mekiva had little time. The mage stopped and cast a spell. Nothing appeared to happen. Then Mekiva realized the troll was stumbling and holding its hands out in front of it as it walked. Moth had blinded it. She had one more chance!

Jaxx pushed himself back to his feet. He took a firmer grip on his ax, but he waited as Mekiva began an intricate pattern of hand movements, something he had quickly learned to recognize as the beginning of a spell. He had made the mistake of interrupting one of her castings; he was still not sure what had been worse, the misfired spell, or Kiva's tongue lashing. The young mage's spells were extremely unpredictable when she got them right. He could only imagine what would happen if she miscast one. He released a brief chuckle, remembering the time she had cast a simple cantrip to make him more difficult to see during a bar fight. He had turned invisible and stayed that way for three days until the spell wore off. Being invisible didn't sound bad right now.

Seconds later, Jaxx's hand trembled. Sweat beaded on his forehead and his skin became cold and clammy. All the hairs on his arm were standing on end. *Wait.* The hairs all over his *body* were standing on end. The air around him felt funny. He noticed that the rain had stopped. His arm quivered. As the muscles twitched, he found it harder to maintain a grip on the old, familiar ax handle. It dropped to the ground at his feet. His eyes went to Brinn, who had dropped his sword. He stepped back away from the blade, joining Moth a few feet away.

Von wasn't sure what was coming, but he knew some was about to happen. He noticed that the rain had stopped. The muscles in his sword arm spasmed. He saw Moth and Raffi toss their sword on the ground, and he knew he needed to get the steel blade out of his hand...fast. Fighting against his impulse to drop the weapon, he stepped forward and thrust the blade into the troll's body.

Mere inches away from the pommel of his sword, a bolt of lightning crashed to earth, knocking him off his feet. He tried to get back to his feet, knowing an injured man was an easy target. Against a human opponent, he might have risked lying flat on his back a few seconds longer. Von knew he did not have the time or the luxury for second-guessing. The struggle to get back to his feet took seconds longer than normal — time which could cost him his life.

Then he realized the troll wasn't moving toward him. The sand-colored creature was staring at something lying on the ground between them. Little remained of his arm but smoking ash in the mud. Von didn't know who was more stunned. Then Mekiva shouted, "get away, run," just before a second bolt struck the sword he'd shoved into the stunned troll. There was a flash of bluish white light, then beast burst into flames. Von forced his body to his feet and stumbled the final few feet to the rock before falling back onto the sand. He lay with his head in Mekiva's lap and watched it burn.

CHAPTER 17

Brinn's voice woke Von from his dazed dream, and he wondered why he was lying on the sand with his head in Mekiva's lap. Not that he minded. It was just his last memory of their time together had ended with her running off to show Gwen a bracelet. That's when he remembered her scream. He had pulled his sword and ran toward the sound, praying to any God that would listen that she would be alright. Then he spotted the sand troll. After that, it was all a blur.

Obviously Mekiva was safe... and she was wearing his bracelet. He could see Brinn resting against a rock, talking to Moth. Raffi was nowhere in sight; but that wasn't unusual. He rarely stayed in one place for long. He was most likely back in camp with Keeyun and Gwen. His biggest concern was Jaxx.

Where was he? He vaguely remembered him blocking the troll's attack and driving it back away from where he lay. There was a large brownish red stain on the ground near the entrance into the clearing. He was almost certain that blood was his. But was it all his? He shifted his weight and pushed up, trying to sit upright. The newly healed muscles in his stomach were tight but worked without pain. Moth could cast healing spells, but injuries like he had received would need much more. Apparently,

Gwen had been there, even though she was no longer in the clearing. Only Rheaaz could have healed the wound so completely. He winced as he gained his balance.

"Take it easy. You were hurt, almost as badly as the first time Gwen healed you." Gwen stood and dusted the sand from her clothes.

Von took her hand as he rose to his feet. "The wounds are fine. I have a bit of a headache. Feels like the Troll kicked me in the head. It could be the heat; maybe I need some water."

"More likely, it's the sun reflecting off the sand. It's so bright. If you feel up to it, we can head back to camp. I wouldn't mind getting out of the sun myself."

Von gave a weak smile as a wave of guilt struck him. He did not know how long he had laid with his head cradled while she sat in the scorching heat without complaint. He took a step, then wavered as a wave of nausea swept over him.

Mekiva grabbed him to prevent him from falling.

Brinn and Moth rushed to assist. With their help, Von could make his way back to camp. He collapsed onto his bedroll, happy to find that someone had moved it into the shadow of a broken wall. Mekiva passed him a skin of water, and he took a few sips before lying back against his pack. Anyone standing nearby could hear the rumbling of his empty stomach.

"Sayed made a stew and pan bread. Do you think you can sit up and eat?"

"I'll manage." He rose to a seated position,

then clutched his head as a sharp pain radiated from the back of his skull toward his eyes. Once the pain passed, he leaned back against the wall, using his bedroll as a pillow.

Gwen handed him a bowl and bread.

It surprised Von how hungry he was. His hand shook a little as he moved the spoon to his mouth, but after a few bites, he felt better.

Mekiva shifted her body so that Gwen could sit down beside her. "Are you sure they were trolls?"

"I have never heard of sand trolls. Especially ones that reacted to fire the way these did." The troll had *burned*. This was another conundrum he didn't understand it. He had fought Trolls before. They didn't burn so much as melt when fire touched them. This troll went up like a bonfire. One second it was there. The next it was a small, blackened section of ground and a pile of hot ashes.

Sayed nodded. "Before the disaster, no one had ever heard of them. They seem to have developed within Adon's Bane. Over the past few cycles, we have seen them within the borderlands. The elders propose they may have bred to where the Red Zone can no longer support their numbers. The trolls we have seen have all been young, usually in pairs like these were."

"Does that mean they were the only ones in the area?"

"Who knows? These followed us away from the oasis. We may have wandered into a different troll's territory. Or there may be none for leagues. It is best we act as if they were all around and stay alert at all times."

"It feels like it was a dream. It happened so fast.

And they were so hard to kill."

The two young women ate a few moments, then Gwen nudged Mekiva, "Ask him."

"He's eating."

"Go ahead," Gwen whispered. "It's not like he can't talk and eat. He does it all the time."

"Fine," she snapped. "Gwen wants to know if you have ever fought a troll before?"

Von looked startled, and Jaxx let out a snicker.

"Yes, I have, and I slayed it, but it was mostly luck."

The two girls leaned forward, not wanting to miss a single word of his story.

"So how did you kill it?"

Jaxx had a smirk on her face. She knew Von had never been close to a troll before. The story was one they had heard in a dockside tavern in Mu. She rose and headed toward the horses. Brinn had asked her to take care of a small problem and now seemed as good a time as any. It couldn't stink any more than what Von was shoveling.

"We were fighting on a knoll I knew well. There was a ledge that offered a view I enjoyed visiting, especially when I had company." His eyes went to Mekiva, and he hesitated. When she didn't react to his statement, he continued. "I was relaxing with a friend when we heard an unusual noise. I turned to look, just in time to see my friend's head land in the grass beside me. There was a huge troll standing right behind me. I threw my body into a roll that got me beyond

SANFORD

the troll's legs. As he turned, I scrambled for my sword, and somehow raised it in time to block the sweep of his claws."

He took a sip of water and gathered his thoughts. "The next few minutes were a blur. I struck blow after blow, but it was regenerating as fast as I injured it. I knew there was no way I could outlast it. It was bigger and stronger, and so far, nothing I had done was working. It had gradually backed me up the knoll. Before long, I would be trapped between the drop off and the troll. That's when I got an idea. It was a long shot, but that's all I had. The troll knew he had the advantage. The sword blows might hurt, but they did no actual damage. I could see the troll gathering itself to lunge at me. I backed away until I could feel the end of the ledge behind me. The drop wasn't far, maybe the height of three men. At the base below the ledge was a mire bog that was full of shallow pools of water. Strange white flowers floated upon broad leaves on the surface, a favorite food of the big bullfrogs I enjoy so much. While trying to spear a few for my dinner, I'd slipped and stepped into the water. Beneath the thin coating of water, there were pools of quicksand. Thankfully, I was near enough to pull myself out using an overhanging limb. The limb had broken but held together long enough for me to reach firm ground."

Brinn grinned, anticipating where the story was going.

"As the troll came running at me, I fell to my knees. At the last moment, I rolled and stuck out a leg. The running troll tripped, falling forward off the overlook. He landed in the quagmire below and sunk almost to his waist. The more he tried to get out, the deeper he sank. In less than a candlemark, it sucked

166

him below the surface."

The two girls' eyes were wide.

Von winked at Brinn and continued. "I often wondered how long it remained alive under the water. Could it suffocate? Or did it die when it starved to death? Maybe it's still alive, regenerating over and over and over..."

Everyone laughed.

Brinn yawned and stretched. "With that in mind, it would be a good idea to clear away anything that might attract a predator. I asked Jaxx to move the horse that the troll killed. I hate to be the bearer of bad news, but it was your bay gelding. Do you feel up to helping move the body?"

"I think do. I need to get my equipment, anyway." Von stood and help Mekiva to her feet. "You can stay here. In this heat, the animal has to stink."

"No. I can handle it."

Raffi laughed. "This I've got to see."

They began walking toward the area where the animals had been penned. After the Troll attack, Keeyun and Sayed had moved the remaining animals to a different location. It was farther from the well, but upwind from the dead horse. As they drew near, they could see Jaxx working near the horse.

Jaxx was determined to move the carcass with no help from the men in the group. It was bad enough he was stuck in this female body until the next full moon. To have to have help to do something this simple grated on her ego. Even if the odor was enough to make her retch, she was determined to move the drassted thing.

Jaxx backed the reluctant mare up to the smelly carcass before swinging out of the saddle. She kept one foot planted on the reins as she slipped the end of a rope around the horse's neck. She attached the other end to the mare's saddle.

Once she was certain the mare would not bolt once she took her foot off the reins, she moved closer to the bloated animal.

Ants had already been at the corpse. They had stripped sections of the legs of its flesh, leaving flashes of white showing. The heat had sped up decomposition. The body needed to be moved now, before the wind shifted and brought the odor straight into camp.

Raffi, Von and Mekiva were walking in her direction. Brinn must have asked them to help her move the dead horse. She appreciated Raffi and Von's help, but there was no way Mekiva could handle the task. Her answer would be to set fire to the carcass and burn it. That was the worst thing they could do. The fire would burn for candlemarks, leaving a smoke trail for any curious desert inhabitant to follow.

She tried to tie a second rope to the horse, running the rope under the body just behind its legs, but Von's quiver and saddle blocked it. Somehow, they would need to shift the body and remove the equipment from beneath it. Maybe Rain could pull it off the saddle? After pulling her belt knife, she sliced the leather strap that held the saddle in place. She hated to cut the girth leather but there was no other way to get it off the body.

Rain did her best to move the bloated animal. Unfortunately, the hot desert sun had deteriorated the flesh. As the horse pulled against the rope, the flesh gave out. With a sharp pop, the bones separated, and the horse's head tore away from the neck. Blood and gore splattered the trio who had walked up to help. The head flew through the air, landing at Mekiva's feet.

Jaxx knew she was smiling now. Mekiva turned to look at her for a moment, then fell down on her knees, gasping and retching. She stayed there for several minutes then struggled to her feet once again, wiping the nasty tasting bile off her mouth. Her eyes went to Von, who looked like he was in shock, broke into tears and took toward where the others were packing up camp.

Raffi shrugged and walked over to the downed horse. The troll had snapped its neck like a dried twig. Mercifully, its death had been quick. This was going to make Sayed angry. The extra horse had been carrying some necessary supplies. Now he would need to rearrange several packs to balance out the added weight the two mules and the goats would need to carry. They would have to move the camp, which meant no sleep in the immediate future. By now, scavengers had scented the blood and were coming that way to investigate. The fire would keep most away until we broke camp and moved on. Some had no fear of humans and would move in within the candle-mark. Those are the ones they needed to avoid. One horse would not feed many if the right pack were eating. Then the idea of a small group of travelers and their animals would be extremely tempting.

She looked at the saddlebags and debated whether there was anything inside they could not do without. Von needed his bow and arrow quiver to hunt with. The water skin was another thing they had to keep. They all kept a small bundle of salt, jerked meat and seed cakes in their saddlebags in case they got separated. She bent to decide if there was a way to slide the saddle bag out from under the body.

"Looks like we may not be moving on after all." Raffi said as he moved closer to help Jaxx. He slid a weathered limb under the horse's body and levered it off the ground. It only rose a few inches, but that enough for her to jerk the back out from beneath the dead animal. They shifted to the other side and repeated the process, allowing Jaxx to free the quiver and arrows.

"What do you mean? You just mentioned how dangerous it is to remain so close to the well."

"That true. But things just changed. See that dust on the horizon. That's a large group of travelers heading in this direction. There are only one or two tribes that large in this area. They are all related to Sayed. Since we know where his tribe is, and it's heading east along the regular trade road, that leaves one of his cousins."

"So, what do we do?"

"We go back to camp and rest. This is the only water in the area." He grinned. "Maybe you can regale them with the troll story."

CHAPTER 18

In less than a candle-mark, hundreds of tents surrounded the tiny well. Most were small and light, barely large enough to provide sleeping quarters for a single man or two, yet each tent was so strongly anchored that the harsh desert storms did little to it. Weavers would spin the coarse goat's hair into a thick thread that was later woven into a tough waterproof cloth. The hairs meshed so well together, that sand could not slip through, In the event of the rare rain-storm, the material would swell and close to-gether in the wet so that only days of continuous rain carried on a high wind could force a slight leak into the dwelling-place.

Unlike most permanent homes, the lee side of a desert tent is always open to the air. If the breeze shifts, the women take down the tent facing into the wind and close up the previous wall. Before anyone noticed it happening, the tents front has changed its outlook and now fac-es toward the most favorable prospect of a cool breeze. In color, they were all similar, a natural mix of camel and goat hair, with little to distin-guish one from another except for an occasional stripe of color or a black goat's hair roof. The no-mad encampment was alive with the combina-tion of noises that animate the desert after dark;

children running and playing, the grunting and groaning of camels, the bleating of sheep and goats, and the occasional barking of dogs. Sloe eyed women sat at looms or spun thread from wool and hair to weave the colorful rugs they traded at markets. Other women tended the smaller children or worked to prepare the evening meal. Most kept their heads down as the group passed, not meeting the eyes of the strangers.

That seemed to be universal among the desert tribes. You might see a woman on horseback guarding the herds, but you would never see one armed for war. They were very careful to show all courtesies to Gwen, but the idea of female mage was unthinkable, and they did not know how to handle Jaxx. She was taller than most of the men, and equally well muscled. Von knew she could shoot as well as any man there. And in a straight one-on-one battle, if Jaxx had her axe, he would wager almost anything on her success.

"How will we find his tent? They all look the same."

Sayed's eyes danced merrily, but he never smiled. "If you ask where a certain sheikh has pitched his tents, they will give you an exact answer, but nothing that would help you locate the tent. My people believe if you need to know, you will know. If not, perhaps you should not be asking."

"So, we will simply wander around until we locate the tent?" Von wasn't certain he wanted to wander around looking at random tents. He tried to see the land through Sayed's his eyes. To the nomads, it is neither desert nor wilderness, but a land of which they know every feature. To them it was not an empty wasteland, but a mother country whose smallest product has a use sufficient for their needs.

"Not quite. Nomads have no need for maps, as the land we travel is constantly changing. The encampment is constantly changing. But we teach our children to look for little things, a rise in the ground, a big stone, the scattered blocks of a building in ruin. Not to mention every hollow or rock formation in which there may be water found, either in winter or in summer. There are marks sufficient for any to follow once you learn the meaning behind the marks. In my cousin's case, we will need nothing to help distinguish his tent from another."

Mekiva wasn't sure that was true. She had been looking at the tents and there was nothing to distinguish one for another. And the people seemed unconcerned about strangers walking past their homes. They followed Sayed as he wove his way through the maze of tents, somehow knowing where his cousin's tent would be without needing to ask for directions. Much as before, as they walked through the tent city, three horsemen paced along behind us, staying just far enough away to be polite, but close enough to intercept us if they found it necessary. Like Sayed, they were lean, swarthy men, dark-haired and heavy-browed, each armed to the teeth, with a menacing aspect that was not softened by a welcoming smile.

We hurried to stay with Sayed, unsure how the nomads would respond if we got separated. Finally, when they were certain they had walked past half the tents in the encampment, he come to a halt before an immense tan tent of with several colorful stripes. Before the tent, armed men lounged on overstuffed pillows of tanned animal skins. They were thick-set, broad-shouldered men, with heavy features of and teeth stained by kafka and the nuts they were chewing.

Sayed called out something in his native tongue, and one man, a handsome young man in full desert dress, the torn cloak slipping from the shoulders, rose to greet him, while the conversation went on uninterrupted. The tips of pointed ears peeked through sable curls beneath his desert head-dress of kerchief and camel's hair rope. He dropped the scarf that covered his face, and it was easy to see why so many young women fantasized about being captured by a desert sheik. He was a tall young man, with a handsome delicate face, a complexion that was almost fair, and long back curls that almost reached his waist.

The two men embraced, talking excitedly back and forth so quickly Brinn could not follow the exchange. The young man said something to the three men he had been sitting with and they began clearing away to move to a different tent.

Sayed motioned them forward. He held the flap open so they could enter.

Brinn began walking toward the open tent and the others followed. He had more experience with the nomads than any in the group. If he felt comfortable, they would trust his judgement.

They passed through the opening into a softly perfumed interior. The main room of the tent was a place of luminous, dancing shadows. Little light passed through the heavy weave of the black roof, leaving the metal firepit as the primary source of light. A heavy aroma of sandalwood and jasmine hung in the air. Behind thick curtains woven in shades of gold, blue, silver and green, the soft strumming of stringed instruments laid out a muted pattern of sound. The interior was sometimes hidden by a column of pungent smoke and sometimes, when a new stick caught fire, it was illumined by a leaping flame.

At the far end of the room, among a bevy of overstuffed pillows, Sayed was speaking to an older, slightly heavier version of the young man he had embraced. He nodded at something Sayed had said, then grinned as Sayed popped a grape into his mouth. Their current cook and guide wiped his fingers negligently on a wisp of silk offered by a veiled maiden, belched loudly and called them over.

One by one, Sayed made the introductions. His cousin's eyebrow raised as he introduced the women. He was familiar with Shii Lakka healers, but the fiery mage and the tall, flaxen haired warrior piqued his curiosity. He was further intrigued when he noticed the thick calluses on Jaxx's sword hand, something that only came through repetitive use. He sensed there was something different about this one, something held back by his cousin. This surprised him, as neither man was in the habit of keeping secrets from the other. He would wait and see before making a judgement. If their friendship was broken over such a minor matter, the price was a large one to pay.

"Would you not sit down and rest? I will have Kafka brought." He clapped his hands, and three young women came from behind the curtains. In minutes, the coffee beans were roasted and crushed, and the coffee-pots were simmering in the ashes. The aroma of kafka, the bitter black beverage of the desert tribes, which they consider better than any nectar made from the fruits of the vine, replaced the sandalwood and jasmine. As in the tents of Abdul, there was a ritual before anyone drank or ate.

A maiden would approach and hand you a cup with a tiny cup, asking "Do you deign to accept?"

You then drink the kafka quickly, in one draught, and pass the cup back empty, murmuring "May you live long and prosper!"

When the tiny cups had gone round once and all necessary phrases of politeness had been exchanged, a normal sized cup of kafka immediately replaced the small cup. You held the new cup without drinking until everyone had completed the ceremony. Unlike the first cup, the women now offered lumps of brown sugar, or honey and goat's milk to ease the bitterness of the kafka. Trays of tiny cakes, cheese, and fruit were passed around.

Gwen picked up a slice of green fruit. It smelled wonderful, but she wasn't sure how it would taste with all the seeds.

Dawood noticed her hesitation. "Kiwa. Try it, it's good. The seeds are sweet."

Gwen took a tentative bite, then smiled and ate the rest. It was quite good, sweet and juicy, as Dawood had said.

"It grows wild in many areas. You will see them. Watch for the stunted gray trees. The fruit is about the size of a crab apple. When it is ripe, it has a fuzzy brown appearance. I am sure Sayed will help you find the ripe ones."

One of the serving girls tittered, and Dawood

waved his hand, sending them back behind the curtain. They sat and talked, sipping on kafka, and nibbling on fresh fruit and pastries. If it upset Dawood to see his store of fresh fruit melt away and his coffee beans disappear by handfuls under the mortar, he showed no sign of his displeasure. He seemed more upset that they would not be staying for dinner. He understood our need to be back at camp, to support the other members of our group and assist if anything made a new attempt on our livestock.

Brinn mentioned the sand trolls and asked if they had encountered many.

"Not so much. We had a problem with one stealing from the flocks during the cold moons. It forced us to hunt it down and kill it. We lost four men that day, and many more were hurt. "

"I am sure it would have been much worse if we did not have a healer with us. Moth has some skill, but nothing to compare with a Shii."

"You mentioned it had followed you from the Ghaib well. It is good that you removed the trolls before we approached the area. You said you arrived just before the second sun passed beyond the mountains?"

"Yes. It was only a candle mark or so before dark."

"This is also good to know. There are certain places my people will never approach after dark—haunted wells to which thirsty men dared not approach. One is the Ghaib well in the rocks. One of my tribesmen swore he had seen a jinni there. He insisted the flocks should not go down to water where it abides." Dawood grinned. "I laughed at him and told my tale of angry spirits. Of meeting a hairy little man who shook a spear and warned me away from the well. I do not think he was djinn. Still, it would be good for my people to walk in groups and avoid being alone at night. And I too, will set extra men to watch over the flocks throughout the night."

"Speaking of night, it is time we should start back to our own camp. Keeyun and Raffi will wonder what is delaying our return. The first sun has set, and the second follows closely. Dawn comes quickly and we need to be on the road again."

CHAPTER 19

The morning broke windless and gray, broken only by the slender beams of red and purple that broke through the cloud cover. The breakfast gruel was simmering over the fire, and Sayed was busy with the last of the pack animals. Over the past week, the group had developed a routine. It would be a candlemark and a half from the moment Sayed awakened until the mule and the oryx were packed and ready. Sometimes we were off a few minutes earlier, but that was a rare occasion.

Today was no different. Same views, same sand, same sun. The thought that that were finally approaching the Red Zone lifted their spirits. The sand was no longer a neutral beige. Areas were tinted slightly pink, with occasional streaks of a darker red that was hauntingly reminiscent of dried blood. One unforeseen side effect was how loose the sand was packed. When riding along a ridge, you had to be on constant alert for sliding shale or sand. This slowed our progress to little more than a shambling walk.

Buck slid sideways, and Raffi tensed, getting ready to throw his body off the gelding if he went down. He hated riding on the sand. No matter how surefooted the horse, it only took one misstep, and the sand could shift, sending the horse and rider sideways. That's the desert, you never know what to expect.

Raffi cursed as Buck gathered his balance again. "Stay close. The sand is loose here. Stay directly behind me. Buck has the most experience traversing unstable land. We can't afford another broken leg."

For once Keeyun didn't argue.

Mekiva sighed and urged her horse forward. For once, Von's mare followed without it turning into a tugging contest. Brinn and Jaxx were riding behind the pack animals. Von was helping Sayed keep the herd in line. After several dangerous falls, they discovered they had a better chance of navigating a nasty section of ridgeline between two hills if they followed in the hoofprints of the horse in front of theirs. It didn't always work, but it was the best option available.

Gwen somehow missed the signal that they were moving and had to trot a short distance to catch up with the others. They rode steadily toward what Sayed had assured them was the west, or at least it was toward the setting of one sun. The other seemed to veer slightly south as it set.

The land had gradually changed, becoming more arid the farther west they traveled. For the last eight days, they had been traveling through the borderlands. It was a hostile land full of long stretches of sandy desert with scrub trees and a spiny plant that resembled a yellowish colored cactus. The mountains notated on Brinn's map proved to be little more than a string of large buttes, some of which stretched miles in the distance. About two days back, they had come across a faint road that was going in the general direction that Sayed had chosen. They had been following it as it wound throughout the desolate county side, hoping that whoever had built it had taken into consideration the need for water. Sayed was right about carrying water into the Red Zone. The levels were falling faster than anyone had expected. Unless they found water soon, they would have to ration.

The double red sun played tricks on everyone. After a while Gwen was squinting from the glare, slightly closing her eyes to help the burning from the heat and the sand; then closing them entirely for stretches at a time, hoping to relieve the red spots that danced across her vision. Even with the white headdress and loose-fitting clothes, the sun was burning her tender flesh. It drew out every drop of moisture from her skin, leaving it cracked and raw.

She imagined Moth and Keeyun had to be miserable. The cousins were from a land that was much cooler, and their pale skin was sensitive to both the light and the heat. Moth had adopted the attire of the desert tribes, but Keeyun refused to give up his pale gray attire.

The handsome young druid was a mystery. He made her skin crawl. She did not know why; he was always polite, if distant. His behavior was nothing like she expected. The men had described him as outgoing and friendly, often playing small jokes on them to ease the routine. So far, she had seen none of those traits. He had not spoken over ten words to her or Mekiva since they started the trip. And it wasn't just the girls. He rarely said anything to anyone. Not even his cousin. Von had mentioned how much he loved playing Gambit, but she had never seen him join the card game. She decided the dour druid was hiding something... but what?

The heat... even Hel could not be much worse; causing faint shimmers of air that wavered as you watched. Von had never been a pious man, yet he learned to pray as he rode, asking for water, then perhaps a breeze, and finally for noise; any kind of sound to break up the monotonous silence. For there was always silence, a silence so oppressive it ate at your soul, bit by bit, until you feel the need to say something, anything, just to hear a sound. Everything is the same, but nothing is the same. Sand, color, wind, rock, ever changing but not changing; it could drive you insane... and often did.

Not that it was much better at night. Without vegetation, the Red Zone lost heat quickly. Within minutes, it would grow cool, then cold. Clothing helped, but not enough. Your body lost heat, bringing tremors and chills that no amount of clothing could block completely. You look for ways to produce enough heat to keep warm. Fire helped, but without wood to burn, there was only enough dried brush around to survive, never enough for comfort. Even the bravest of souls failed in the face of the bane lands.

Only Sayed seemed unaffected. Of course, fear is something a Tabruk or Zarrni has trouble understanding. But thirst was something they all understood, and as the days passed by since leaving the oasis, they were all worrying.

Brinn called out to Von, "tell Raffi to start looking for a shelter. We need to give the animals a chance to rest and cool down."

Von urged his horse forward. "Raffi, Brinn said find a place to hold up."

"Sure. I'll just conjure up an oasis."

Von grinned. How Raffi could keep a sense of humor in this heat was a minor miracle. He had to concentrate to fight the urge to snap at everyone.

The second sun had risen a full hand's width above the distant horizon when Raffi finally spotted what they were looking for: a small overhang of rock that was almost a cave. It was difficult to spot it from the ground and it would be almost impossible to see it from the air. It was deep enough that they could move the horses under cover, so it would protect them from the heat and any Xyvelix flying overhead.

Jaxx and Brinn looked around carefully, but other than a small hole at the back of the overhang, there were no signs of an animal making this its home. Not that they had seen any animals larger than a lizard since leaving the borderlands.

After Sayed removed the mules and goat's packs and stacked them up against the far wall, he built a small fire and set a pot of stew to simmer. The animals were finishing their daily ration of grain and settling in to rest a candlemark or two.

No one talked much. Gwen's stomach was rumbling, and she exhausted. The intense heat drained energy faster than the body could replace it. Without water, her leg muscles cramped, making it hard to keep her feet in the stirrups. She looked around, expecting to see everyone sleeping, but they were all wide awake and staring out at the desert.

"Did I miss something?"

"Nothing anyone can put a name to. Just a feeling. Like something is about to happen, something you have no control over."

"Maybe is just because we are all hungry. How long until that stew is ready, Sayed?"

"Not long now. I'm about to bake up some flatbread to eat with the stew. Perhaps you are right, and once we all got some food in our bellies, we will want to get some sleep." His warm brown eyes twinkled merrily, and he winked.

I be... he has a sense of humor.

One hen had died from the heat. Sayed had added onions and herbs to the chicken, along with some dried vegetables, and created a stew. The aroma was mouth-watering. They ate quickly, for we were all hungry. The heat would only get worse later in the day. Gwen felt as tired as she had been before her brief nap. And now she was feeling the same odd tension as the others.

Moth wiped his bowl and packed it away before turning to Brinn. "I think I'm going to climb to the top of the rock escarpment and look around. It keeps nagging at me, that I don't know why I feel this way."

Keeyun stood. "I think I will go with you. I can't get comfortable and I'm making it harder for the others to rest."

Moth's eyes scanned the horizon, looking for movement or anything that might explain the intense sensation he had been feeling. He paid little attention to the monotonous view around him, searching instead for something that did not fit. Nothing caught his attention. He turned to study the land behind them. In the distance, near to the sheer cliff face they had followed on their way to Nona, he spotted what appeared to be a low-hanging storm cloud. This surprised him, as rain clouds stayed high in the sky. A cloud bank of that size should have prevented sunlight from reaching the ground. Even the brief showers that occasionally sprung up near the homestead would cause a marked decrease in the temperature.

"Does anything about that cloud look strange to you?" It wasn't unusual to see clouds. Every day a storm hung heavily upon the desert, clouds of blue and gray and silver, swirling with the hot midday sand. The cloud should have been too far away to affect them. The air was charged with electricity; the hairs were standing up along his arm and head.

"It's strange that it's so drassted hot. Never saw a rain cloud get darker when it was raining. Usually they lighten up."

"I've never seen one where the water would fall to the ground and then turn around and rise back up to the clouds, either. Maybe it's not rain. But what else could it be?"

"A herd of animals, but it would an enormous herd to kick up that much dust."

"Maybe Sayed will know something about it. It's heading this way."

"I'll go get him."

In a matter of moments Keeyun was back

with Sayed.

He looked toward the clouds and blanched almost as pale as the cousins.

"Mother of us all! I thought there was something about that sensation that was familiar. We must hurry. There's not much time. Run!"

He didn't wait to see if they followed.

Moth looked at the cloud and noticed it seemed to be moving in their direction. "I think we need to get undercover like Sayed said. Theres something about that cloud I do not like."

Reaching the overhang Sayed began calling out, "Everyone must help. Hurry! We need to pack the animals now. We have little time."

"What's wrong?" Brinn asked.

"Shaitan! Dancing djinns. We need to prepare the horses." He began loading the packs on the restless animals. As the pressure rose, they began milling about, breathing harder, eyes wide and rolling.

Von looked puzzled, but he gathered the equipment.

The girls were not sure what they should do. Brinn noticed.

"Make sure the animals are secure. It's a sandstorm. Like a tempest at sea except it's not water. It can strip the meat off the bones of an animal in moments. I've lived through one and that was one too many. We have to find something to help break the wind." It was Brinn's words that finally drove home the terrible danger that threatened them.

Sayed was running as he moved from animal to animal, snapping long lines to their halters. Then he removed the long scarf he wore around his head and tore it into two long strips, then tore them in half. "Here. Take these. Cover the horses' faces. Make sure to protect their eyes and nose."

"There's only four pieces."

"Then use your clothes. They won't do you any good if you are dead. The goats, too. Protect them or we will lose them."

"Is there else anything we can do?" Mekiva asked as Gwen dug through her clothing.

"Find a long rope and tie them all together. When the storm hits, they will go crazy and try to run." He fastened the goats' heads together by their horns, then covered their heads with several blankets to help keep them calm. He hobbled the Oryx, who were lying beside the back walls of the cave.

"Gather all the bedding and all the water. We will put the animals at the back against the wall and huddle together with them. That might help them stay calm once the storm arrives."

Brinn had been looking up at something above the shallow caves opening. "Jaxx, Keeyun, and Raffi need to help me. I think we can shove that big rock off the side of the escapement. It will block some of the wind. Sayed can finish up here with Von and the girls' help."

With all four pushing, they could move the stone enough to flip it over the edge. It fell straight down, blocking most of the opening to the overhang.

"I don't think there's enough room to get the horses by the rock." Jaxx kept his eye on the rapidly approaching cloud bank. It was moving faster than he'd expected.

"We will worry about how to get the animals out after the storm has passed."

They quickly slid down the rock and made their way back into the protection of the rocks.

Through the opening, they could see the horizon, which appeared to be moving closer and closer. Flashes of lightning moved across the face of the cloud. Bits of sand whirled in the air outside the overhang. An instant later, the sun and the sky disappeared from view.

The sandstorm took on the appearance of a dense black fog; the thickness broken occasionally by bright flashes of light. They easily felt the increasing pressure, recognizing the sensation that had been a constant itch all morning. The shriek and moan of the intense winds broke the silence of the desert. As the wall drew closer, it was easy to see that what had appeared like flashes of light were gigantic columns of sand, twisting and turning as they rose high in the air, creating fantastic shapes that glinted and reflected the bits of sunlight that broke through from above.

Gwen noticed a continuous low-pitched hiss and looked around. The fur on Twist's body was standing on end, making him look like a puffball with wings. He had crouched just inside the hole at the back of the cave. His wings were tight against his body. Fear had caused his pupils to expand, making his eyes look dark and wild. She had never seen the Mir-cat act this way, and that scared her more than Sayed's words.

Instead of the cooling wind they expected from a storm, the surrounding sand grew hotter. As if the world held its breath, everything grew quiet, and then the whirlwind struck their shelter. The air became thick from the murderous deluge of finely ground rock. A cyclone of dancing debris instantly surrounded the cave, swirling columns of hot sand and intense bursts of winds that funneled particles of grit through the narrowed opening. The dust-laden air made it difficult to fill their lungs enough to breathe. Wind roared and thunder crashed, but no water fell. The direction had shifted and now it felt as if their tiny spot of safety placed them directly in the teeth of the storm.

They huddled together behind the big rock beneath their bedding, holding tight to the ropes that helped control the terrified animals. The ground around them swirled and funneled beneath their feet, rising and falling like the swells of the sea. They had pulled all the extra clothing from the packs, providing makeshift shields for their face that afforded little protection. Somehow the stinging, heated particles found ways inside, penetrating ears and nostrils, and burning lips until they bled.

Brinn was worried. He had heard that remaining motionless in sandstorm meant death; for wherever the wind met with an obstruction, it piled up in huge mounds. More than the story told of hunters who had thus been buried alive. Yet to move seemed to invite death, and the sloped escarpment allowed most of the sand to flow up and over instead of piling it before the opening.

Despite the protection of the overhang and the additional boulder, the sand flew everywhere. Before long, everyone's eyes were red and irritated, the lids crusted and swollen.

Mekiva's throat was raw and swollen. She

was certain she had never been this thirsty in her life. Every breath she took, she choked on dust. Raffi and Jaxx had both stressed the need to conserve their water; not knowing how far they would need to travel before they located a well or oasis. Despite this, it tempted her to use some of the water to wash the grit from her mouth and eyes. It was a waste of water. The flying particles of sand and grit would replace anything she removed in seconds. She wished she had learned a shield spell. There was one in the big grimoire, but she had left it behind at Brinn's after copying any she thought she might need into her personal spell book. Using her ability to manipulate the wind could make it worse.

No one knew how long the elements had buffeted them. Brinn had been told that such tempests were usually of short duration. It seemed as if he had spent half the day wondering if the storm would bury them alive before moving on.

Jaxx and Von wondered about something similar. Had Izabal manipulated the weather in order to rid herself of unwelcome complications? The sorceress would not forget the blow to her ego... or her plans.

During one breath, the wind howled throughout their small haven, the next breath it was silent. The sand was no longer being thrown against them by the hot tempest. It took a while for their minds to accept the idea that the storm had passed.

Gwen was the first to break the silence. "Well, first I'm almost drowned by water and now I'm almost drowned by sand. Is it just me or does it seem like someone is trying to tell me something?"

Everyone laughed.

"Facing a gale at sea and drowning seems a pleasant way to go when compared to choking to death as your lungs fill up on hot sand." Jaxx once again wondered why she had walked away from a comfortable berth aboard the Sea Wyvern to start a freight hauling business.

Sayed decided he had waited long enough. "Praise be to Ao. I need a drink of water." Without waiting for any of the others, he walked back to his mule and removed the cloth covering her face. There was still a thin dusting of fine grit on her coat, but the cloth had protected her eyes and nose from the worst of the storm. Taking down one of the big water skins, he poured a small amount into a cup, drank about half, and then offered the parched mule the rest. Then he carefully dusted much of the sand away from her eyes and wiped out her nose and mouth.

After observing Sayed's actions, the others set out to make the animals as comfortable as possible. It was amazing how fast the frightened horses settled down. Water and a grain bag worked wonders.

The storm had blown shallow drifts of sand throughout the overhang, some almost as tall as the smaller goats' back. This did not seem to bother them. The hungry goats no trouble scrambling onto the drifted sand to reach the cracked corn Sayed had placed there.

By the time they had cared for the animals, they had all recovered a measure of strength from the exhaustion they experienced immediately following their battle with the elements. The two women had carefully brushed the particles of sand from their hair and clothing and were now using scraps of cloth and water to clean the sand and salt from their faces.

The men had gathered by the big rock. They were debating how they were going to move it now that the storm was over. There was barely enough room for the men to squeeze through. There was no way the horses were going anywhere.

Mekiva smiled. She was too tired to walk all night, anyway. If they had not moved it by tomorrow, she'd offer to help. She rolled her cloak into a cushion for her head, lay down next to Gwen, and fell into an exhausted sleep.

CHAPTER 20

"Twist! Where are you? We are ready to leave." Mekiva called out for her Mir-cat, but the flying feline was nowhere in sight. As he got older, his absences had become more common. But he always located Mekiva when he was ready to return. He was probably out looking for one of the reddish-brown lizards he was so fond of. They had seen no sign of life since they entered the Red Zone, but Twist had no problem finding something to eat.

Gwen wasn't worried. Twist was no longer a pudgy little kitten. He weighed as much as Brin and Jaxx together. He was much too large to ride on Mekiva's shoulder and could easily carry her if necessary. She did not know how he could fly. His bones were not hollow. She knew that after the last time, he got hurt. His wings did not look strong enough to lift his weight, yet he flew easily. He could also adjust his weight so he could ride behind Mekiva without straining the horse. She slapped her mare lightly, moving her to the side so she could tighten up the cinch on her saddle. An unusual sound caught her attention. Gwen looked around. Nothing. Then it came again, a faint cry, almost like the wail of a baby.

"What is it? Did you hear from Twist?" Brinn

asked when Gwen reacted to the sound. He glanced around, expecting to spot the flying pest approaching from an angle that would prevent anyone from spotting him until it was too late.

"No, it's something else. I hear something crying." The keening sound, coming unexpectedly from nowhere, had unnerved her. She continued to listen, searching around with the others for its source.

Then she exclaimed excitedly, "It's coming from over there." She pointed to the hole in the back of the overhang they were using. "Maybe someone was hurt during the sandstorm. Sayed said that his people knew safe places that are passed from father to son. There could be another entrance that got blocked by sand. It could be hurt and need help."

"It's been an entire sun cycle. Anyone injured would have died from loss of blood by now. But we can check it out just to be sure."

Raffi volunteered to look and Keeyun tagged along because he was bored.

Moving closer, Keeyun crouched by the opening in the back of the cave, almost buried by the sand. With both men digging, they were able to clear the opening in minutes. The entrance was small, much smaller than anyone could easily crawl into, so Raffi volunteered to check it out. Duaars could see fairly well in the dark, but he took along a lantern in case he needed the extra light. Born to a family of five sons, all who loved crawling through caves, the cramped confines of the tunnel didn't bother him; even though he preferred the open air. He crawled on his stomach into the dark interior, which soon opened up into a small grotto. The cave appeared to be a living space, with a few baskets of dried berries and nuts stacked alongside a small store of wood and kindling for building fires. Someone had used stone and mud to craft a small fireplace, complete with a turnspit; however, the ashes inside were cold. A second, smaller passage exited the rear of the tiny cavern; blocked by a tumble of sand and rocks and broken scrub. The mournful cries seemed to come from beyond the blockage. Raffi squirmed and wiggled his body into the opening, but he could not maneuver his arm enough to move the rocks and dirt. It was just too tight a fit for his wide shoulders. Frustrated; he backed out to the main room, calling out to anyone behind the blockage.

"Hello!! Is there anyone inside? Can you answer me?" There was a slight rustling sound, and the cries increased in volume, but he could not recognize any type of words, only sound. The desperate cries increased, as if the trapped person knew help was only a few feet away. Raffi concentrated so intently on the cries, hoping to recognize the language being spoken, that he failed to hear anyone approaching until a small hand tapped him on his shoulder, causing him to jump. Startled, he struck his head on the low ceiling, letting out a sharp curse, then quickly shut up as Gwen slid into the small cave beside him.

"Move out of the way and let me try," she suggested. "I may not be as strong as you, but I'm much smaller."

"First, help me move this rock. Then we will decide if it's safe for you to go further in." Raffi took the small rope he used as a belt and wrapped it around the larger stone blocking the passage. Then, after working his way back beyond Gwen, he gestured for her to start pulling. With her assistance, the two loosened the rock and slowly slide it out of the rubble; followed by a small amount of dirt and dust that fell as the ground settled. The falling debris wasn't enough to worry the astute duaar, so he allowed Gwen to slide a little farther into the tunnel. The sides and ceiling seemed to hold well, so Gwen proceeded to the next obstruction, a sizeable chunk of a shattered tree limb wedged sideways across the opening. She cautiously tugged at the branch, but it was jammed in tight and would not budge. What was worse, it was also too close to the ceiling for her to try chopping it out with any kind of axe.

"I think I can dig under it and crawl through, she said to Jaxx, but I'm going to need the lantern. Can you light it and pass it back to me?" The flickering light was too dim for her to see what was making the cries, but the wailing increased as the light shone down the passage, allowing her vivid imagination to conjure up loads of unpleasant images before she got it back under control. Despite her fears, she could never get so close to someone trapped inside, and then leave them there to die. Inching her way along on her stomach, she reached out into the darkness, feeling with her hand, hoping to locate the trapped person.

"Hello! Can you hear me?" She called again and again, but her only answer was the frantic whimpers and sounds of movement, as though someone was struggling to escape.

The broken stones and sharp spikes of trees snapped during the storm made the arduous task of crawling through the dark, narrow confines even more threatening. Alone, in the dark and narrow opening, Gwen's imagination ran wild. Apprehen-

sion magnified the sounds of her harsh inhalations and pounding heartbeat. She stopped and
took a deep breath to stop her panic attack, then
pressed onward; determined to rescue whoever
was trapped within the honeycomb of wreckage.
The dust in the air irritated her nose and throat,
bringing on a strident barking cough that allowed
Raffi to follow her movements. Still, the fear of
the tunnel breaking up around her grew as she
crawled further into the partially collapsed area.

"Maybe I should go back, she thought to
herself. It's too far, too tight, I can't do it." She
had just about talked herself into giving up when
her hand grasped something warm and furry
that moved away from her touch while crying
out in pain. Confined into a small area, the small
creature thrashed around, unsuccessfully trying
to escape.

"Rheaaz, guide me! It's an animal," she
called back to Raffi, "what should I do now?"

"Gwen, freeze!! Don't touch it!" he shouted
urgently. "If the animal is hurt, it may bite. Move
slowly and pull your hand away, then back out of
there." For once, Gwen didn't argue. She slowly
withdrew her hand while crawling backwards
away from the animal.

"Help... please... help." Startled, Gwen froze
again, not sure if she had really heard the barely
whispered words spoken in broken common.
She leaned a little closer to the animal and asked,
"Can you understand me?"

"Yes, hhhhurt," came the response from the
darkness. "Hurt bad, help", it begged softly, its
voice rough and scratchy sounding as though it
had gone without water for some time.

"Jaxx, it's not an animal after all. Whoever it is, he's trapped and in pain. I'm going to see if I can get him out." She slid as close to the trapped body as possible, then began pulling away any sharp pieces of broken plants and rocks within reach. The trapped man must have been wearing a heavy fur coat that was entangled in the debris from the slide. In fact, the storm drove one branch through the coat and pinned him to the ground. She could see dried blood around the stick and on the ground near his body. "Brace yourself, she said, this is going to hurt." With one foot against a large tree root for leverage and she jerked the stick out.

"Arrrrghhhh!" he screamed loudly as the stick came out. Startled, Gwen belatedly realized that the stick had been driven into his flesh under the coat. Blood seeped from the area around the hole where the stick had protruded. "I know it hurts, but I need to do something about the bleeding. Try to stay still." She brushed aside the fur near the wound, noticing it was already wet and sticky from older blood. Probably dried to the wound too, she mused silently. *Nothing I can do about that now.* Shrugging, she muttered a quick prayer to Rheaaz and laid her hand over the wound. Almost instantly, the flow of blood stopped, and the small man stopped thrashing around so much.

"I know you hurt, but you must stop fighting me. I need you to push with your legs or I'll not be able to get you out." Gwen could feel the little man bunching his muscles under her hand to prepare for pushing while she pulled. She took a tight hold of his coat and tugged; with his help, she could move him a few inches closer to the opening. "This is going to take a little longer than I thought," she said to the trapped man. "But once I get you free of this blockage, Raffi can help me pull." She braced her foot against a tangle of roots and tugged again; sliding his body into the mouth of the small opening she had cleared. "Just one more time and you should be free, so really dig in and push. Now!" she said, dragging the man through the opening and into the main tunnel, free at last. She rolled backwards to rest; her breath coming in shallow gasps that caused Jaxx to hurry forward in case she was injured.

"Are you alright?" he asked. Splashes of scarlet and clay brown covered most of her clothing.

"Yes, just exhausted. I think he just passed out." The little man's long, heavy overcoat was matted and sticky from the wet and drying blood, preventing her from seeing the extent of his injuries in the dim light.

"I guess it will be easier to examine him after we get his coat off. Raffi, would you hand me your knife? I'll just cut it away; it's ruined by all this blood and muck, anyway."

Holding Raffi's knife in one hand and grabbing the heavy fur in the other, Gwen started to cut the wet fur coat away from the unconscious man. Blood flowed down her arm as the sharp knife sliced into the coat. The man twitched wildly and moaned in pain, subconsciously jerking his body away from her hand.

"Raffi," she said, backing slowly away. "I think you had better come here and look at him; something is wrong. His coat is bleeding."

"You mean you cut him while trying to cut away his coat?"

"No, I mean, the actual coat is bleeding. It's really bleeding, like you would if I cut your arm."

"Wait a minute, let me get another light." Raffi crawled back to the entrance of the tiny cavern; sticking his head out of the hole to talk. "Can one of you give me a lantern with some oil in it? The one we have with us is empty and Gwen needs light to work on the injured man." Minutes later, he was back. He held the lantern overhead and as the light fell across her patient's face, Raffi almost dropped the lantern. Gwen was tenderly holding his hand and praying to Rheaaz for the recovery of something. But it mystified him exactly what kind of something it was. *Drasst! What should I do? The beast could turn on her.* His eyes stayed focused on the pair in front of him as he calmly inched his hand closer to the long knife hanging on his belt. *Drasst. I gave it to Gwen.*

"Gwen," he whispered, "I'm not trying to scare you, but did he bite you or scratch you or anything like that?"

"No, of course not; I told you already that he's not an animal, but a man."

"Not exactly a man, I think." *Perhaps he's some type of hybrid? But unlike any animal I've ever seen before.* "Maybe it would be best if we just leave him here to awaken on his own."

"Don't be silly. I'm going to finish healing him. He didn't attack me when I pulled the stick from his shoulder, so I think I'll be fine. It had to have hurt, even with my gentle touch." She giggled softly and then placed her hand tenderly on Raffi's shoulder.

"For someone who's traveled all around like you have; you are still such a boy about some things. It's my duty to help whomever I can, without judging.

That's why Rheaaz graced me with my gift. Now either come over here and help me or go. But leave the lantern behind. It's your choice." She turned back to the torn and bloody body, raised its head onto her lap; and then she began to pray.

"Rheaaz, this is one of your creatures. He did nothing to deserve the pain he has received from the storm. Please grant me your blessing, and heal him of his injuries, so that one day he might return the favor unto another deserving soul." The light from her hand grew steadily, covering the strange body in a pulsing glow that gradually grew in strength, until it suddenly flared brightly, and then faded all at once.

"Thank you for your gift," Gwen intoned solemnly as she lowered its head back to the ground.

The bloody figure was breathing deeply and no longer moaning in pain. For the first time, Gwen noticed his eyes were golden, with slotted pupils, like a hippogriff or a dragon. He gazed up at her and smiled weakly, his large pointy teeth overhanging his mouth. Then he closed his eyes and slept, this time the deep natural sleep so necessary after an illness.

She untied her water bottle and placed it beside the sleeping man. It wasn't a lot, but it was the best she could do. Then she followed Raffi out of the cave.

CHAPTER 21

Now that they were deep inside the Red Zone, the small group pushed forward in short stages only, traveling early in the day and late when the cool air began each night. It was easier to sleep in the shade of rocks or inside tents during the day. Von now understood why the animals were so comfortable passing in and out of the homes of their masters. It was important that they become accustomed to behavior inside and recognize family spaces. With no trees to provide shade, the animals needed the tents to protect them from the relentless heat of the twin suns.

Just before sunrise on the second day after the sandstorm, they saw signs of untouched ruins. From the ridge, the path down the back side of the massive pile of red sand and rocks looked to be a two candle-mark ride, but it took most of the day to wind their way down the loosely packed desert silt to the ancient road below. The two camels, then Von's horse, smelled the water and increased their pace. It was clear they were nearing the source long before anyone could see the haze of liquid evaporating in the afternoon sun. The oryx broke away and ran for the pool. Seeing the oryx pass on its way to the water, the mare fought to follow, pulling against the leather reins as he fought to keep control.

Von looked around the clearing and sighed. It was not a pretty spot, this little rock-strewn glade where the narrow trail forked away from the main road. The brackish water with its green scum film made his stomach roil. The oryx were not content to wait, and drank with loud gulps, eager to slake their thirst. The horses did not want to get close to oryx but wasted no time once they the sated birds moved to graze on the green scrub nearby. The goats spread out around the edges, with several wading into the pool to drink their fill.

Von wondered why Raffi and Keeyun had let the animals drink first until he realized most of the green film was gone. He figured an underground stream must feed the pond, as the level remained the same regardless of how many animals drank.

Once the animals had their fill, the rest of the party drank. Then Sayed filled a pail for cooking and sat it beside the remains of a prior fire. The girls portioned out enough for two basins and then washed their faces and hands with obvious pleasure. Moth and Keeyun watered the chickens and the remaining duck, then began filling the various waterskins and bottles. The chances of them finding another fresh water source were not good.

The tension in the faces of his friends over the past few candlemarks had relaxed. Whether they attributed this to surviving the sandstorm or to their safe arrival at the waterhole, he could not determine. But the bitterness had vanished from Jaxx's cheerful voice as she offered to help Sayed feed the animals. She brushed down the horses after Sayed slipped bags of grain over their noses and listened to the subdued laughter of the others as they argued with Raffi over whose turn it was to help prepare the evening meal. Raffi lost and Von winced, remembering the last time his friend helped cook dinner. He sat with his back to a flat rock and watched the kindling of the fire, Raffi's less than deft manipulation of the bread dough, and the steaming of the tough dried meat in the pot before he added the softer ingredients. It was good. The bread was hard on the bottom, but the Oryx enjoyed it. And there could have been a bit more of the soup, but what there was of it was tasty even if it could have used a little more salt.

The packs were removed, and everyone worked together to get the tents erected, using the limited shade the atrophied trees provided. None were much taller than Jaxx or Raffi, with narrow spikes instead of leaves, but they blocked a lot of the sunlight. There were clear signs that at one time there had been a town of some size around them. Unlike the ruins in the borderlands, these building had lain untouched since the battle that created the wastelands. The broken foundations of buildings buried in the sand showed unlimited salvage possibilities. Brinn looked pleased as he wandered around the ruins, looking at the busted blocks buried in the sand. "Once we locate Von's family treasure, we can return with a crew and excavate some ruins. There's no telling what is waiting to be found."

Keeyun was not as enthusiastic. "All I see is shattered, mud brick homes. Maybe there was a temple in town? There are usually a few gold pieces used for the service. How will you know where to start looking? Seems like a waste of coins that could be better used elsewhere. I haven't seen anything that points to treasure."

Moth frowned. He had been on more than one of Brinn's speculative treasure hunts. Usually, they were lucky to break even, much less make a profit. Once or twice, they had got lucky and found a hidden treasure. Brinn reminded him of a hungry dog. Once he got his teeth into the meat, it was almost impossible to get him to give it up. His eyes had that same sparkle he'd seen too many times before. He'd expected Key to back up Brinn, not complain about wasting time.

"We've risked a lot more to make a lot less. No one escaped the blast. There's sure to be at least one or two caches to be found in a town of this size."

"Let's wait until this search is complete before we plan the next one." Moth shook his head and walked away.

The girls were so tired they didn't notice Moth's odd behavior. They were full, and sleepy and ready to head to the tents to rest.

Sayed gave the animals a rinse before allowing them to graze on the green saw grass and bushes that grew near the water. "They need to rest as long as possible. Grazing on the fresh grass will give them the strength they will need. This is likely the last chance for water before we reach the center of the bane land."

"Does that mean we have to carry enough water for the rest of the trip when we leave?" Gwen wasn't sure it would matter. Even if they filled every empty container, it was doubtful there would be enough for everyone. That would mean rationing again.

Brinn was talking to Moth about the possibility of returning to dig for unclaimed treasure when Moth suddenly looked up and around the oasis. The enigmatic mage held his finger in front of his mouth, signaling for silence. The expression in his eyes was troubled. It was little more than a quiver, a feeling of imminent danger, but it had his nerves on edge.

Brinn narrowed his eyes, looking around. As far as he could see, it was the same red color, sand, rocks, a few dried out plants, more sand. Absolutely nothing caught his eye. The skies were empty, with not even a to cloud to break up the haze. Maybe it was because he had been staring at the same landscape for too long? He closed his eyes and took and deep breath, held it for a count of ten, then opened his eyes and looked around. Nothing. "We need to set a guard tonight. My trouble bump is itching. No use taking a chance."

Brinn frowned. "Much as I hate that itch, it has saved our ass more times than I can remember. I will talk to the others and set up a rotation,"

CHAPTER 22

"Jaxx. Wait up, I will walk with you."

"If you like." Jaxx wondered what was up. Everyone was antsy since Brinn, and Moth set up a watch rotation. Over the last year, she had come to appreciate Moth's gut instincts. If he said he had an itch, they all looked for trouble. "I'm going to climb up the bluff. I need to get the lay of the land before it gets dark."

Raffi would rather have been playing cards or sleeping. "Yeah. I forgot you got first watch. Why did you join the pool? There are plenty of us to cover the night."

"Why did you get in? My eyes are as good as yours. And Von pulled 3rd mark. He can't see twenty feet until the moon comes up."

"Yeah, but" His face squirmed as he fought to come up with the words he needed.

"But nothing. You don't think I should stand guard because I'm a female now? Just because I look different doesn't mean I can't pull my weight. I can out-shoot everyone but Keeyun. And my ax doesn't care that I have long hair and softer skin."

"That's not it. I just think you are pushing yourself too hard to prove you can do anything in this body you did in your other. That ax has got to be hard to swing now."

"It is. But I will manage. Be honest. It bothers you I'm not a man. You were fine with me as long as I had the right tools hanging between my legs. My using an ax has nothing to do with it."

"Hmmm. Honesty. Let me think about how I should answer this," Raffi said. "You're a beautiful woman. Men would drape you in jewels just to see your smile. But you wear men's clothing, and openly carry a sword. I have to admit that bothers me. Sometimes I see you working out and I find myself thinking that you would be better suited to warm my bed than fight by my side. Is it so hard for you to understand my uncertainty?"

Jaxx knew she wasn't feeling emotional. Raffi's answer had been intended to provoke a reaction, and it would be best if she pretended, she had not heard the question. Ignoring him seemed like her best defense. His answer was not the response she had expected. She had to think about her reply. "Yes, this is different. You know that among the Duaar, they expect women to pull our own weight. They teach us to rely on our own abilities instead of a man. The best swordsmen in my father's guards trained me. That I was really a female may have entered his mind, but he never allowed it to affect my training. My parents expected me to train the same way the boys trained, and I obeyed."

"But fighting men with an edged weapon... I think that's the part that bothers me. My nightmare is waking up with a knife in my chest because a woman was having a bad moon day."

"That's what I mean. Only a man would think that way. Being male for so many years has helped me to understand the way your mind works. I don't think it's the fear of a sharp weapon. If a woman kills a hen for dinner, she uses a knife. A sword is just a longer knife. It's me killing another person with a blade you find offensive. And I don't blame you. I killed a man for the first time less than a fortnight after leaving my father's household. Well, I killed a Gynark raider who thought he could sell me. Either way, my actions cut creature short the life of a living, thinking being. I made the decision that my life was worth more than his; and I acted. And I can't even tell myself it was for food."

"There is truth in your words. I thought nothing about it when we fought our way from the prison. In my mind, you were a man under a curse. Now I'm adjusting to the idea that you are actually a woman and the man's body is the cursed form. But it's more than the sword. You talk as a man would, planning strategy and defense; and your swordsmanship is improving. Von treats you as a partner, not as a female to be sheltered from harm." Raffi hesitated, "and lately Brinn has included you in our plans; as though you were a man."

"That's good," she said with a smile. "I expect to be included. It would disappoint my parents if I did not pull my weight. My father is a hard man; but fair. He taught me to do the right thing, no matter how difficult that thing might be. Honor is something he understands, vengeance too. But my father isn't here. I am. So, you are going to have to make do with me. I may not have as much experience in this form as I do in the other, but my heart is just as willing."

"I understand the gist of your tirade. You're a valuable member of the team, and an unusual asset. Your mind doesn't look at things the same way the other women do; but that's a good thing. It gives you a unique perspective. It could be the edge we need in a fight. No one will expect it. The rest is a personal issue I'll have to deal with."

"Thanks. That's all I can ask for. Von and I are happy working being a part of this team. Its feels right."

Raffi laughed. "The question is what you are looking to get out of this relationship? Only the insane risks their life for nothing. You may do a few crazy things, but you are not a foolish woman."

"Maybe I want to find a place where I don't have to constantly peer over my shoulder for assassins."

"That place does not exist." His heart wasn't really into all this verbal sparring. "You need to accept reality. You will always be a target, especially if anyone discovers you are the heir to the throne."

Jaxx froze. *How did he know that*? She looked, but Raffi was no longer standing behind her. She needed to talk to Von and get his opinion. It would have to wait until the end of her shift. She shrugged and started climbing. If anything were going to happen, it would be right after the second sun had set. The attack would come while the shadows would make it difficult to distinguish between a fixed object and a moving one.

Raffi watched her make her way to the top of the bluff. He realized he had been pushing Jaxx but had told himself it was only for her own good. Now he wondered if he had overlooked her feelings while trying to protect his own.

He decided he needed to be alone for a while and think.

———————

Jaxx had been happy to draw the first watch. She was even happier when Brinn had arrived to relieve her.

This meant she would be last to lie down. She would get more sleep since the others would talk for at least a candlemark before slipping away to their bedrolls. As soon as her relief showed up, she headed straight to bed. After arranging a sack of grain to use as a pillow and doubling up one blanket to lie upon, she pulled the others over her lanky, curvaceous new body. Then she lay and listened to the sounds of the night. There had been lots of dead trees still lying in the same condition as when they fell, and someone had gathered a lot of it. The dry wood burned with a clear flame, and occasionally snapped out a red spark. The animals were quiet, most grazing happily on the fresh growth. Mekiva slept soundly, but Gwen was restless, turning and shifting position. It tempted Jaxx to walk over and check on her, but she knew that would disturb the sleep of the others and bring on unwanted questions. Questions she wasn't ready to answer. With star light on her face and the chilly nighttime wind tickling the hair on her brow, she lay and thought of the strangeness of it all. Sometime later, she fell asleep.

CHAPTER 23

Brinn concentrated his attention on the pile of eroded rocks, but nothing moved. The shadow he'd seen was not human. He was certain of that. He scanned the area around the campsite, but other than sandy scrub and a patch of stunted cactus, there was nothing in sight. It must be his imagination. Everyone's nerves were on edge. He could see Twist heading that way. He had something in his claws, most likely a lizard or a hare. As the Mir cat approached the camp area, he began flying faster. He swooped over the fire and dropped his catch, then continued to climb, rising higher than the bluff. Then he plummeted toward the ground, his speed increasing as he fell.

———

Twist's speed did not slow until his claws struck the hidden watcher. He lashed out, bloody strips flying as the razor-sharp tines dug deep furrows through feathered flesh. Once he had a good grip, he flew upward, jerking the gangly watcher up in its toes. The winged demon yelped and swung at the Mir-dragon with both hands, cursing aloud. Twist was almost level with Brinn when he opened his claws and darted away. The scout screamed threats at the Mir cat as he flapped his wings, only to discover they would not support his weight. He cursed as he fought to stay aloft, the sound alerting everyone in camp that something was happening. His angry tirade ended abruptly as Brinn sent an arrow deep into his chest. His tattered wings gave one weak flap, and then he fell. There was a puff of dust when he struck the ground.

Brinn immediately nocked a new arrow in his bow. The dead scout was definitely a Xyvelix; a buff-colored male with deep gouges across what remained of his forehead. The scout had been holding a bow when Twist struck him. He scanned the area nearby, searching for movement.

The scout would not have been by himself. It was the partner he hadn't seen that worried him. The winged demons were cautious, preferring to attack while their targets slept. For them to come out this early in the evening meant they believed it was going to be a short, easily won fight. That usually meant there were a lot of them nearby. His eyes scanned the sky.

———

No one could have missed the scream. Raffi scowled, dropped his cards, and reached for his sword. As he rose to his feet, a dark shadow broke away from a pile of rubble and ran toward him. Instead of flying, the spine benders wings were tight against its back. He ran on his back legs with three claws extended before him, his beak gaping wide.

Raffi's eyes went to his bow, propped again a rock a few feet away. Spine benders were easy to kill, their chest offered no protection to their heart. But a thick chitinous shell covered the rest of the beast, like a beetle. That's what it reminded him of, a beetle with patches of fur. Sayed said the Xyvelix kept them as pets. His eyes darted around, looking skyward. If there was a spine bender in camp, there would soon be more. Like the first, this one was not trying to fly overhead. He took two steps forward and drove his blade into its chest. The spine bender's eyes went wide, and a puzzled look came over his face. Then he fell.

As if its death was a signal, at least a hand full of the drasted beasts flew toward the camp, no longer concerned with remaining unseen. Von jerked around at a high-pitched scream and saw a Xyvelix covered in flames diving toward the pool of water. Less than a man's length away, it gave a strangled cry and collapsed to the sand. The feathers continued to burn, his light brown skin already blackened and cracking. He did not know who cast the spell, Moth or Mekiva, but was happy to know the others were prepared for a fight.

He needed to find a defensible location, preferably one where he didn't have to watch his back. Looking around, he spotted a likely spot and headed that way. He could see at least a dozen of the avian creatures flying in his direction. There had to be at least that many he missed. In the distance, he saw two horses running away from the camp. Seconds later, one of the demons flew off, carrying a goat.

Sayed wasted two or three arrows trying to bring it down before turning to fight off a pair of the spine benders. One of the beast's claws had dug a deep furrow along his thigh, before he drove his belt knife into its heart. The other beast was dragging its wing behind it as it fought to pull a struggling nanny toward the shadows. Sayed hit it twice, but the arrows bounced off its carapace. He gave up trying to save the goat and concentrated on two of the human hybrids that were trying to corner a mare. She landed a solid kick, sending one avian to the ground near the two oryx. The voracious oryx tore the stunned birdman apart, eating feathers and all.

Von knew he had little time. Dropping his pack on the sand, he removed his bow from his shoulder and strung it. The petrified stump in front of him was all that remained of a once majestic Alder. Now only about three feet high, the petrified tree offered him some protection from the front, as the large boulder protected his back. It also gave him a convenient place to lean his quiver of arrows. He took out four and stuck them point down in the soft ground beside him. Now satisfied he was as ready as he could be, he tried to relax.

When the main attack came, it surprised them all. First, a flight of arrows ripped through the air, a pointed announcement of what was to come. Most passed overhead doing no damage, but one glanced off Von's shoulder, leaving a shallow groove that bled more than it hurt. He knocked an arrow and waited for a target. He was wondering if he might have overreacted when a pair of sword wielding demons dropped from the rock wall behind him. He got off one arrow, striking the Xyvelix on the right, then grabbed his sword, knowing instinctively the left side swordsman would not hesitate or check on his partner. In the next confusing few moments, he somehow deflected the demon's obsidian blade before slashing his sword across the beast's throat. The flat of the injured beast's sword struck his hand, numbing his fingers. He panicked as his blade fell to the sand, and dove for the startled birdman. As his fingers closed on the Xyvelix neck, his face broke into a wicked grin. He continued to bend the birdman's head back until he felt a snap as the neckbones separated. The dying demon drove a shirt blade into his side, slicing through the fat and muscle below his ribs.

Von gasped at the pain, grit his teeth and limped back to where he'd dropped his bow.

Moth had settled behind a pile of rocks, hoping to get a better view of the shallow area where the girls had been sleeping. The two archers saw each other at the same time and released their arrows. The shattered stump blocked the arrow fired at Von, but Moth's shaft struck its target, and the Xyvelix fell, mortally wounded. He went to his knee as arrows from many directions hit the stump and the big rock, knocked another arrow, and looked for another target. The girls were on their own. He looked around for his cousin, but Keeyun was nowhere in sight.

The Xyvelix and their pets had wormed their way closer to the camp than anyone expected. Brinn kept his arrow trained on their movement, hoping for a clear shot. He had experienced battle with the wily scavengers several times in the past, but never this many at once. The first hint of his imminent danger was the arrow lodged in his side. He fell forward and rolled, gasping aloud as the shaft broke away, and landed in a half crouch. The rock offered limited shelter, but it allowed him to get off a shot at one of his assailants. The sly pair had landed at the back of the bluff, coming up behind him. Finding himself outnumbered and on his knees, he released the arrow and swung his bow like a staff, knocking the knife from the hand of the first Xyvelix, but the second drove his blade into his left shoulder. He pulled his boot blade and prepared for the next attack.

When it didn't come, Brinn dropped his bow, clamped the knife between his teeth, and struggled to remove the sword sheathed at his side while mentally thanking Mekiva. She must have spotted the Xyvelix and cast a spell. The winged demons could not move. He watched their eyes as they struggled to overcome the spell that held them frozen in place, but their bodies refused to respond. Brinn did not know how long Mekiva's spell would last, but he was not prepared to leave armed enemies behind him. One of the panicked birdmen hands remained frozen overhead. The second was balanced on one foot, the other leg frozen in mid-step. His intent was to cut their throats, but the abject fear in their eyes held his strike. Instead, he removed all their weapons and then he pushed them off the bluff, figuring they had a fifty-fifty chance of surviving the fall. At least there didn't appear to be any more nearby.

He was losing blood, and that was never a good thing. The blade in his shoulder helped keep the wound closed, but it made using that arm next to impossible. It was also impossible for him to reach the handle to pull it out. A black fog was growing before his eyes. His legs trembled, and he wondered if he should feel something besides cold. That made him smile. He hadn't noticed the suns going down. Twist appeared beside him and licked his face before lying down beside him. He sagged against the winged cat's body, enjoying the warmth.

Jaxx motioned the trio of Xyvelix forward, "Here birdie, birdie, come on, let's dance. I've been told I need to practice. I figure the three of you might equal one decent swordsman." She waited patiently for the three-armed demons to approach. As the first birdman flew past her position, she swung the heavy battle axe, burying the blade into its wing and back. His flight became an irregular flutter. The blow must have damaged his spinal cord, as he flew into the bluff wall with a grunt of pain and collapsed. The second Xyvelix wings beat furiously, moving him outside Jaxx's reach but in an excellent position to attack when his partner did. Jaxx had lost sight of the third beast and that was always dangerous. She shifted position, trying to put her back to a protected area. Unfortunately, that moved her into the range of a hidden archer. As the arrow struck her shoulder, she stumbled, started to scream, and realized she needed to swing her ax. The Xyvelix to her right had attacked as soon as his partner took the shot. Its wings whipped out and back, propelling it directly at Jaxx. The ax blade bit deep into his chest. His face turned white. He took a step toward Jaxx, and they collapsed side by side.

Gwen saw Jaxx fall and knew she had to help her somehow. The injury wasn't life threatening, but it had entered just to the right of her arm, and it appeared as if she was having trouble getting a breath. She tugged at Keeyun and pointed, indicating she wanted him to help her reach Jaxx. He grunted and waved her that way, before slicing his blade through an archer's string and bow. He flipped his sword beneath the next birdman's sword, twisted his wrist and grinned as the blade went flying. Before the startled avian understood what had happened, he struck, removing its head. From the corner of his eye, he could see Gwen taking care of Jaxx's wound. Satisfied she was in no immediate peril; he went looking for a new target.

Mekiva was tossing balls of ice at the winged demons, watching them grow larger the farther they had to travel before slamming into the target. She knocked five from the air and then looked around, surprised. They were gone as if they had never been there to begin with. She looked around but the fight appeared to be over. Then she noticed Von sprawled out on the ground beside two dead Xyvelix.

"Gwen, I need you!" she yelled as she ran.

The tired Shi'i healer ran as fast as she could. She hated to leave Jaxx, but she was stable. It was not likely the Xyvelix would return soon. Kiva moved out of her way as she ran up. Begging Rheaaz for her patience, she concentrated on the tissue around the blade and pulled it free. The magical energy quickly cauterized the blood vessels and began rebuilding the damaged tissue. Pain tore through her body and her concentration faltered. Mekiva held her upright as she lay her hands on Von's side once again and urged Rheaaz's waves of soothing healing to flow through his shoulder.

Moth and Raffi had moved Jaxx into the tent to rest. Now they were standing nearby watching as she healed Von. Instead of dispersing the excess energy into the air, she held it inside in case any of the others had minor injuries that needed attention.

"Where's Sayed?"

Keeyun shrugged. "He was worried about the animals. He said one of furry beetles had been dragging a nanny when it was killed. The goat had run off during the attack and he wanted to look around in case she was on the other side of the water grazing."

"He loves those goats. I'm certain he would prefer they took a camel. Or both oryx."

Raffi laughed. "He would pay them to take an oryx. I see him coming now. Looks like he didn't find the goat."

Gwen turned to look, as Sayed exited the trail leading from the desert water hole. He stumbled and grabbed for a young tree, somehow remaining on his feet. As he struggled back upright, she saw blood running down his side, staining the off-white material scarlet.

"Sayed's hurt." She rose, took a few wobbly steps toward him, then froze in horror as the jovial cook coughed up blood, choked, and fell to the ground. The shafts of three black arrows rose from the back of his blood stained trobe. From across the clearing, it was hard to say of if he was dead, but he was definitely dying.

Then she gasped as an arrow buried itself in her chest. Von somehow caught her before she hit the ground. "Drasst! Now what do we do?"

CHAPTER 24

Brinn sat up with a gasp, his face pale, his heart slamming in his chest. His head was pounding, and the intense sunlight was not helping matters. The twin suns were high overhead. He tried to slow his breathing long enough to get an idea of where he was and what was happening. Someone had wrapped his side with bandages. The arrow was gone from his back, but he could still feel the pull when he moved. It was healing, but not healed. How much time had passed?

Moth crouched down to talk to him. "How are you feeling?"

"Worse than when that wyvern spit vitriol at me. That was all on the outside. I hurt in places I didn't know could hurt."

"It was close. When Twist found you, he called Mekiva. He was busy licking the blood away from the knife blade in your shoulder. I examined the wound, expecting to find an open cut, however, the blade was keeping the wound closed. You had lost a lot of blood and that worried her. I got the arrow out and used my last healing spell but all I could do was stabilize the damage."

"How long have I been unconscious?"

"Two sun cycles."

Two. That meant Gwen could not heal him. Or she was in no shape to heal anyone. "I recall nothing after I killed the two Xyvelix. What happened?"

"We won. Well, Mekiva won. When she saw the arrow strike Gwen, she lost her temper. Remind me not to get her angry. She cast a spell and froze the Xyvelix and the spine benders."

"Yeah, I saw them freeze, but did not know what happened."

"You don't understand. She didn't freeze then temporarily. She froze them solid. Like statues. They are all still frozen." He gave an involuntary shiver.

"All of them?"

"Everyone. Over two dozen Xyvelix and twice as many of their pets. They are still standing exactly as they were when the spell struck." He paused to let what he said sink in. "We carried the ones inside the camp out into the desert. Left them standing in a hollow between two dunes."

"The spell will wear off and they will be out for revenge."

"I'm not sure if this spell will wear off. She only said one word. No."

"No?"

"That's all. I have seen nothing like it. I've heard of the will and the word, but I have never met a mage that could enact magic without a ritual spell and a focus. She scares me."

"What about the others?"

"We lost Sayed. It's going to be hard to tell his family. They were extremely helpful to Raffi and the boys. That's not all the bad news. Gwen's in bad shape. I gave her the last healing potion, but they had dipped the arrow in some kind of poison. She was too weak to heal herself, and too sick to pray. Last night, her body glowed. Mekiva was certain she had died, that Rheaaz had called her. She was wrong. The girl lives but she is still very weak. Her wounds are closed, her injuries healed. But she is still fighting the poison."

A stricken look flashed over Brinn's face, and his eyes darkened. He lay back on the pallet. "Find Sayed's pack. He mentioned he carried a small leather case with anti-venom. There's a snake that many of the tribes milked for venom. They spread it on their weapons. The poison doesn't kill, but it slows the body's functions, making it hard to think, or breathe. Chances are the avians used the same venom."

"I guess we need to make some decisions. But not now. You need to rest. I will look for the antivenom. The other injuries are minor. I will take care of what I can. The rest can wait.

Moth regarded the supplies thoughtfully. They had lost a horse and all but three goats. Two white and a white and brown one. This puzzled him. When he went to talk to Brinn, there were only two white goats grazing by the pond. The brown and white one was nowhere in sight. Keeyun was not in camp, nor had he been seen since he gave Gwen the antivenom. It didn't take a genius to suspect that the two things were related. That same nanny had been grazing near Brinn while they were talking earlier that afternoon. A druid could take the form of an animal if necessary. Keeyun had once changed into a reindeer and pulled Moth's sled across the ice after the polar bear killed the real deer. His gaze went to the animals, then he looked around in every direction, even though he knew there was no possibility of anyone slipping up on him. What he couldn't understand was why his cousin would spy on them. He could have joined the conversation. There was no logical reason for his cousin to change his shape. He couldn't be hungry; he'd eaten two plates of the beans and fry bread.

"Need some help?" Mekiva asked. "I'm all packed and ready to go."

"No. I'm about finished. We loaded most of the big things on the oryx' pack frames. I just need to balance the load for the goats and have the packs ready to load. That will make it easy to leave in the morning." He reached for his belt knife and realized it was still lying next to his whet stone. "Mind lending me your knife. I left mine beside my bedroll."

Mekiva pulled her knife and passed it to Moth.

Moth eyes widened. "Where did you get this knife?"

"One of the winged demons embedded it in Brinn's back. I didn't think he needed it any longer. Brinn tossed all the frozen bodies off the bluff." She looked puzzled. "Why do you ask?"

"It's a Savaii blade. My people give them to a young man when they come of age. My father gave this knife to Keeyun just before he died." Moth raised his shirt and showed her an almost identical knife in a pouch hanging around his neck. The only difference was one sigil carved into the handle. "See this? It is Taoyuan, my name in my native tongue. This rune says Keeyun."

"I'm sorry. I did not know it belonged to Keeyun.

He never mentioned losing it."

Nor did he mention plunging it into Brinn's back...

The evening sky had darkened to shades of orange and sienna, with touches of shading toward purple, when everyone gathered for dinner. Von had volunteered to cook and while the meal wasn't to Sayed's standards, it was edible. Twist sprawled upon the flat rock Von had used for cover, enjoying the final few bites of the creature he's snagged for dinner. No one could identify the bloody beast, and there was not enough of it to risk angering the Mir cat by taking enough to do a taste test. Twist seemed to enjoy his meal. Moth winced as the sharp crack of the thigh bone snapping was followed by the sound of crunching cartilage. Upon finishing his meal, he began grooming his golden-brown fur to remove any trace of the gore his food had left behind.

"We need to decide. Do we turn back or continue? Normally, this would not be a question. Once we begin a search, we continue. But this is different. Sayed was our guide."

Jaxx nodded. "Until you mentioned spotting the ruins of a large city from the top of the bluff, I would have agreed it was time to give up and go home. Now I feel like we are moving the right direction. Is it smart to turn back with our goal in sight?

Von nodded agreement. However, he stayed out of the conversation since it was his family treasure they were searching for. Until Sayed died, it had seemed like any other expedition.

The Xyvelix had no connection to his uncle or Izabal. No one was going to appear and steal away another medallion. And he had seen no sign of another traveler since camping with Sayed's cousins. It was best he remains neutral and let the pragmatic members of the group determine their destination.

Moth sat next to Keeyun, listening to everyone speak. Brinn had already decided they would continue. They were too close to give up. The company had invested too much into this project to take a loss. Without Sayed to guide them, returning would require rationing water, but they could handle it. Much as he hated to admit it, Twist was becoming an asset instead of a pain in the ass. The Mir could spot something edible from high in the sky and often shared his catch. Before he let Mekiva go thirsty, he would discover where the water was located.

Raffi cleared his throat, and Brinn looked his way. "You know my opinion on giving up. There's nothing I can add to the conversation. I would like a word with you later. I'm going to check on the horses." Keeyun looked at him but did not say a word. Raffi stared back. Key's blank faced gaze was giving him the creeps. He didn't wait for anyone to answer before he walked away.

Moth took advantage of Raffi's distraction to study his cousin. Something was nagging at him, something he couldn't put a name to. It wasn't just his behavior. Key was moody. He could be going through one of his 'distant' episodes. It wasn't that. It was something else. Something important. Before he could get an idea of what was off, Raffi walked away, and Key turned his attention back to Brinn and the debate.

"I asked Moth to get an idea of what supplies

we have and how long we can risk staying in the city once we arrive. He gave me a general idea. It's not great, but it could be worse. He sorted through our meager rations and calculated how many days we could survive on the limited amount of food and water that we were carrying with us. At the current rate of consumption, the rations would last about a week. We could butcher a goat and give ourselves a day or two longer, but we need them to carry supplies as long as possible. There are still four hens. Between the eggs and the meat that might give us another 4 days. Less than three weeks total. Worse come to worse, we could all go on half rations of food and water which would stretch it out a moon cycle. Not much time to locate the ruins, find the hidden treasure and return."

No one looked especially happy at his words, especially after Raffi added, "And we need to factor in the demons. They could come back. The meat they took won't last long and our animals are a tempting target."

Mekiva felt it was time to join the discussion. "This might make it easier. Gwen is doing better. Sayed's antivenom was the key. The poison was not lethal, and she slept off the effects once we neutralized the toxin. She is resting but I'm certain she will be ready to continue in the morning."

Raffi grinned. "We took that under consideration when we came up with the number of days we can spare before we have to head back." He held up his hand. "Five. The city ruins look to be at least a day's ride away. That's doesn't leave a lot of wiggle room."

"You are saying we have five days to reach the ruins, locate Von's family treasure, and gather anything we can sell for a profit. If Twist can locate anything extra, that's great, but we can't depend on it. Then we have to give up and return home."

"That's the gist of it. Get as much rest as you can because we have a hard ride ahead of us." He turned to Moth, who had moved to his side as the meeting ended, and everyone wandered off.

"I need a little of your time."

Okay. Here?

"No. Somewhere we won't be disturbed. We need to have a serious talk about Keeyun."

"Keeyun? Wha.."

"Later. It will wait. Let's find Raffi and talk."

Brinn could not believe what Moth was saying. Key had been acting strange, but he was young. He might resent the way he had taken Von and Jaxx under his wing.

Raffi disagreed. There were times when Jaxx irritated him to the point he wanted to scream. Now that he, was she, it was even worse. A woman had never provoked him the way Jaxx did. "Maybe Key was having trouble handling the female members of the party?"

Moth shook his head. "That's not all. It's not like Keeyun to avoid a fight. This makes three times he's vanished instead of fighting. Something's wrong. The first time I made excuses for him, thinking there wasn't a lot a druid could do. But the second time, there were plenty of plants growing at the oasis. I did not see him use a spell. And he missed a shot

Gwen could have made. Instead of being the best archer in the group, he's now one of the worst? It doesn't add up."

"Could he be upset that Gwen is a healer and he can only cure minor wounds in humans? That might be why he didn't try." Brinn did not want to believe Keeyun was intentionally avoiding his responsibilities.

Moth's eyes reflected his concern. "No. Keeyun would have given his life to keep Brinn alive. Instead, he let Gwen heal everyone. He didn't even offer to help. That is not like my cousin."

Raffi chimed in. "Now that you mention it, it surprised me he didn't try to heal the horse. That was a minor fracture. I've seen him heal bones snapped in two or three places. Instead, he slit its throat. "

Moth's eyes widened. "That can't be! Keeyun asks forgiveness every time he pulls a fish from a pond. There's no way he would let an animal die without need. To simply slit its throat. Are you certain it wasn't already cut?"

"Completely. I was standing less than a stride away." Raffi had spent many years working with Keeyun. He should have been able to read his thoughts from the slightest hint of facial cues. He was wrong. The young druid had kept his face fixed and emotionless as he took the horse's life.

"It could explain the knife. Perhaps he could not stand to hold the blade after he used it to take the life of the horse?"

"No." Moth shook his head sadly. "They left

the knife in Brinn's back during the fight. I have that knife. He killed the horse after Brinn was stabbed. He must have used his boot knife on the horse."

"There's got to be something we are missing. From this point on, watch him. I want to know where he goes, and what he does. This personality change happened after he left to find Tyro. He has never talked about what happened when he found him. Now might be a good time to ask."

The three men looked at each other but no one knew the answer to the puzzle.

———————

From his position in the knee-deep grass, the goat watched the three men talking. They were keeping their voices low, so he could not hear much of what they said. He recognized his name when Brinn blurted it out and raised his head in time to lock eyes with Moth. That was not good. The white and brown billy grazing near the camp took a few more bites of the tough Sawgrass and then wandered back toward the rest of the herd. After a few minutes, it waded into the water for a drink. No one was paying attention when he moved to another spot to graze. The next time anyone looked at the herd, he was gone.

CHAPTER 25

Gwen knew something had happened as soon as she opened her eyes.

The grim expressions on the faces of the men did not bode well. Whatever happened during the night, it was something that upset the entire group. She looked around, realizing Keeyun was not present. He could be working with the animals, but she somehow knew that was not the answer.

"Where is Keeyun?" she asked as Von passed the final bowl of porridge to her.

Von shifted nervously and the other men looked at each other.

Finally, Brinn cleared his throat and said, "No one knows. He vanished during the night." Brinn and Moth seemed equally disturbed by Key's unusual absence.

Xyvelix? Or one of the hairy beasts? "He could be in danger! Why are you just sitting there? Shouldn't we be trying to find him?"

"He knew what he was doing when he left during the night. He waited until we located the ruins of the city before vanishing."

"That doesn't make sense. It must have been the demons." Mekiva could not understand why no one was worried about his safety. Especially Moth. He was always talking about adventures he'd shared with his cousin.

"They would have taken an animal before attacking an armed man," Jaxx replied. She had her hone out and was sharpening the edge of her ax. She had never been comfortable around the pensive druid, but her body reacted physically to his presence. Whenever he was around, goosebumps covered her arms and the hairs stood on end.

Brinn sighed and lowered his eyes. "That would have been easier to accept. He took his horse, his equipment, and enough food and water to survive the trip back to civilization."

"He also took Sayed's mule," Raffi added. "That means we will have to share the supplies the mule has been carrying." The proclamation did little to relieve the tension in the room.

"He said nothing to Moth? That's strange. It's hard for me to accept he simply disappeared while we were sleeping." Mekiva's expression revealed her doubts. It seemed odd that the stoic Mage did not seem to be disturbed by his cousin's unusual departure. It was almost as if he'd expected it to happen. But why?

Raffi was more pragmatic. "It could be worse. He could have slit our throats as we slept." He sat his empty porridge bowl to the side and stood. "The tracks led directly to the edge of the ruins and continued into the desert. He was not in a hurry, but his path was clear." He'd followed the tracks for a candlemark before returning to camp.

"You don't really believe that do you?" Jaxx appeared, startled by Raffi's words.

"I don't know what to believe anymore. I saw him kill that horse without the smallest amount of remorse. Something happened that changed Key's personality, and it's not for the better. The man I know would never leave without saying goodbye. He would have packed up, taken his share of the salvage and rode out, but he would not slip away like a thief in the night." The cynical Duaar seemed badly shaken by Key's sudden departure. There was a fleeting touch of bitterness and anger reflected in his eye before they softened and showed the pain he was hiding by his terse words.

Brinn knew there were things about Keeyun's sudden disappearance that made little sense, but they could not devote a lot of time to discovering what he was hiding. The odds were against him making the crossing alone. There was nothing he could do about it, and for now, he would have to live with Keeyun's decision. The amount of food and water he had taken would affect the time they could spare to hunt for the hidden treasure. For now, they would concentrate on that, and give him the benefit of the doubt. He stood and stretched.

"Let's get started."

Brinn drew rein and pulled his gelding to a stop. He pointed to a trio of fire-blackened stones on the ground. "That's the first man made grouping I've spotted. From this point and further in, the rubble appears to have been part of a large city. It looks like the closer we get to the center, the less damage the buildings sustained from the blast." He scanned the surrounding terrain. At one time, there had been rolling farmland that extended for hundreds of leagues in any direction.

"See that line of stones? Someone had to have gathered them. They place them along the edge of tilled fields to differentiate between farms. If you look closely, you can see how the ridge and furrows followed the edge of the meadow. I'd bet a gold ryl if we could move the ash, we would find the skeletons of the laborers working in the fields when the accident occurred."

Brinn was right. The signs were so obvious once they reached the edge of the desert, no one failed to recognize it. Until then, most of the paths that crisscrossed the area showed signs of abandonment but had still been easily recognized as roads. Now, even the trails were heavily overgrown with scrub and weeds that gradually disappeared until only the memories remained. As far as the eye could see, there was nothing but ash and dust, all with an eerie red tint. But the haunting remains of the once great metropolis were even worse.

From the mountains beyond the desolation, the ground sloped gradually away to the north and north-east. The general track of the mountain range was from south to south-west. It rose abruptly out of the plains and carries upon its crest a series of ruins, most likely the shattered mansions of the city's elite or guard towers. The center of the ruins held several damaged buildings with multiple existing floors. That the ruin should stand as it had stood for over a thousand years, uninjured save by the wind and sands, increased the prospect of the group finding treasure. It was quiet. Eerily quiet. It was as if someone had taken a giant bucket of ash and dumped it over the center of a city, allowing it to spread out from the center in a circle that covered everything within so thickly nothing could live. It reminded Mekiva of the times she had delved deep beneath the ground in an ancient cavern that had never been explored. This was a similar feeling of loneliness. No animals, no birds, no insects, nothing.

Mekiva ran her fingers through the fine ash that covered everything like a dark gray blanket of virgin snow. "At least we know Keeyun is not in front of us. It looks like no one has been here since the explosion destroyed the city. There's sure to be treasure hidden here, but I don't see how it could your family's treasure."

Von replied but did not really answer her question. "There are many stories that hint at the location of family treasure. Supposedly, my ancestor was a powerful mage. The treasure belonged to him. Unfortunately, no one knows what it is or why it's so valuable. No one knows exactly where it was hidden. We don't even know his name or when he lived. But everything points to this city. Who knows how the elders got it here? Anyone that could answer that question has been dead for generations. But I am confident it is still here."

"We have too many coins invested to go back empty-handed. If we don't find your family treasure, there's sure to be lots of salvage to be found," Moth said. "It looks like everything is still where it was when the explosion occurred."

"Look behind you," Brinn replied. "We are the first to walk these streets in ages, maybe even the first since the disaster." He pointed back along the path they had taken entering the city.

Their footprints showed an obvious trail through the previously pristine ash and dust. "It's good to be first, but anyone following will have no trouble finding us."

"Let's not tempt fate then. We need find a defendable building. One that still has a roof, if possible. It's got to be cooler inside than out here."

Jaxx was curious about the tracks of a small animal in the sand nearby. She followed the tracks, finding several of plump rodents grazing in an open area nearby. Using the leather laces that held up her spare boots, she made snares. With any luck at all, they would have a hot meal before too much longer.

She heard the beast before she saw it. The low-pitched growl carried well in the silence. It was much too large for her to have missed it as it approached. Now it crouched on an undersized ledge above her head, its mouth awash in bright white teeth. Taller than most men, it was covered with long, sand colored fur, just like the small one Gwen had healed after the sandstorm. The beast was heavily fleshed and full muscled; she could see the ripple of its muscles as it maneuvered on the ledge. Keeping a close watch its position, Jaxx backed slowly, but she still looked around expectantly just in case more came sliding around the corner.

It followed her movement with its oversized green eyes. Jaxx felt like a mouse being watched by a cat. *I wonder if it plays with its food like a cat.* For a brief moment she imagined she could hear it laughing. Her mind instantly urged her to start running. But she collected her wits and stood as still as possible, knowing that movement could entice the animal to strike. The beast might attack regardless, but she did not want to do anything to encourage it. If she was lucky, she might get in one or two blows before the creature tore her apart.

The creature failed to signal its intent before it pounced. The beast's weight pinning her chest and shoulders to the ground, landing hard enough to knock the breath from her gut. Her stomach churned as the scent of blood and meat wafted into her face. She resisted the urge to scream and struggle, intuitively knowing that this would anger the beast. For a few heartbeats, they stared eye to eye. Then it huffed out a breath of rancid air and calmly walked away as though she was no longer of concern. Muscles in its back legs rippled as it pushed off the sand and leaped straight up, catching its claws in the uneven face of the rock. Then it immediately launched itself upward again. Three more lunges carried to the top, where it stopped long enough to gaze back at the young woman lying in the sand before vanishing into the rubble.

"Jaxx! Did it hurt you?"

"No, I am fine. It seemed more amused than mad."

"Anything strong enough to survive this far away from borderlands is something that none of us want to anger. But now you see why we said stay close together. Keeyun and Raffi both missed it. That makes it one very dangerous animal."

"I do not think it was an animal. I think it was intelligent."

"Intelligent? I've never heard of an intelligent race that fits the description."

Raffi looked like he was thinking. "I wish

Gwen had been here. The animal you described could be an older version of the thing she pulled out of the rockslide after the sandstorm."

"Could they be lairing in the ruins? If so, there must be water nearby."

"There are many buildings still standing. The creatures could live inside them. We can look for a communal pump or a fountain. But that can wait for another day. It's going to be dark soon. We need to get undercover." He pointed up a side street with a handful of buildings that looked less damaged than the ones they had passed. "Von, go with Raffi and check out a few of the larger buildings. Find one we can use as a base camp."

Raffi shouldered the half-filled pack he had been sitting on and picked up his ax. It surprised him how angry he was. Jaxx could have been seriously hurt, even killed. He had no idea why it mattered, but it did. He kicked his way through the knee-high dust and ash, wondering how the scattered patched of grass survived the heat without water. The bushes were almost the same burnt umber color as the ash they stumbled through.

Raffi passed the first couple but stopped before the third block and stucco building, signaling he wanted to check it out. Moth agreed. The first large chamber was obviously natural, except for the pens and mangers for animals that had been fashioned out of the stone. The skeleton of a cow stood before one manger; half chewed hay still trapped inside the skull's teeth. A narrow passage carved through the rock led into a smaller room, set up for normal living. Another passage in the far wall led to sleeping chambers. A tiny skeleton lay in a wooden cradle, bottle still in hand. Nearby was the skeleton of a mature woman, most likely the babe's mother. Her clothing crumbled to the touch. Atop her skull, dark hair had been pulled back into a loose bun. She remained in the same position, perched on a footstool while carding a basket of wool, one hand on the carding comb, the other holding raw wool. The flesh had long since rotted away, yet no one had disturbed the bodies. Like the cow in the first room, they remained frozen in time, exactly as they were when the explosion occurred.

The next house held a trio of skeletons dressed in tanned leather boots and colorful clothing. The men were sitting around a fire pit in the center of the room. In the ashes of the pit stood the essential coffee-pot. One cup lay broken on the floor, bony fingers still clasped tightly around the other two. Across from them a humped back skeleton cooked rice over the same firepit.

"Go tell Brinn this one will do. There's nothing to draw attention, and it's in decent shape." It pleased Raffi that the third house proved was empty. For once, there were no bugs crawling across a table and no spiders spinning webs in the corners. The old corn husk mattresses had long since rotted away and time had turned the dried rushes on the floor to threads. In less time than expected, they could clear the building and attached stables. One pleasant find was the well in the kitchen. The pump needed to be greased before it moved easily but being able to have fresh water was worth all the unexpected work.

Von returned quickly, leading Brinn and rest of the group to the building. It was a fight to drive the stubborn pack animals away from the short wiry grass and ragweed that grew along the street. Despite their efforts the animals managed to stop and grab a mouth full or two before entering the stable for the night.

There was no hay left in the racks above the mangers, but the weary animals were content to munch on grain and the brush they gathered before settling down for the night. They appeared to be happy to be inside the stable area and remained quiet as long as they kept the oryx penned on the opposite side of the stable.

While Gwen and Mekiva cooked, Brinn had sent them out to drag the ash with cloth, spreading the ashes so that it was not so obvious from the sky. It would not fool a tracker, but it might prevent someone flying overhead from following the prints right to the camp. The roofs would hide them from view and allow them to get a good night's sleep. No one complained. It would be the first night inside a building in almost a moon cycle.

Come sunup, they would begin the search for the wyvern.

CHAPTER 26

Raffi cracked one eye, groaned, and rolled over, hoping the insistent shaking would stop. It didn't, so he opened the second eye, saw that the sun was barely up, and shut both again. The shaking stopped but the damage was done. Eventually, he pried himself from his bedroll and sat up. No one else was sleeping in the small room. The murmurs of sound coming from the main room were enough to tell him it would not do any good to lie back down. He sniffed, catching a whiff of hot kafka brewing. Time to gather his scattered thoughts and pull himself together.

In less than a candle mark, they were moving away from the building. Brinn decided it was smart to leave the animals inside the building stable out of sight while they searched for the temple.

Mekiva had cast a cantrip that would help keep anyone from discovering the camp. While she could not make it invisible, it caused the eyes to drift away without focusing on the building. It may stop no one, but it made them feel a lot better about leaving the animals alone.

To the south of the building in which we had sheltered, the land rose. On top of the rising ground was another ruin, an oblong rectangle of masonry, built of large stones carefully laid without mortar. At one corner, a crumbling stair led to a rooftop patio. The slope of the hill brought it almost level with the surface of the ground on the east side. Raffi stood on the patio and striding the surrounding land. He spotted a building with column bases along the outer side.

"How about that building? Looks like a private mausoleum."

"Looks as good as any other." He pointed to a narrow lane that climbed up the side of a butte. "We can check a few but the real prizes will be up there."

The private crypt held six sarcophagi, two along each of the remaining walls, the other two sat lengthwise down the center. The face of the buttress was quite plain, though some of the scattered fragments were carved with birds and a flowing vine pattern. Brinn had removed the cover to one sarcophagus, removing a ring and a sack of coins but no one wanted to loot the remaining coffins.

"Why are all of you just standing around?" Raffi asked as he sat atop a stack of rubble just slightly lower than Mekiva's head. "There is no one close by to worry about. I have checked anything large enough to hide anything dangerous. Let's go find this treasure."

For the next candlemark, they traveled the remains of what must have been, at one time, a flourishing waterway. The dry streambed was a swath of cracked mud and sharp rocks cutting into the soles of their boots as they walked. The sand filled channel was the quickest way to reach the center of the city since they would have needed to skirt or circle around the piles of rubble that filled the overgrown streets. Some rocks and debris remained, the shattered rubble of a building that overlooked the water and had fallen that way when the explosion happened. Once they had to cross the rotted remains of a waterwheel, all that remained to show what had once been a prosperous gristmill. It was unlikely, but possible if they made the effort, they could find the millers' lockbox somewhere under the ash that coated the ground. The worse part of the climb toward the upper city was when they left the dry riverbed and began making their way along the switchback. On the pinnacle of the plateau stood the remains of a dozen stone mansions, the guard tower, and three temples. Here at the apex of the storm, it was hard to imagine the power that had ripped throughout the city before destroying so many leagues of lush farmland. The wizards had stood at the two highest points, one upon the guard tower and one at the tip of the temple as the spell storm grew in intensity.

Mekiva tried to picture what it must have been like during the battle and resulting spell storm. She could close her eyes and see the colors, the flashes of lightning, the prismatic displays, the tingles of magic building in the surrounding air, until finally it all came apart in an explosive whirlwind of colors and explosive energy. They had probably thought themselves invulnerable, high above the ancient bastion of humanity in the valley below.

Jaxx came over the crest faster than Raffi, so she was the first to spot the temples. She signaled to the others and waited behind a tumble of stone blocks to see if there was any sign of activity near the building. "Do you think that's what we've been looking for?" She let her eyes move from Brinn to Von to Mekiva as she spoke.

The winds had died down, allowing them an unrestricted view of the terrain that surrounded the peak. The heat reflecting off the red desert sands was stifling; despite the light breeze blowing across their faces. The combination of bright sunlight and blue sky temporarily allowed her to forget how tired and hungry she was. The temples in the distance were not the only structures standing, though they showed fewer signs of severe damage. The stones weathered, probably a combination of damage sustained during the conflict, and the natural degradation from the elements during the passing years. She dreaded the walk to come; but she knew darkness came swiftly as the twin suns sank beyond the horizon; bringing with it a bone deep chilliness to the night air. The temple was shelter... and possibly the end of their lengthy search.

After a reasonable amount of time had passed with no sign of any living creature, Brinn nodded, and they began moving once again.

The tired group entered the clearing cautiously, looking about as if they expected to be attacked at any moment. So far, they had been lucky. They had spotted none of the winged demons flying over the city as they traveled through it. Everyone kept one eye on the sky as they walked. They were much higher and closer to the comfort zone of the Xyvelix. No one forgot about the hairy creatures. They did not know where either laired. An empty city of ruins offered plenty of prospective homes.

"Which do we check first?" Jaxx asked. Her eyes scanned the area. "I vote for the biggest one. Big temples usually mean big money. I've never seen a poor priest." What she really wanted was a bath. It was a long shot, but there might be water inside the temple. Many were built over natural springs and had pools for ritual cleansing. Her desert clothing kept most of her body protected, but she was still itchy and uncomfortable. She could only imagine how miserable the others felt with nothing to protect their faces. The men had stopped shaving long ago, but their sparse beards only covered part of the exposed faces; leaving their eyes and forehead raw and blistered.

Raffi looked around, noting any ambush locations. Other than the line of fresh cat tracks in the ash outside the door, there were no signs of an animal making this its home, so he crossed that problem off his list. Most animals preferred small dark holes, not big open spaces. The ghastly line of bleached bones lying in the ash outside the temple was interesting. Either the temple sacrificed calves to the twin gods, or they had taken livestock as offerings. If the area was using farm animals as tithe, there might not be a lot of wealth hidden inside. It was already late afternoon. They had stopped to check out any potential location of treasure and had gathered quite a lot of coin and jewelry. Even if they never found Von's family treasure, the salvage would be enough to make the trip worthwhile.

Gwen refused to pick up the jewelry and coins near the bodies. "It makes me feel like a grave robber."

Jax rolled her eyes, but Mekiva went to her defense. "You don't have to gather anything. Unless you find some gold, you want to donate to Rheaaz's temple." Everyone else was now carrying enough coin and jewels to keep them in comfort for many years.

Jaxx ran her fingers through the fine ash that covered everything like a dark gray blanket of virgin snow. "It looks like no one has been here since the temple was destroyed. There might be a secret family treasure hidden here. But how are we going to find it? We do not know what we are looking for."

Von didn't really answer her question. "I remember my mother telling me stories. Some of those story's hint at the hiding place — but no one knew exactly where it's hidden. Every sign we have come across has been the same wyvern, all leading to this city. Someone went to a lot of trouble to carve them for them to mean nothing. Who knows? Anyone that could answer that question has been dead for cycles. But I'm confident it's here... somewhere... just waiting for us to come and claim it."

"How can you be sure if you don't know where it was hidden?" Mekiva asked. "It all sounds good, and you may be right. We can't overlook the possibility that someone discovered it a long time ago."

Von said nothing.

"Look behind you," Moth said. "We're the first to walk these streets in ages, maybe even the first since the war."

"Let's not tempt fate then. It's got to be cooler underground than up here." Jaxx shouldered the empty pack she had been sitting on and walked over to the only flight of stairs still accessible. She did a quick search of the area around the entry ramp, finding nothing to pique her curiosity. It would be safer, and far more interesting to investigate below. She nudged a lump of sand with his foot, uncovering the bleached white skeletal remains lying just beneath.

Raffi bent over and picked something up off the ground beside her foot. "Look at this." Lying just beneath the shattered skull was a tarnished necklace of beryl stones set in silver. "We will be rich if we do nothing but pick up what's lying around the ruins in the ash. These old ruins are full of undiscovered booty, just waiting for a deserving party, like me, for instance, to find them. Everyone died at the same time. No one removed anything. Surely a temple as big as this one has a treasure room. Let's go find it." Whistling cheerfully; Raffi led the way into the unknown darkness.

Gwen moved to follow him, but a chill down her spine made her hesitate. Some inner intuition was warning her to be careful. She looked around but didn't see anyone or anything out of the ordinary. She tried to shrug it off, but it persisted. Everyone else was walking toward the ramp that led down into the temple. The only one outside was Twist. She hurried to catch up with the others.

The ramp led down into an entry chamber, where the priests would listen to petitions and decide whether the petitioner could enter the temple. Depending on the amount of the donation, a lessor priest would see the faithful in a small anti-chamber or the high priestess in the main cathedral of the God or Goddess.

"If this is just a vestibule, can you imagine what the central chamber must look like?" Raffi remarked as the small group stared in wonder at the riches that surrounded them.

No one bothered to answer.

In awe, they looked around. The hallway stretched about a hundred feet before opening into a marble enshrouded vestibule. The walls were as tall as three men, sheathed in cream-colored marble and decorated with an elaborate motif of inlaid gold. An ornate glyph in ancient dialect decorated the wall. Mekiva could read a few words, not enough to hold a conversation

"You're right. It was a temple of Rhoma and Rhema, the twin Gods of Luck." Mekiva's parents worshiped them, but the temple near her home was not as ornate.

On the far wall, matching sets of gilded double doors hinted at further riches just beyond. The floor was as beautiful as the walls, a checkerboard of cream and black marble. In the center of the room was a mosaic set with thousands of tiny jewels. The gems had been laid out to form a picture of Omission from a perspective high overhead. How the artists knew the exact layout of the three main continents was a mystery since there was no know spell that would allow them to see the land from above. The marble pillars that support the roof bore similar decorations; though only in two small sections, like bands that divided the length into thirds.

"I've been in cemetery's that made me feel more comfortable," Mekiva said to Gwen after they had all searched the vestibule at the bottom of the staircase. "This place would make the dead cringe. It seems more like a crypt than a temple with all the bones scattered around."

"We know," Brinn said with a grin, "we could all tell from the shriek you let out when that skeleton fell into pieces."

"How was I to know there wasn't anything holding the bones together? One touch with the tip of my finger, then whoosh, everything hit the floor."

Everyone knew the story. The thaumaturge Azaar de'Brantos and the Elementalist LaSaundra the White had waged a war that had seemed unending until Azaar had miscast a spell designed to remove LaSaundra's ability to manipulate the environment. The results of that miscast had been instantaneous and overwhelming. Besides the immediate destruction of both mages, every living thing within the spell's scope had died instantly. It was as if time stopped. Everything remained exactly as they were at the time of their death. Without living insects and other scavengers to take care of the bodies there was nothing except time and the desert winds to affect the remains. Now the bare skeletons were all that remained to remind them of the once bustling city... a few bones; a few scraps of clothing—anything made of metal or jewelry.

Jaxx and Raffi made a game out of the treasure hunt, and Von had quickly joined in the fun. They could tell Gwen wanted to play, but she was hesitant to do anything that would upset Mekiva. Instead, they sat with Moth and Brinn and kept score. Too many images haunted their minds to even consider hunting for treasure left behind.

Skeletons of priests kneeled at prayer in moldy cassocks. Mothers held their children at their breast or by the hand. Kitchen staff sat at tables preparing meals, many of their hands still gripping a knife or the bones of a fowl. Here, protected from the elements by stone and earth, the remains of the faithful had slowly rotted where they died.

The halls of the temple were easy to negotiate. Behind the main temple area there were three halls laid out in an H: one directly behind the chapel, one on each side. Gwen crossed herself from habit as they entered the chapel area of the temple. Not that she was overly concerned with religion or anything. It wasn't a temple dedicated to Rheaaz. It just seemed the right thing to do. Her mother had taught her the fundamentals as a child. Gwen had absorbed the Shii-lakka doctrine and rituals at an early age but had never become a member of a temple. Her father was more realistic. Once his children were old enough to know wrong from right, he allowed them to make their own choices and then respected their decisions; even when it led them away from his own values. Not that her adopted parents weren't great. They'd always treated her as if she was their blood daughter. However, neither understood her choice to become Shii-lakka; and both made it clear they considered it a mistake. The temple chapel brought back many of Gwen's happier childhood memories of life before her birth parents' deaths had shattered her illusions. She was pleased when Brinn insisted they move on to the other areas of the temple.

They investigated each hall at a brisk pace, stopping along the way to carefully check out each room they came across. After a cursory search, they made their way back to the kitchens off the main temple area and set up camp for the night. Von broke up a small table left behind when the temple was abandoned and built a small fire. They would welcome warm food after the disappointing day.

"We'll need more wood to make it through the

night. Raffi, think you can round up something to burn?"

"Why does it always seem to be my turn to look for firewood?" *Not that he minded. There had to be firewood or coal somewhere. The temple had to burn a lot to keep so many priests warm.* "Maybe there was an exit beyond the pantry?"

No one answered so Raffi shrugged and began to pull his boots back on. *If he didn't find a storage area; he was certain to find a few more tables to burn. It gave him an excuse to explore.*

"Raffi's right, he gets drafted for firewood duty all the time. Stay there and relax," Jaxx said. "I will get some wood to burn."

"I'll go with you," Gwen offered unexpectedly. "I can help carry it back. It would be wonderful to have a hot meal." She looked at her, wondering if there might be more to the offer. Jaxx found it hard to look away from her pale green eyes. She remembered the time Gwen almost drowned and blushed at memories of her naked body.

"I'd enjoy the company," she said.

Just as Raffi had expected, there was a sturdy metal clad door complete with a well-worn bar lock at the back of the pantry. It only took a few seconds for Gwen to pick the lock. The door opened into a small walled courtyard. One section had been divided into several bins: each overflowing with lengths of neatly chopped firewood. There was also a bin with coal but no bucket to transport it. Much of the wood had been exposed to the weather and had rotted away; but there was more than enough remaining to supply the needs of their small group.

"Looks like it won't take us as long as we thought to gather wood," Jaxx remarked. The sky was clear and the stars bright. She thought of ways to prolong their return.

"If you are in no hurry, I'd like to sit for a while before going back." She spread her cape out over one of the sturdier looking scrap piles, and then motioned for Gwen to take a seat with a courtly bow. They sat and watched the stars twinkle, enjoying the peaceful silence. Overhead, a pair of bats danced an impromptu ballet across the rising moon; a scene so beautiful it took Gwen's breath away. The air was heavy with hints of the storm gathering just beyond the mountain ridge. It would break before moon fall, bringing with it the chance of rain.

"We might better gather the wood and head back inside. The storm looks like it's going to break soon," she said.

"There's time," she said confidently, "two candlemarks at least."

"How do you know?"

"I just do," she replied.

"So, you're just guessing?" Gwen stated wryly.

"Nope. It's experience. Watch the bats. See how they're still foraging for food? If the storm was near, they would head for shelter. They don't have to see the storm to know when it's nearby. If the insects are moving about, we still have time before it hits."

She sounded so smug. Gwen contemplated her words in silence. "What are you so pleased about?"

"I'm just content", she replied, her voice unexpectedly soft; an expression in her eyes that Gwen found strangely hypnotic. "I'd forgotten how good it felt to just sit and take in the world around me."

"Liar" She lifted her head; her green eyes flashing defiantly in the moonlight.

Jaxx studied her for a second or two; smiling as she blushed. And then, slowly and calmly, she pulled the woman into her arms. Her lips were firm and as she pressed his mouth to Gwen's. Her lips lingered for a moment more before pulling back and breaking contact.

Gwen tensed at the unfamiliar sensation roiling her stomach. Only when she finally sat back did she allow herself to breathe once more. She tried to smile, but her mouth refused to obey her mental demands. *I will not faint. I will not run away.*

"Cinnamon and honey," Jaxx murmured softly. "You taste so sweet; I wanted to savor the moment." She had expected something more, but other than a faint tingle, she felt nothing she'd hoped for. Just as before, there was no intense rush of lust, no sudden urge to make love to Gwen. It was pleasant, but nothing like she'd hoped to feel.

Gwen's face showed nothing of how she was feeling. "It's all right. Just give me a second to gather my thoughts." She was breathing softly, in slow deep inhalations. "It would be best if you don't do that again."

Jaxx's heart lightened as a wave of relief washed over her. She hadn't been prepared for this. Nor had she considered her own response to Gwen's word. She lowered her eyes to hide the confusion she was feeling. "Do you mind telling me why?"

Gwen looked at her uneasily, wondering if she'd somehow misread Jaxx's intentions. "I'm Shii-lak-ka", she whispered as though that should explain everything.

"What has that to do with anything?"

"Shii- lakka are... different. I'm only a novice; I haven't taken my final vows. But the Goddess has accepted me as one of her own; she grants me the ability to heal. You saw the scars. They are one burden I must bear in exchange for her blessings. It mattered little to me; yet now, I doubt my decision for the first time. Before my next birthday, I must take my vows. That means I must remain unsullied by another's touch. It's not allowed."

Jaxx stared at her as if she couldn't believe what Gwen was saying. She had been looking for a graceful way out and it was an excuse she could grasp. So why did it hurt her feelings? Emotion lent a hard edge to her voice as she spoke. "Choose a romantic liaison or Rheaaz? I don't need over one guess to figure how this scenario ends." She was silent for a minute. Then she started gathering wood from the bin. "Looks like I was wrong about the weather; the storm is closer than I thought. We need to go in now."

Gwen watched her walk away. She tried to stay strong, but her emotions got the best of her. "Jaxx, wait!"

Jaxx heard her name, but she kept walking, ignoring Gwen's calls. Quickly, Gwen gathered her own bundle and followed. Neither spoke, instead they'd walked silently, side by side but not touching. Gwen glanced at her once or twice and was shocked by the hard bitterness showing on her face.

"Jaxx-------"

She raised a hand, seeking to silence her.

Gwen sighed but didn't argue. She couldn't blame her at all.

Jaxx's head was throbbing. No matter how hard she tried, she couldn't concentrate. There was something about her, --- she couldn't get that kiss out of her mind. Even though nothing had really *happened* since the river; she'd felt like they'd somehow agreed... a promise of sorts, of their future intentions. True, Gwen had said nothing in actual words; she'd just assumed their relationship would grow stronger as time passed by. Instead, it was all wrong. She felt no attraction to Gwen at all. When she was a man, she had felt nothing for the women she had spent time with. She'd convinced herself that she would have to feel something now that she a woman. So why did she feel the kiss was wrong? Was it because of Rheaaz or because woman did not attract her at all?

Von knew there was trouble brewing as soon as Jaxx and Gwen returned. Gwen was distraught. Jaxx looked like she could chew iron; the air thick with tension as she dropped his armload of scrap wood without saying a word.

Moth and Brinn looked up from their cards, puzzled by the sudden tension in the room. Raffi ignored everyone. He allowed a brief quiver of his lips as he fought to keep the grin from his face. Instead, he tossed a coin into the pot and took a card, using the game as an excuse to avoid the situation.

Gwen kept her veil pulled up and her hood low so no one could see was struggling to keep the tears away. Somehow, she had to avoid Mekiva; one look and her friend know something was upsetting her. Better to put it off until tomorrow. She would, she supposed, get quite a tongue lashing from Mekiva when the others weren't around. Gwen felt her lower lip tremble as the tears slid down her cheek. Now she was over-reacting; Mekiva was certain to notice.

Instead of joining her by the fire, Gwen turned away after adding her meager load to the night's stack of firewood.

Mekiva stirred the pot of stew a few times but didn't ask questions. Gwen's behavior puzzled her. She wanted to ask her what was wrong, but she was obviously not ready to talk about it. She had pasted a big smile on her face, but it looked fake... as if she was overcompensating for something.,

Von was dead set on ribbing Jaxx. "That's a tiny handful of wood, after such a long absence. Did you have to wait for the trees to grow?"

Jaxx lifted one dark eyebrow. "Is there a question in all that rambling?" she asked frostily.

"I'm just curious. What kept you away so long?" Von continued; unable to see that his questions were making matters worse.

Jaxx answered Alex's questioning gaze with a challenge of her own. "Exactly the same thing you and Mekiva do every time you disappear from camp," he said dryly.

"And what exactly was that?" Mekiva inquired archly. She felt her heart drop into her stomach as Gwen's face paled. Immediately, she regretted asking that question. As much as she wanted to know what was going on between the miss-matched pair, she valued her friendship more.

Jaxx was more amused than angry at her petulant manner. For a moment it tempted her to tell them everything; just to enjoy the look on Gwen's face. Unfortunately, she really liked her and wanted to keep her friendship. Gwen was already suffering, and nothing she could say would make it better. It surprised her that Raffi was not saying anything. He could be a sadistic jerk. Raffi would relish using that tidbit of information against her, taking a minor mistake and turning it into illicit grope session. She shrugged.

"Absolutely nothing. We gathered wood. I'll take first watch," she stated. "I'm not tired; it would be impossible for me to get any sleep right now. I don't know if it's excitement or just pent-up frustration. I just know we haven't found any real treasure."

"Yeah, I thought we would have found something by now," Von said, hoping to diffuse the tension. "We covered the entire temple today. If there was a wyvern, we must have missed it. The runes have been correct so far; there has to be a clue here somewhere."

Gwen rose from the rug where she had been praying and made her way over to the group of friends sitting nearby. She listened to them talk for a moment and then spoke in her usual quiet voice. "Perhaps we have all been trying too hard. The sigil may be hidden or placed in a less obvious location than the ones we found in the underground passage. What if it's not here in the main temple? There are two smaller ones. We do not know to what gods they were dedicated. Or even if the treasure was hidden inside a temple. It could be in one of the mansions or even the guard tower."

Brinn agreed. "Tomorrow is another day. Me-kiva is already in her bedroll, and it would be smart for us to join her."

No one argued.

CHAPTER 27

"This is a waste of time," Brinn said as Raffiel disarmed another deadfall. Raffi had already found two hidden trapdoors and disarmed them, taking only one small nick on the side of his hand from a sharp rock as he jerked back away from the spring. Fallen stone and dirt blocked the first hatch and it only dropped a foot or so. The second trap was still dangerous. Water from a treacherous underground stream had eaten away at the floor of the pit and the current would sweep away anyone falling inside. They had warned everyone about getting too near the trap with the hidden stream. The water was still eating away at the foundation, and it could collapse. They were currently exploring the second smaller temple and had found nothing to suggest a wyvern anywhere. "Drasst it! I give up. I'm ready to head back to camp and relax."

"Yeah, I thought we would find some sign in this one," Von replied as he entered the area the other two men were searching. "We covered that other small temple in one day. We must have missed the clue somehow. Every sign points here. Tomorrow, we can move to the buildings around the edge of the upper city. There has to be a clue here somewhere."

Brinn and Raffi locked eyes, and Brinn nodded. "I know you want to find you family treasure. But we need to seriously think about calling it done and heading back to the compound. The weather is going to change soon, and it's going to get cold... things will start freezing. We can always return in the spring." He hated to see the light dim in Von's eyes, but it was time to accept reality. And the reality was that they could not stretch the food out any longer and have enough to make it back to the borderlands unless they started back in the next day or two.

Von didn't like what he was hearing. Not that he hadn't been expecting to hear it all day. He turned to follow Brinn and Rafi back to camp. They were still using the priests' living quarters as their main camp and used the kitchen to prepare hot meals. Once they had discovered the pumps in the kitchen still worked and the water was pure, there was no reason to move. Moth had left earlier, heading back to the business district to feed and water the pack animals they had hidden in the ruins of the lower city. The animals were not happy about being kept inside, but as long as they provided food and water, they tolerated being penned up. Twist's hunts had provided fresh meat for the oryx, and occasionally something they could add to whatever pot was simmering over the fire in the temple.

Jaxx had been a bitch earlier, snapping at Mekiva and Gwen over tiny things, then stomped off, telling no one where she was going. When she tried to have a serious talk with Mekiva, she'd ruined it by letting lust push out all common sense. She was lucky the good-natured mage was speaking to her at all.

Von looked around, noting that she was somewhere in the temple, but he did not know where. The best thing for him to do was to keep his mouth shut and his mind on finding the family treasure. So why did he feel like the storm was just starting?

CHAPTER 28

Jaxx felt rotten. She'd snapped at Gwen for no reason and did her best to ruin everyone else's evening. *What was love, anyway? Everybody wanted it, yet no one seemed to know what it was. She hadn't really put that much effort into finding love while a man. Why should she expect anything different now that she was a woman?* That was a question she needed to answer before it tore apart her friendship with the others.

She needed something to keep her mind occupied, so she returned to the main shrine to scrutinize the stone altar. There was something about it that didn't feel right to her. It was only a feeling, but that same instinct had saved her from trouble many times in the past. Besides, staying busy would keep her mind off her other problems.

She felt a slight sense of relief as the door to the sanctuary opened immediately. From the doorway, she had an unobstructed view of the entire room; a rectangle space, about fifteen spans long and about six spans wide. The floor was all open space; except for the altar and the two giant statues of Ligarza and Yaaga placed on either side of it.

There wasn't anything special about the dais; a raised, flat-topped slab of some shiny black stone set on a rectangular base of a similar material. The slab's surface was polished smooth but pitted from the blades wielded by the priests during the religious ceremonies. Jaxx could see hints of rusty brown stains still present in the pits, and she wondered exactly what they had sacrificed to appease the twin gods. It was doubtful a few cows would satisfy the blood thirsty twin gods.

Running his hand along the base of the altar, Jaxx noticed a slight depression in the stone. Kneeling down, she tried to see inside, but her body wouldn't fit between the altar's base and the marble statues resting on pedestals on either side. She solved the problem by lying face down on the altar, then sliding headfirst toward the ground directly in front of the opening. There was just enough room for her to line her eye up with the depression. Sure enough, there was a wyvern glyph inscribed within the depression... an exact match for Gwen's copy.

She ran back to the kitchen and began waking her sleeping friends. "Hey! Wake up! Come to the room with the two statues. I think I may have found it!"

Everyone rushed through the temple doors, certain Jaxx was injured and perhaps dying. Instead, she was reclining atop the altar, lying back against one of the carved statues, grinning smugly.

"Who died and made you queen?" Von didn't appear impressed by her attitude. Mekiva was about to turn around and head back to the kitchen area when she noticed the shadowed opening directly behind the altar. She was certain it wasn't there when they checked out the room earlier.

"I knew there had to be rooms we had not seen," Raffi didn't wait for an answer, walking forward as Jaxx slid off the backside of the altar. In anticipation of their needs, she grabbed a burning torch from the iron rack beside the door, and then waved them forward and led the excited group down the narrow stairs through the darkness with the ease of familiarity. She had not waited for their arrival before exploring the newly discovered passageway.

Raffi was practically dancing along the newly discovered passageway as he followed close behind Jaxx. His pace quickened with expectation as they neared the end of the passage. This was the most promising find so far, and he was certain Jaxx had found what they were looking for.

"Ligazra's icy tits!" Raffi reached the door and froze, stunned by what he saw inside.

Raffi's reaction to the hidden room did not disappoint Jaxx. Nor did the gasps and cries from the others. Everywhere they looked, there was treasure. Religious icons and temple regalia hung from hooks on the walls. Stacks of golden serving trays, bowls, mirrors and other ceremonial instruments rested near jars and flasks of perfumed oils and unguents. They stacked chests of jewelry and sacks of coins around the room. The pack animals could not carry a tenth. But it was the dark opening at the back of the room that drew everyone's attention.

Jaxx grinned and motioned them forward into a short passage. Jaxx halted at the end; using her arms to block them from entering the dark room. "Don't try to enter, you can't. Every time my light went out. It becomes harder to breathe the farther in you go. I finally gave up after making a score of attempts."

Despite the light from the torch, the interior of the hidden chamber was pitch black.

Von shivered. The room made him uncomfortable; not warning him off, but also not welcoming him inside.

Moth paused just beyond the glow of Raffi's torch and cast a reveal magic spell. The room flared brightly for a breath or two, then faded away to blackness once more. Obviously magic at play. He took a deep breath and spoke the words of a dispel magic spell. Nothing happened. "Someone powerful spent a lot of time building the wards around this room," he muttered.

Brinn nodded at his words. The room appeared to be empty, but something unseen was causing his normally thick skin to prickle, a feeling he commonly felt only when he was being scried. He gave the others a chance to try before he asked Mekiva to dispel the ward. The girl was powerful, but her lack of control scared him.

Mekiva concentrated, but nothing happened.

"Maybe it doesn't like you. Let me try." Von took two steps, then stopped. The room seemed to swallow the light from his torch, the flickering beams shrinking until the room was dark once more. His breathing was heavy and strained, loud in the chamber's silence. He took one or two uneasy steps forward before he began gasping for air. Facing death in a fair fight was one thing; suffocating in a pitch-black room was entirely different. Defeated; he meekly retreated to the entrance.

"This is going to be tricky," he conceded.

Raffi laughed bitterly. "Ligarza be damned. I had my heart set on finding the treasure, and then returning triumphantly to rub it in. I couldn't make it over four steps into the room." He crossed his arms across his chest and looked from Brinn to Moth to Mekiva. They all looked perplexed. "The closer you get to the pedestal, the harder it is to breathe," he said. "That must be why the torches keep going out. They need air to burn, and I think the air diminishes the farther in you go."

"I can do something about the light problem," Mekiva offered. "It won't solve the air problem but it's one step in the right direction."

"Another glow stone?" Jaxx asked eagerly.

"No components; sorry. But I don't need any for this." She rubbed her hands together briskly and spoke a short cantrip; then clapped once. At first nothing happened; then hundreds of tiny sparkles of light materialized around her open palm. The pale amber motes of dancing light swirled and came together only to fall apart; continuing to shift in size and shape. Their light steadily grew in intensity until the room was lit well enough for human eyes to see without strain or discomfort. With a flick of her wrist, she tossed them into the room. Almost immediately, the tiny motes faded.

"That's strange. It's like it dispelled the charm. It's a paradox. A barrier to magic, except the barrier itself must be magic. My dancing fireflies can't move any closer, but the light itself can pass through. It's only after the source of light attempts to move inside the barrier that it's affected." She quickly repeated her earlier cantrip. The yellow sparks continued to circle around the edges of the room but did not enter the area near the idol. "At least we can all see inside."

The hidden room wasn't small, but they had no trouble clearly seeing. The most prominent feature of the hidden chamber was a carved marble platform on which a second stone altar rested. On either side stood eight severed heads, long devoid of flesh, each positioned on stakes driven into the rock. Where the skull's eyes had rested, fiery opals the size of hen's eggs had been set.

The ceiling was low, maybe inches above their heads. Centered in the room was a slab, a rectangular block of stone worn smooth by years of use. Atop that slab, someone had placed a coffer of heavy dark wood. The carpenters' pride of workmanship was clear throughout the elaborate carved motif of birds and flowers. Here and there the artisan had highlighted certain areas with hints of silver and gold; and all the hardware appeared to have been molded of the same metals. The ebony must have cost a fortune. Atop the platform, streams of brightly colored energy danced; rising like heat off the hot desert sands. Seated in a raised bed of gold was an enormous red jewel.

Brinn let out a low whistle as his eyes landed on the gem.

"Wow, I can't wait to get a closer look at that ruby. It's got to be as big as my hand," Jaxx chortled. Her face lit up in anticipation.

"Or maybe your heart," Raffi replied. "We found Von's treasure. Now we just have to figure out a way to reach it."

"True. There has to be a spell involved." Moth appeared puzzled. "But I've never heard of a magic spell to block magic; it seems like it would cancel itself out. At least we know the spell has limits. Mekiva's glows work, at least as long as they stay outside the dark zone."

"That solves the light problem, but what about the lack of air?" Jaxx asked no one in particular; preferring to get everyone's opinion before offering her own.

"Let's see how close we can get to the pedestal before running out of air," Von said.

Gwen gingerly moved aside so that he could once more enter the room.

Mekiva cast another cantrip and directed the glows movement as Von walked forward. By the second step, the air was diminishing. Two more steps left him dizzy and gasping for air. He quickly returned to the outer chamber.

"That answers that question," Brinn said. "As long as we stay out of the room, the light spell works. Once anyone enters the room, the spell fails regardless of its source."

"I think it's tied to the floor," Moth added. He pulled out his spell book and began flipping pages.

"Why do you say that?" Brinn asked.

"Because we held the torch inside the room and the light didn't go out. It began fading after Von stepped into the room itself. It was the same with the glows."

"That means we have two distinct problems, no magic and no air," Mekiva stated. "My glows can produce enough light, but how do we enter a room without touching the floor. As soon as we entered the anti-magic field., it would disrupt any spell I cast."

Moth agreed. He had scanned the room and

Mekiva was correct. The wards affected nothing until they were in the room. However, ... "There's more to it than that. I tried to call the stone to me, and my spell failed. Then I tried a switch places spell. This torch disappeared, and the lights flared, but then it reappeared in my hand. It was as if I have never cast the spell."

"Could the stone itself diffuse magic? Could that be why Izabal wants it?"

"It's possible. I do not know how that would benefit her, but I'm not a sorceress. My magic is traditional and the two are nothing alike."

Gwen had been watching the others as they experimented with the magic field. Jaxx, Raffi and Von had all tried to enter and failed. It reminded her of something, but she was having trouble remembering what it was. Something about her brothers. And the time they spent exploring the caves near her home.

"Mekiva, can you cast that light spell again?" Gwen asked. She had an idea, but it would only work with Mekiva's help.

"Sure, it's just a simple cantrip. It doesn't take much effort. But why? It'll just fade away once anyone enters the room." She lit the room once more.

Gwen studied the room, growing excited. "I need you to trust me on this. I think I know how we can work around this. I'll be right back." Without explaining further, she ran back up the stairs.

"Do you need any help?" Jaxx called after the running girl.

"No; just stay out of the room until I return."

"Drasst, missed again!" Raffi slammed his fist onto the top of a nearby chest as the iron hook hit the floor in a shower of sparks. Somehow, they had to get the homemade grappling hook over the heavy beam. They had all made attempts and failed. Some had come close, but the space between the ceiling and the beam was too narrow for the awkwardly shaped hook to pass through. Gwen's idea was a good one, if they could get it set up, but so far, it had just wasted a lot of time.

Moth got an idea. "Jaxx, do you still have that lightweight length of spider silk?"

"Yes, but it's not long enough to reach the beam."

"True; but I think I can make it work for something else. Would you go get it and bring back a few other things?" The two men talked quietly for a moment, then the Duaar hurried away. She returned carrying a small bag, as well as a crossbow scavenged from the remains of a dead guard.

Moth wasted no time explaining his plan before putting it in motion. He used his knife to carve a slit near the end of a bolt. Once he was satisfied it was large enough, he threaded the end of the thin spider silk through the hole; then tied it securely. Then he removed the hook from the climbing rope and tied the two lines together. With a self-satisfied wink, he sighted carefully, then shot the bolt over the beam and into the wall beyond. It struck the stone and bounced back toward the doorway, landing just a few feet inside the door.

"Now we just need to snag the line with the grapple and pull it back to us," Von crowed.

"Not a bad idea," Raffi said, "except for one small

problem. Where are we going to get another rope to tie the grapple to?"

They solved their problem by tying the grapple to the other end of the rope they'd used. It was simple to catch the line near the bolt with the grapple and pull it back to the edge of the room; then secure it to the door frame. Once they had the line securely set, it was apparent there was only one person small enough to make the crossing.

"What if the rope breaks? Or she falls. How will we get her out?" Mekiva wasn't so sure Gwen was the right person to make the attempt.

"We have the rope. We can pull her to safety before her air expires." Von squeezed her shoulder, letting her know everything was going to be all right.

Gwen wasn't worried. She's spent a lot of time hanging from a similar setup while exploring with her brothers. She'd rigged the makeshift rappelling harness herself and knew that it would support her weight. The heavy strip of leather slid smoothly over the rope, allowing her to pull her body over to the altar without ever setting foot on the floor.

"What about air? How will you breathe? Mekiva asked as Gwen hooked herself into the rappelling harness.

"If I'm right; that won't be a problem." Gwen replied. "But if I'm wrong, get ready to pull me back. But this is the important part. Once I touch the Gem, it may trigger the spell that removes the oxygen... or worse. I can only hold my breath for a minute or two. It will be up to you to pull me back to the room's door before I pass out. Better make sure the boys understand because we won't get a second chance." She began pulling herself hand over hand along the rope system stretched across the room. Once she was centered over the pedestal, she stopped, then released a latch that enabled her to slowly lower herself toward the surface of the altar.

She took a big breath and held it--- then reached for the heart.

"Never realized how much I appreciated a simple length of rope," Jaxx said as she wound the heavy rope up and tied it to her pack alongside the spider-silk that already hung there. "And that pulley thing you used. Maybe we're in the wrong business. We could make a fortune selling them. Once we get back to Cabrell we really need to talk to an artificer or two."

No one was paying the chattering Duaar a bit of attention as she rambled on about future plans. Gwen was resting and Mekiva and Alex were examining the softly glowing ruby in Brinn's hand. Just like a real heart, it seemed to pulse, radiating a soft rise and fade from pink to scarlet. Realizing she'd just spent the last candle mark talking to herself, Jaxx slumped down by Twist and pulled the Mir cat's head into her lap.

"You don't mind listening to my rambling, do you, Twist?" Jaxx asked as she scratched between the Mir-cat's ears. Ever vigilant for any excuse to get his tummy rubbed, the furry dragonet purred to show how much he appreciated Jaxx's attention before rolling onto his back in a blatant, catlike plea for more. He had no use for a pulley system, but Jaxx could talk about it all day as long as she kept up the delicious finger movements.

"I wonder why everyone is so intent on finding this," Mekiva asked Von. "It's a pretty bauble, but I was expecting something more."

"Pretty bauble? It is beautiful! It has got to be worth a fortune. I have never seen a ruby of this size. It solves all our startup problems. With our share of the money from the sale, we can buy two, maybe even three wagons, and teams to pull them."

"I'm still wondering why your uncle wants it so badly. He can afford to buy several gems like this one. There has to be more to it; something we don't know, that would make it all clear."

"Let's worry about that later. I'm starving and ready to for dawn feast. I'm way to wound up to go back to sleep." He passed the gem back to Mekiva, and she tossed it to Gwen.

Gwen wasn't sure what she was supposed to do with the giant gem. She wrapped a scrap of cloth around it and dropped it into an inner pocket, then turned to follow the others out of the temple.

CHAPTER 29

Moth tossed the last bundle of bedding to Von, then settled down next to Mekiva to catch a quick nap before they started out on the long trek across the desert. Now that they had found the gem, everyone was excited about leaving, so it was easy to get them all started on preparations for the long trip home. At first Brinn tried to delegate the different jobs; then gave up after he realized no one was listening to him. The bulk of responsibility for breaking camp fell onto his and Raffi's shoulders. Brinn was still recovering from the injuries he'd sustained during the Xyvelix attack, so he couldn't lift much. Gwen had healed most of his injuries, but it would be a long time before he came close to having his strength back. Gwen was busy with Mekiva on some secret project that brought them both to hysterical giggles every time he looked their way. Mekiva needed to rest and pray before she would be of any help in an emergency, so Brinn excused her from the preparations.

Moth had decided packing the remaining food and filling the water containers would be his responsibility. He gathered up all the water skins, filled them at temple pump, then stacked them nearby. They had plenty of water, but food was a different story. Their supplies consisted of the goats, a few hens, some jerked beef and trail rations. Twist could find enough lizards to keep him happy, but no one was looking forward to sharing his meals. Once they left the red zone Twist would soon supply them with fresh meat, but for now they would just have to continue rationing. Still, it was not long before the entire group was packed and ready to start out. Eagar as he was to leave, Moth still knew a moment of regret as he thought about his cousin. He did not know what had caused Keeyun to leave so abruptly. It bothered him that Key had not cared enough to say goodbye before he disappeared.

He still needed to make the trip down to feed and water the animals. With any luck at all, this would be the last time he had to make this trek. He would take Raffi and bring the string up in the morning.

As he walked along, he could not shake the feeling that he was not alone.

"I think it is going to be all right. I realize it might be a little hard for you to believe, but Mekiva cares for me. I want to ask her to bond with me once we get back."

Jaxx stopped him before he walked away. "I think you might be making a big mistake. You are both too young to be making any commitments."

"I have a peculiar feeling you might be right." Von said with a weary smile.

"Then don't go through with it. It's not worth taking a chance like that for a possibility. What if she does not feel the same about you? Imagine how you will feel if she says no? The trip back will make you miserable. You would have to face her every day knowing she does not care."

Von shifted his weight from foot to foot. Then he adjusted his ax. Nothing helped. He had been avoiding this conversation long enough. But now they needed to talk about it. He closed his eyes and breathed in and out a few times. Gradually, his racing heart slowed, and he grew calmer. He had stalled long enough, so he blurted it out. "Why didn't you tell me you were really a woman?"

Jaxx appeared surprised by the question. "I don't know. Maybe I was happy being a man. Maybe I was afraid you would think less of me. Mostly, I was afraid of seeing the same look in your eyes I see now."

"Aggravation?"

"More like contempt. And a certain lack of trust you can't help from exhibiting. I'm still the same fighter. I'm simply shaped a little different."

There was a tone of soft mockery in Von's voice as he answered. "Has it ever crossed your mind that you hurt me? How could you not trust me enough to share your secret? Instead, I find out from Raffiel that you are not only a chimera. You are also the heir to the throne of Duaara. That's a lot to absorb."

Before Von finished talking, Jaxx's mug was airborne, smashing against the plaster wall.

Von wiped drops of ale from his forehead. Jazz had missed his head by a matter of inches. "Hey! What the hells was that for?"

As quickly as Jaxx's temper had flared, it vanished, only to be replaced by a slow trickle of salty tears on one cheek. "That's why. That look. They had my memory changed. At least, I think so, I'm still woozy on the details. I have often imagined what I would do if someone found out who my father is. In my dreams, everything was black and white; and I knew exactly what I would say and how I would do it. Now I face a reality that paints a picture that's not so clear. More shades of gray have appeared than I originally planned for."

Von could not help but grimace. Not once could he remember Jaxx ever mentioning his father in a kind way. She must have experienced a type of Hel he could only guess at.

"We have been friends too long to let this come between us. But promise me, no more secrets."

"You have my word." He paused. "Not that it's my business, but I agree it might be good for you and Mekiva to clear the air. It getting to the point everyone is noticing the tension."

Von's brown eyes twinkled merrily. "You're right. It's not. But I will talk to her, anyway." He laughed as Jaxx gave him the familiar three-finger salute he hadn't seen in some time. He started to fire back, then changed his mind. A small frown crossed his forehead, but then he turned and walked off without another word.

Jaxx rolled her eyes. Humans lived so short a time that they rushed headfirst into situations that were incomprehensible to the long-lived duaar. She would never consider a bonding, at least for another fifty or sixty cycles. Till then, she was just going to continue to enjoy the company of as many... She stopped and realized she did not know. She wasn't attracted to women and had never thought about another man. In her mind, she was still male, and that was the problem.

She wasn't two souled, her kiss with Gwen had confirmed that. So, what was she?

Von was fighting himself. Over the last few nights, he'd had several opportunities to talk to Mekiva about their future and had let fear of rejection prevent him from doing it each time. Strangely, what disturbed him the most was the idea that she might laugh at him. He grimaced at the thought, just in time for Raffi to enter the room and catch a quick glance at his face before he changed his expression. Raffiel cocked an eyebrow in a silent inquiry but Von shook his head. Now was not the time to discuss it. Raffi nodded once, agreeing to wait, but he made herself a promise to corner Von sometime soon to discuss the burgeoning tension between him and Mekiva. For now, he just wanted to eat his evening meal and relax. They had to be ready to leave by dawn.

Brinn passed the second bowl to Raffi and sat down to eat. The two men sat without talking until most of the meal was done. He looked like there was something on his mind.

Finally, Raffi turned to speak. "Go ahead and say it. You won't be happy until you do."

"You realize the problem you have with Von has nothing to do with his ideas. You resent the fact that he and Mekiva have finally acknowledged what they feel about each other, and you still have not got up the nerve to talk to Jaxx. It's affecting your judgment and not in a good way."

"Wha... Jaxx? What makes you think..."

"It's a little late to start playing dumb now. I've known you too many years."

"There's more on the line than my injured pride,

you know. I need to tear down some of the walls she's built. That means getting her to open up about what happened."

"Then talk to her."

"I don't think Jaxx is ready for a conversation like that. She's having enough trouble adjusting to the idea that she was never a man. Adding another complication to deal with could be enough to break her."

"Have you told her who you are?"

"No! And you will not tell her. I will figure out a way to ease into that conversation soon, but not today."

"Will there ever be a good time to talk to her? You may not have another chance. That way if something happens and we don't make it out of here; she will at least know how you feel about her."

"Then let's make sure we make it home."

———

Von fumed silently as he wandered along the main corridor of the temple, hoping to find Mekiva so they could talk. Jaxx infuriated him more now than she did after a drunken binge. She was being obstinate. Why not trust his judgment? Because he'd almost gotten them killed in Mu was no reason to say he wasn't ready for a relationship. Anyone with half a brain could understand why he ran from his last engagement. There was little chance of a successful union if her father was trying to kill him. Lost in his musing, Von almost passed the room where Mekiva was sitting. Once she realized he was standing by the door, she motioned for him to join her.

"Want company?" he asked as he approached the place she was searching.

Mekiva nodded but did not reply. She shifted over so that he could sit beside her on the broken pedestal.

"You look so serious." he said as he sat down beside her.

"I was just thinking." She sighed. Von was surprised by how tired she looked. She'd aged too much during the quest. She was still a beautiful woman, but there was a shadow in her eyes that had not been there when they met in the market less than a cycle earlier. Next to him, she was little more than a wisp of a girl, but that slender form was molded from adamantine.

"Not a pleasant memory?" he asked. He tried to put his emotions in his voice but wasn't sure if she could tell how he was feeling.

"That's not it. Just... all of it... everything that's happened since we left Cabrell." She replied, dropping her eyes from his face so that he could not see the tears brimming there.

He leaned closer and turned her head up so he could see her face. "I know it's been hard on you and Gwen."

"Life is like that. You think you have it under control, and then it throws something else at you." He realized he was babbling, but he did not know what to say. It was a battle he'd never fought, and his only defense was his words.

"Jaxx... I've yet to see anything that he, make that she, cannot defeat. But she's a lot older than you are. She's already been through the dragon's fire and survived."

Mekiva sighed, a sound so quiet Von almost missed it. He felt his legs go all rubbery again as her arms wrapped around his neck and her lips moved closer to his face. She was so close he could feel her breath against his face as she spoke.

"I always knew we'd make it here," she whispered. "I admit it wasn't easy. I've discovered that my trust wasn't unfounded. No matter how dangerous it was, how deadly the creature, you have always been there to protect me." Mekiva's blush deepened as he continued to stare deep into her eyes. She shifted uneasily. "Don't you think it's about time you kissed me again?"

Von did not answer; he pulled her closer into his arms, and then slowly brought his mouth down over hers. For a moment, it was as if time stood still, her lips soft and yielding under his. Then her touch inflamed him, and passion took over, driving all concern for tenderness from his mind. Startled, Mekiva pulled away and reality came rushing back like a wave crashing onto a beach.

Mekiva placed her hand over her mouth in surprise, and haunted, almost panicked expression in her eyes. Then, before Von could stop her, she was up and running away.

"Wait! Mekiva wait! Give me a chance to explain." He reached for her arm, but she pulled it away and continued running down the hall toward the others. Von felt as though a rogue mule had kicked him in the stomach. His eyes brimmed with tears, but nothing came out. This was not how he wanted the conversation to end. He felt lost, as if everything he had cared for in the world had suddenly disappeared, leaving him totally alone. Crushed, he slumped down to the floor, put his hands to his head, and let the tears fall.

Mekiva really needed to stop thinking about Von and decide what she was going to do with her life. Her options were limited. She could locate an Elemental Master and petition to become a student. That might be a problem. She had no idea where to start her search. The school had made it clear they did not want her back. There was no way she was returning to her father's home. Even if she fell to her knees and begged his forgiveness, he would never allow her to continue her studies. If she was being honest, he would much prefer her quietly buried in an unmarked grave, with her younger sister confirmed as his heir. Memoria had always been her father's favorite child. Mekiva often wondered if her father was really her father. She was certain he had wondered the same thing. With his swarthy complexion and jet-black hair, he had trouble believing her fair skin, freckles and red hair had come from his loins. Nor was red hair common in her mother's family. It had appalled him when she had mentioned her aptitude for magic. He threatened to have her placed in a convent until she swore off her wicked ways. Mekiva climbed out the window and down the outside trellis that cold and rainy night, taking only her cloak, her personal jewelry, and a change of clothing on her horse. She had stopped at the top of the hill to look back at the light in her bedroom window, figuring that someone would miss her by now and come to search. After a candlemark, the light went out, but no one seemed to care. After a chilly night shivering in the damp beneath the remains of a fallen barn, she had mounted her horse and set out for Cabrell and the school. That was six cycles earlier, and she had never regretted the decision. She fought back a grin at the memory of the girl she had been, then laughed aloud. She liked the woman she had become, even as she wondered what her future might bring. She's worry about that when the time came. For now... she was tired and needed to get some sleep. Too bad there was no way she could relax with her emotions in turmoil. When they started this adventure, it was supposed to be a lark, something to fill in time before the next semester of school started back. At the back of her mind, she had considered it the last chance for Gwen to have some fun. It offered a chance to change her heart-sister's mind before she before pledged the rest of her life to the temple. She hadn't thought about the repercussions of their actions, and now Sayed was dead, Keeyun was missing, and they would be lucky if they made it back to Brinn's compound with no further loss.

Glimpsing the few solitary glimmers of light that drifted down from the landing above, Mekiva increased her stride, impatient to be out in the warm sunlight once again. She wanted to lie back and soak in the heat while she could. The last sun would pass beyond the northern mountains soon. The desert cooled down faster than she'd realized. On the landing she paused, drinking in the silence of the empty ruins. One slow deep breath, exhale and watch how the heat made her vison blur. Then pull her cloak tight around her shoulders and step out into the open air. The sun felt fantastic after being inside all day.

The shock of the arrow striking her shoulder spun her around and down onto her back in the ash and dust. She vaguely heard the faint whirring of the second arrow as it passed over her body and struck the ground a few feet behind. Then, just before she fainted, she heard the scream of a furious Mir cat followed by an even louder, terrified shriek that suddenly stopped in mid-cry.

CHAPTER 30

It had been a long day. Moth was covered in mud, urine and Oryx droppings. The crazy birds had rushed the gate when he opened it to feed them and knocked him down. Then they ate all the forage he had gathered to feed all the animals. It took him an extra candlemark to gather enough to feed the rest. He stunk. His hair was sticking out like twigs and his clothes would never come clean. First, he wanted a bath, then he was looking forward to a hot meal and relaxing. A shrill screech and the terrifying growl of a furious Mir cat plummeting toward the ground with all four sets of claws extended removed any chance of that happening.

Twist's body trembled as he held his position, motionless as only a cat can stay just before he attacks. His nostrils flared as he drew in the slightly sweet, slightly oily scent of the hidden demon scout. He was close but not so close that the scout could see the Mir crouching in the shadows on the ledge above the entrance to the temple's atrium. Two steps more and the giant cat leaped...the downward sweep on his wings propelling him higher and higher.

The flying cat covered the distance in seconds. The terrified Xyvelix tried in vain to throw his arm up to block just as Twist struck. Blood poured from multiple gashes made by his claws. Trap-like jaws delivered a powerful strike to the archer's head that ripped it away from his shoulders, cutting off his scream. The headless body crumpled to the floor in a bloody heap not ten feet from Moth who had not even realized the Xyvelix was nearby.

He lifted her body and began walking down the ramp into the temple. Mekiva needed immediate care, or she would not make it. The arrow was still in her chest. Fron the angle of the shaft, he knew the arrowhead had to be close to her heart. He cast his only spell, hoping to stabilize her until Gwen could heal the damage.

Von was running toward him.

Moth was ready to pass the young mage to him. He was younger and stronger; he could more easily carry her weight. He needed to get his body under control in case there were winged demons in the area.

His body was quivering by the time Von appeared. His brain had reacted automatically to Twist's attack, sending waves of adrenaline through his muscles. Now, with nothing to fight, his body was struggling to overcome its own survival instinct by twitching uncontrollably. And itching. The irritated mage was scratching every available surface raw in his haste to burn up the excess adrenaline in his system.

"Take a right at the corner and keep running until you get to the room above the main shrine. We should be able to hold them off from there." Raffi braced himself against the door, using his body weight to hold it closed long enough for Brinn to reach the corner. Once the others had disappeared from view, he moved away from the opening so that Jaxx could get a better swing at whoever stumbled through it.

Brinn continued to hack at anything that came within reach of his sword. Since the demon had injured Mekiva he had been holding the doorway while Gwen healed her. The slowly growing pile of dead bodies made it difficult for the bird men to rush his position. Like ants, the spine benders simply climbed over anything in their way. There was still an occasional arrow to dodge, but now the besieged group was facing the winged warriors, one at a time.

It was amazing how fast everything had changed. Less than a candlemark earlier they were heading across the open courtyard toward the ramp leading down into the main section of the temple. Now, thanks to Twist's vociferous warning, they had escaped the Xyvelix trap and found themselves in a running battle with the odds heavily stacked against them.

Moth and Von had carried Mekiva to safety. Now they were back to lend Jaxx and Brinn a hand. Moth's antics had broken the tension as he attempted to maneuver his arms to reach places on his body that itched uncontrollably. There had not enough Xyvelix to burn off all the excessive hormones.

"Everyone is behind the barricade but us." Brinn twisted sideways to avoid the thrust of a knife, then slapped the blade from the Xyvelix had with the flat of his sword before kicking it back away from the narrow opening. The winged demons held a significant advantage in the air, but inside the temple, the birdmen's agility was restricted. "If we go now, we can hold them at the entrance to the sanctuary long enough for the others to escape. Why don't you let Moth take over for a while and give your arm a break?"

"No thanks," Jaxx said as they continued to back slowly down the hall. "I think I have finally convinced them how dangerous my axe is. If we swap positions, some of them may decide to take a chance on getting past your blade." She smashed the spine-bender with the back of her axe, then drove the shape spike on the end of the handle into its breast. The hall in front was empty for now, but it was only a matter of time before the birdmen renewed their assault.

Von grinned. "Not that I want to disparage your ax technique, but I haven't seen an arrow fly for a while. Think it's possible they gave up?"

"Think the sun is going to come back up? There's no fracking way they have given up. It might take a candlemark or two, but they will be back."

Mekiva wrapped her arms around the trembling Mir, trying to reassure and calm him after his experience. She ran her fingers through the gore filled ash on his coat to remove any clumps before they hardened, then pulled him close and nuzzled him, heedless of the coppery smell of his blood-soaked fur. Twist licked her face and laid his muzzle against her cheek, then began his fifth examination of her body, just in case he had missed something the first four times. The adolescent Mir-cat had fought and killed before, but never had he lost control. Even when hunting for food, his target was always given a chance to run. That was what made the hunt fun. He had no memory of killing the human bird hybrid. When the arrow struck Mekiva, he felt a burst of intense pain, then it stopped. Convinced of her death, he plummeted from high above the temple, claws outstretched, his desperate plunge slowed by the thrashing of the surprised Xyvelix wings as his talons dug deep furrows into its body. He shifted his weight as he ripped and tore with all four paws. One brief growl escaped before his razor-sharp teeth closed around the winged warrior's neck. Hot blood gushed into his mouth and dripped from his fangs. He enjoyed the birdman's screams as he ripped the muscles from the skull and shredded the wings with his back claws. He reveled in the crunch as his teeth shattered the creature's spine. The winged demon did not have a chance to raise his weapon before it was over. Then Twist went hunting for another.

Most of the surrounding buildings were silent and dark when Twist returned. Blood stained his thick golden fur dark red, almost black. One hip was gashed, and the broken shaft of an arrow hung from his shoulder. Gwen healed all the cuts and washed away the blood after assuring Twist that Mekiva was asleep and not dead. Gwen had promised she would be fine. Twist trusted Gwen but still refused to leave her side, even after she wakened.

———

Raffi spent the last few minutes explaining his plan; using the ground to draw a rough map of the temple so that everyone could visualize it as much as possible. Now all they could do was wait and hope it was not a waste of time. "We have little time to prepare our defenses. Whoever sent the Xyvelix will soon realize their warriors will not be returning. They will not bother sending another scouting team; instead, they will send all the warriors available in hopes of over running in the temple. They think they trapped us with no way out."

"There can't be many left to send. We had to have killed fifty between the attack on the herds and then at the oasis in the desert. Not to mention all the spine-benders we killed before they realized they had no protection from out weapons." Brinn wasn't used to Raffi assuming control of the band. He realized by spending more time at home with his family, the others began looking to Raffiel for direction. Funding this trip had been a risk, however, he couldn't overlook the possibility of a great return on his investment. They had found enough coin and jewelry to make a profit, but nothing close to what Jaxx had located in the hidden storeroom. He looked at the loose skin on his hands and sighed. It was time to step back and let younger men take the risks. This would be his last treasure hunt.

Moth looked worried, but he'd worried about every fight. "Don't be fooled by how few you saw. By now, the scouts will have sent messengers out and called in every available warrior. We can count on at least twice as many, every certain he'd been born to exact revenge for a nest mate's death. Even if we kill their leader, they will simply keep fighting until a new flight master is chosen. Not that it's a guarantee they will leave then, the new flight master may decide to carry on with the hunt."

"We should have an advantage if they enter the temple. They will have to walk to locate us. Many of the halls are not wide enough for them to extend their wings. That should give us plenty of warning. I see no reason to block every access to this area. We need to keep the exit through the storage room as an option. Us having one way out is worse than them having only one way in."

Mekiva had been sitting quietly to the side as she listened to Raffi go over his strategy with the others. They both asked excellent questions, but she had to admit Raffi's logic was hard to find fault with. He had been dealing with desert tribes much longer than any of them. Now she found herself in a quandary that could lead to problems in her burgeoning relationship with Von. Still, she had to speak up.

"Von, you know I trust your judgment and most of the time, you are correct. But not this time." Her voice took on a softer, silky tone as she continued. "We are part of a team. We have to stick together, or we will all fail. Now is not the time to let your pride interfere with your judgment, Raffi's is the best plan."

For a moment, there was an awkward silence that hung in the air, and then Von answered begrudgingly. "I still think we are making a big mistake, but if everyone else feels Raffi is right; then I surrender. We go with his plan. I may be stubborn but even I recognize the rule of the majority."

"I am fed up with all of you," Jaxx added. "Neither of you will admit the other might be right. Can't you all work together to produce a plan that will help us all? You remind me of dogs trying to decide who will run the pack. Just sniff butt and let's move on."

Mekiva slid her end of the last trunk into place, dusted her hands on her robes, and sneezed.

"Bless You! "Jaxx said automatically then laughed at the puzzled expression on Mekiva's dust-streaked face. "It's just something we say back home. Not that a blessing or two would not hurt right now."

Mekiva nodded her agreement as she lowered her body down to rest against the back of the trunk. Finally, everything was in place, and they could relax. In her opinion, they had spent way too much time preparing for an attack that may never come. Time they could have spent on the long trek home.

Gwen pushed a small table against the door of the inner chapel and then dropped beside Mekiva with a little huff of contentment. Raffi's plan was a good one, even if Von could not see it. Now there was no way anyone could come up the main passage to the priests' quarters. It would be much easier to defend the one side entrance that remained open if the Xyvelix tried to attack. The holes were too small for the spine benders to get through, and that made her feel better.

Mekiva was daydreaming, enjoying her first moments of complete relaxation since she had been injured. She had just gotten to the point in her dream in which the handsome man, who looked remarkably like Von, had kissed her soundly when Gwen's voice sounded loudly by her head, driving any chance of a happy ending right out of her mind.

"Did you hear that?" Gwen asked. She used a finger against her lips to ask Kiva to remain quiet and then listened. *Nothing*. Still, without warning, every hair on her body now stood on end. She could not shake the creepy feeling that she was being watched. She turned slowly around, then froze as Mekiva screamed. Jaxx leaped for her, cutting off her cry with her hand over her mouth as she dragged the struggling girl's body down to the ground to lie beside her.

"Quiet!" Jaxx hissed between clenched teeth. "Don't talk, don't make a sound; I do not think anyone saw us. If we are careful, we should be able to reach the hall before they know we are here. Crawl. Stay low behind the barrier."

She didn't wait to see if Mekiva and Gwen were behind her. The two birdmen were focused on the main entrance, not the men working inside the three-story sanctuary. They were all on the top floor, but the bird men could easily fly up.

Mekiva continued to watch the winged warriors as Gwen crept along behind Jaxx. Once they were safe, she edged her way back out of the room. It was only a short distance down the hallway to where the others had been working. By now, Jaxx would have alerted them. Somehow, the Xyvelix had slipped past Twist and Raffi and entered the temple. But how? They had blocked the outer doors from the inside and she knew they had not passed them. She looked down at the floor and the only tracks in the dust were the expected footprints. They had blocked all the cross-access hallways and most of the doorways to direct the birdmen toward a working deadfall. Instead, they were the ones caught without a way out.

"Do they have magic users? Something that allows them to teleport?"

"No. I would have felt a disturbance if someone had teleported in. Chances are there is a hidden entrance into the temple, something we missed. They've been here a lot longer, there's no telling what they found, and we missed."

"How they got in is not as important as how we are going to get out. "Von replied grimly. "The same barriers that we built to keep them out work just as well to keep us in."

Raffi wanted to deny Von's statement, but then he decided it would only make matters worse. He was only being realistic about the situation they were in.

"At least we have food and water." Mekiva said. "And a good supply of weapons. Maybe we can just wait them out?"

"If we can get past them and reach the priests' quarters, we might stand a chance of surviving. It's also possible that one of us can slip out and get food and water to the pack animals. Of course, that will be redundant if the oryx get too hungry and attack the other animals."

Mekiva was quiet. She had not given the animals a thought. They would need them if they hoped to survive the return trip across the dead zone.

"I doubt they will allow us that opportunity. Instead, they will keep pressing us until we get desperate and make a mistake. Then they will overrun us."

"We can always take the fight to them. Perhaps some of us will have the chance to escape." They could all hear the steady clamor of the birdmen as they cleared away the debris that had been so painstakingly piled to block easy access to their location.

———

With one Xyvelix before him and two others

heading his way, Raffi knew he was over-matched in a fair fight, so he broke a few rules. Rolling to the floor, he tossed a handful of dusty ash into the winged warriors' face, and then he followed it up by sweeping his legs along the ground. His kick landed solidly on the birdman's right knee. It squawked and stumbled backwards, blinded by the ash and unable to balance on the injured leg. The Xyvelix flailed about with his sword, not striking anything but keeping the bigger man from getting too close.

Raffi knew he had to act fast before the half-maddened creature's vision returned. It might not be a real denizen of the lower Hels, but he now understood why the desert nomads called them winged demons. Jumping hastily to his feet, he stabbed out randomly, striking the raider in his side and dragging the blade through its ragged leather jerkin. The blade came away with a wet smacking noise that sounded loud in Raffi's ears, momentarily distracting him enough that the birdman managed to Twist away. It held the blade in one hand while grabbing at his bleeding side with the other, using the wings to balance. As it turned to allow another Xyvelix to move into position, Raffi lunged, driving his dagger deep into the feathered warriors' unprotected throat, and ripped it across toward his ear. Surprise, then fear crossed the raider's face, before it fell heavily to lie in a rapidly spreading pool of his own blood.

Before another swordman could move near enough to strike him, an arrow struck it. Within seconds, a second followed, driving the beast man to his knees. The third Xyvelix retreated beyond bow range.

Raffi edged his way over to Von. The young adventurer was perched on a small bench behind an overturned trestle table that was blocking the doorway. He had a knocked arrow in his bow and several more leaning against the bench. Von nodded once to acknowledge the Duaar's presence, then returned to watching the Xyvelix behind the blockage.

Brinn knew the Xyvelix would allow none of them to leave the ruins. If Moth was still living, we would be in the kitchen area, since that was the only source of water they had located. Without water, there was little chance they could survive. They could go a day or two, maybe longer without eating, but not without water. The Xyvelix faced the same constraints, but they may have located a nearby source of water. They had lived in the red zone for many years. The local sages thought they were the descendants of survivors that never left the Bane, mutated by the wild magic that escaped during the battle. Others felt they had migrated there from another land and had no way of returning home. Regardless of where the raiders came from, they were a problem that could not wait.

"We have to decide. We are three levels above the chapel floor. The marble is beautiful, but it would break bones if we had to jump. We need to figure out a way to get down there before they realize they have us penned up here." Brinn threw his body sideways as a stray arrow narrowly missed impaling his left shoulder.

"Great, so how do we get down to the main sanctuary from the gallery; it's too far to drop."

Strangely enough, it was Gwen who offered the best solution. "We use a rope and slide down. If we move now, two of us can hold the Xyvelix at the entrance to the sanctuary loft long enough for the others to escape."

"Does anyone have gloves with them? We should be able to slide down the rope much faster than climbing from one toe hold to another."

"I'll stay behind and delay the demons as long as possible. Once everyone is down, we can work our way to the priests' quarters."

Raffi nodded. "The two of us can prevent them from following for quite some time. Jaxx can scout ahead and Brinn can make sure everyone stays together. Once you get down; run far and as fast as you can. There's nothing to use for cover once you enter the main hallway until the turnoff to the priest's quarters. The best we can hope for is that you get a big enough lead. So, hurry!"

"No, you need to go with the others," Von said. "There's only room for one bowman. I don't intend to let them get close enough to use my sword."

"Brinn can help anchor the rope. Once he's on the ground, he can help Jaxx keep the passage clear." She slid the length of spider silk around one banister and dropped the rest to the ground below. Then she tied a complicated knot in the rope, jerking it twice to ensure it would hold. Jaxx had pulled on thick leather gloves and was waiting to be first down the line.

Raffi started to argue but one look at the determined set of Mekiva's face assured him it would be a losing battle; one they could not afford right now.

Twist paced back and forth along the base of the crumbling wall. His tail jerked impatiently each time one of the birdmen's arrows slammed into the wall near Mekiva.

Jaxx gave Twist's back one last reassuring scratch, then pushed him away. It was difficult for the stubborn Duaar to accept that they expected her to walk away from a fight, but she finally gave in and reached for the line. Brinn assisted her over the banister, and then everyone watched as she slid to the ground below. Once down, Jaxx quickly rolled to her knees, preparing to stand and fight if anything threatened the group.

Gwen signaled for Brinn to follow Jaxx. The older ranger slid down, landing easily. He raised his arm to signal he was okay, then hesitated as a single Xyvelix stepped into the doorway, a loaded crossbow in his arms.

Jaxx saw the raider enter and charged that way, only to fall flat as raider fired. The barbed shaft passed over her body. Brinn spun to his right, attempting to dodge the oncoming projectile. He wasn't fast enough. The bolt buried itself in his left shoulder, slamming the older man to the ground. He groaned and lurched back to his feet, but there was no way he could fight.

Jaxx used her axe to brush the birdman's weak attempt to parry her blade with the crossbow before whipping the pointed end of her handle straight up, slamming the Xyvelix under the chin and driving the sharp metal tip up into its brain.

Then she ran to help Brinn.

Brinn had fallen back to his knees. The motion jarred the blackened bolt, sending waves of pain shooting down his shoulder and spine. He continued rocking back and forth from the pain, trying not to cry out loud. His eyes watered and his head felt like brownies were dancing a jig. Seeing him down on all fours was hard on everyone, but especially for Gwen.

Raffi could see his friends' concern. "Gwen, you go next. Wrap your cloak around the rope to protect your hands, then just slide. Brinn needs you. I'll be right behind you." The tiny Shii' healer did not hesitate, quickly sliding down the rope.

"Hurry." Jaxx whispered when Gwen stood beside her. "Brinn really needs your help. His shoulder is in awful shape and he's losing blood. Can you do something for him?" She kept her eyes on the open door as Gwen moved to help Brinn. Jaxx knew they had to remove the bolt before Gwen could heal the wound. She also knew Brinn was strong-willed, but she had seen much bigger men brought to their knees from less pain. But she had to guard the door or someone else could end up in similar or worse shape.

Raffi immediately grasped her conflict. "Stay where you are. I will handle it." He turned to Brinn. "This is going to hurt like the hells, but I'll try to make it fast." He handed him a piece of leather to bite down on, then took a good hold on the bolt and pulled it through his shoulder. Brinn's scream echoed throughout the sanctuary for several seconds, then he passed out.

Gwen did not give Raffi a chance to move away before she was on her knees beside the unconscious dwarf. Raffiel could feel the warmth radiating from her hands as she petitioned for and received the ability to heal once again. The warm glow of healing grace spread rapidly down Gwen's arms and into Brinn's torn muscles, knitting the torn tissue and removing the swelling and pain. Gwen ran her fingers lightly over the fresh pink scar, amazed at the ability Rheaaz had granted her. To be a healer was every novice cleric's greatest desire. The many years of study necessary to leave the rank of apprentice were just the first of several requirements that had to be met before becoming a healing cleric. Somehow, she had skipped the training and could perform a healing that many high-ranking clerics would fear. Reyna offered her thanks to Rheaaz, bowing her head to show she honored her Goddess, even in this place that was so far from a scene of comfort and healing.

Opening his eyes after the world around him had once more become solid; Brinn let his vision to return to normal before dragging himself into a sitting position. He was tired from losing blood, but his arm felt almost as good as before he injured it. There was a new scar, and the weal would always pull when he swung his sword, but as long as he favored it until it healed completely, he could use it.

Mekiva knew their time was rapidly running out. So far, Von had held off the raiders, but he had to be tiring. And even with so many dead, they were cunning foes. They could not keep pushing their luck, they needed to join the others. She was happy to see that Brinn was standing, but he was still in no shape to fight.

"Mekiva! Get down the rope. I can't hold them much longer." Von's voice was terse and higher pitched than normal. Something was wrong.

"I am not leaving you alone. Once the Xyvelix realize we're getting away, they will rush in all at once. We need to go down together. Come now, we don't have time to stand around arguing about it."

Jaxx was already moving down the hallway, away from the temple. It was up to her to prevent them from running into another trap. She just hoped that Mekiva's plan was as good as Mekiva thought it was.

Von wiped the sweat from his forehead. No one had tried to get past him for several minutes, so this was going to be the best opportunity they would have to escape. With luck, they could be down the rope before the raiders realized they were gone.

Mekiva had the rope in her hands, as if she was prepared to slide down. She sat down on the edge of the banister, careful to give him room to slide in beside her. She was about to slide when Von grabbed her arm and jerked her over the edge, his arm entangled in the line.

Von heard, rather than felt, the dull thud of the crossbow bolt striking his side as he swung from the crumbling ledge. He knew he had to protect Mekiva from the latest onslaught, but the pain in his side made it difficult for him to move. He pulled himself back up the rope to just below the crumbling ledge where she dangled. Immediately, he received two more hits, one glancing off his thigh and a more serious blow to his chest, right below his heart. Gritting his teeth against the pain, he snapped off most of the wooden bolt in his chest, thankful that it had hit a bone on an angle and not reached his heart. "I can't make it down the rope. I think I'm going to fall instead."

Mekiva grabbed his shirt. As they fell, she intoned the last words of her spell and they both disappeared.

CHAPTER 31

Darkness greeted them when they reappeared in the hidden courtyard behind the temple. Mekiva was happy she had missed the wood pile. There had been little time to visualize their destination before the jump, Teleporting blind was dangerous, and they were lucky that they had missed any of the objects in the storage courtyard. Once again, the teleport jump had made Von nauseated. The ground seemed to fall out from beneath him and his stomach spun round and round. Then the pounding of his heart slowed to a gentle thud, and everything started spinning. He slid to the ground, holding his as best he could chest to prevent the arrows stub from jarring with the ground. His side was numb, and a steady trickle of blood continued to flow down his right leg.

"Looks like one of them got off a lucky shot," Mekiva muttered as she leaned over to examine the wound. Von sat on the ground, unaware of how many arrows he had taken. Only one was bleeding freely, the other two speared to have clotted. There was a small amount of oozing around the shafts, but nothing serious. She would need to get them out, but first she needed to calm him down. "The others got down before birdmen overran the ledge. Everything is going to be all right now. Take a minute and rest. You will feel better, then we can rejoin them."

Von's voice was raspy as he struggled to take a deep breath. "I will be fine in a minute. Just give me a little time until my dizziness passes. Then we will head back up to the others." He slipped farther toward the ground. Mekiva grabbed his arm and tried to keep him on his feet, but he was too heavy. She had one minor healing spell memorized, but nothing sufficient to heal internal injuries. They had been depending on Gwen for healing. Now she realized how dangerous that was. Moth could heal some wounds, but his ability depended on the whim of his barbaric God. He could also neutralize poisons and make water pure. She needed to do some research and learn a few healing spells, just in case. But that would not help Von now. She was about to cast the cantrip she had memorized when she remembered the tiny vial, she had in her belt pouch. They had used most of the potion when Brinn was hurt during the battle with the trolls. But there was still a small amount left in the vial. It might not heal him, but it might be enough to stop the bleeding and keep him alive until Gwen could finish the job. As he drifted into a light state of consciousness, she probed the two shallow wounds. As she expected, the arrowheads had not broken through the muscles. She jerked the heads back through the entry wound. The final arrowhead was deeply embedded. Removing it might do more damage than the small amount of healing serum could handle. She left it in place and address the shaft instead.

"Von, this is going to hurt. Be ready." She used her knife and cut a grove around the shaft, then snapped it off. The movement jostled the head, and the wound began bleeding harder. "Here. Drink this." He didn't open his eyes.

Realizing any further delay could endanger his life, Mekiva tilted his chin up and opened his mouth. She held the open vial inside his mouth and let every drop drain out, rubbing his throat to help him swallow as much as possible.

Just as she hoped, the smaller wounds closed, and the blood stopped flowing from around the remaining shaft. His color picked up and the lines between his eyes gradually faded away. He was far from healed, but at least he was not in immediate danger.

Satisfied it was safe, she once more leaned down to the young man lying on the ground, took a solid grip on his arm and tried to him sit up. He wavered for a moment, then froze as her arms wrapped around his neck and his lips moved closer to hers. The kiss didn't last long, but the promise was there.

She sat down beside him, moving her face until she was so close, he could feel her breath against his mouth as she spoke. Her silky lips warmed him and urged him closer. He flinched as her body brushed against the broken arrow sticking from his chest, but decided it was worth the pain. After too short a time, they broke apart. The hungry expression in her eyes had faded to one of concern.

"Teasing witch," he protested. His frustration was obvious, but he knew she would not consider any more cuddling.

Mekiva ignored his comment. She was not looking forward to seeing the way Von suffered while walking across the uneven courtyard. Once they were inside the temple, the floors would be level and smooth. If she had to drag him, she hoped he held out until they reached the slick marble floors. Right now, Von was feeling somewhat stronger, but that could change.

She watched as he closed his eyes and steeled himself against the pain before he took the first step. The area around the arrow throbbed with pain but he knew he could go on. They had been lucky so far. None of the flying Xyvelix had discovered the covered storage area and come to check it out.

Once they reached the passage that led back to the priests' quarters, Mekiva felt better about their chances. That changed at the next corner.

She stopped walking. Von was leaning against her shoulder and looked up to see why she had stopped walked. He saw the two Xyvelix and knew they had to move fast. The birdmen had their backs to them, but the smallest sound could draw their attention. Step by step, they retreated down the tunnel. Mekiva silently thanked the unknown masons that had worked so hard to build the remarkable underground passage. Because of their habit of requiring perfectly level floors, they could walk backwards without fear of stumbling on uneven pavers in the darkness.

The pair must have been assigned guard duty. They were standing just inside the hallway where the hall crossed over the secondary hall that led to the main entrance of the priest's quarters. The two guards fidgeted restlessly as they peered into the dark hallway; shifting their weight from left to right to keep their muscles loose, as though an attack was expected at any time. Occasionally, one would spread his wings as much as possible within the narrow confinement of the hall. Besides their own natural armament, they armed each birdman with an oversized halberd. The heavy weapon had an axe blade on one end and a sharp spear pick tip on the other. In a fight, it could slash or stab; besides acting as a tool to block most sword blows. They obviously did not feel the halberds would be enough to protect them in battle, so they must have been in the group that attacked them in the main vestibule earlier.

The small side passage that led to the kitchen was only a short distance down the hall, but unless you knew it was there, it was easy to miss it. The swinging door blended seamlessly with the walls, and there was no handle. You simply pushed on a certain rock, and it opened. However, there was no way they would not notice them hobbling in that direction. So far, they had avoided detection, but Mekiva knew their good luck streak was bound to end sometime. It would be suicide to take on the two guards one on one. Now, with the addition of Von's injury, any serious combat would probably lead to at least one of them being severely hurt, or possibly killed. She needed to find a better way, or at least find a more defensible location in which to fight.

She set her small backpack on the ground and began digging through it.

"What are you looking for?" Von hissed.

"These," she said as she pulled out a bundle of small scrolls. She began unrolling and reading them one by one. After four, she worried there was nothing there that might help. There were two left when she found a possibility. It would be close. The spell was only temporary, and she did not know how long it would last. There was always the possibility that one of the other Xyvelix might notice and come to check them out. But it was the only chance they had. She put the scroll to the side and put everything else back into her backpack.

"What does it do?" he asked. "We don't want them to know we are here."

"Get ready to move fast. The spell will make them blind, but I don't know how long it will last. They designed it for humans, not Xyvelix."

"Yeah, and there might be others close enough to come and check on them when they discover they are blind." He was leaning against the wall in the corner. Every so often, he would peep at the two guards. Nothing had changed.

Mekiva began reading the scroll aloud. Once she reached the last word, she stopped talking. She would have to step out into the hall to cast the spell. With any luck at all, they would never see her. She glanced at Von, and he smiled and blew her a kiss.

Taking a deep breath, she stepped into the hall and spoke the final word. The scroll crumbled in her hand. Both Xyvelix began calling out and moving around. They had their wings stretched out and their arms extended out in front of their bodies. She had a good idea what they were saying, but no idea how long before someone came to help.

Von was already moving down the hall. He was resting his weight against the wall and taking small steps. She hurried to catch up. She was not worried about reaching the door, she was worried about being shot by her friends when they tried to get inside. She caught up to Von just as he pushed the stone to unlock the door. It moved about three inches and stopped. Something was blocking it.

Von immediately began calling out to Moth, but he was too far away to hear them. Brinn noticed the crack between the wall and the door and was already moving toward the door when he heard Von calling Moth.

"I need help now. We need to get the door open. Von and Mekiva are outside." He grabbed one leg of the table and tried to slide it away from the opening. Von was pushing on the stone door while Kiva monitored the blind guards. That's when she realized they were out of time.

"Von, move aside. I need to see into the room." She stepped in front of him and pressed her face against the crack. It wasn't much, but she could see into the room. They could hear voices growing closer. She did the only thing she could. She grabbed Von's hand and teleported again.

As soon as she materialized Mekiva snapped out, "Shut the door." She let go of Von's hand and he collapsed. Brinn quickly slammed the stone door shut, removing any possibility of the approaching birdmen spotting the opening. Raffi helped him push the table tightly against the door and then they added anything else they could find. There was always a small possibility one of the approaching Xyvelix had noticed them standing in the hall.

Gwen and Moth were already working on Von's injury. She took a step toward them and then the room began to spin.

Moth worked his way through the long-shattered debris of the city toward the building they were using as a stable. Brinn had suggested he attempt to reach the animals instead of Jaxx or Raffi, even though they both volunteered. Brinn's suggestions were his way of manipulating his best friend into doing something he didn't really want to do. He had to concede he was the best person for the job. Raffi hated working around the Oryx, and Jaxx was still getting used to her new center of balance.

Their conversation had not been long.

"Are you sure this is a good idea?"

"No. But it's the best one I have."

"Twist says all birdmen are gone."

"Still want you to go."

Moth had rolled his eyes, but he'd reached for his pack.

It had taken him longer than expected to work his way down to the building. The southern sky was already shifting from purple to pale gray. He was tired, hungry, and thirsty. The animals were in worse shape. It had been three days since the stock had been fed, or watered. By now, the oryx were considering the other animals as a source of meat. The penned animals would know they were in danger. He increased his pace from a slow, cautious walk to a jog. The path he was following was still in decent shape, sun baked dirt and relatively free of potholes, though it could not be considered a solid, well-maintained road.

He was glad the birdmen preferred to remain above street level. As he approached, he could hear faint sounds of movement from the building. The sour odor of urine and manure wafted to him on the morning breeze. There was no way they could hide the building any longer. He would have to move the animals to the temple as soon as the twin suns went down.

But first, he needed to get them fed and watered.

———

"Brinn did not look happy about us leaving the kitchen to look for Twist. He's certain the Mir-cat followed Moth down to the stable. He enjoys hunting the small rodents and lizards than have been foraging for grain dropped by the horses and the camel since we arrived." Brinn had a valid point. The sun was up, and the winged demons could come back. Stealing a private minute or two would not hurt, but Von was doomed to disappointment if he thought she intended allowing anything more than a kiss or two. Raffi was guarding the main entrance, and Jaxx was helping Gwen pack up the last few things. They were ready to leave as soon as Moth arrived with the animals. Raffi didn't expect to see him before the twin suns set that evening. He would feed the animals well and make sure they had enough forage to keep them quiet for most of the day.

Von laughed. "Brinn knows exactly what we are doing. He's just mad because his wife is back at the compound." He grabbed her and swung her in a circle, laughing as she pretended to be alarmed. Then he bent to kiss her, pulling her body close against his. They cuddled and kissed and cuddled some more. Gradually his kisses deepened and Mekiva began wondering if perhaps they had more time than she originally thought. That thought was interrupted as a familiar itch began running across her skin. Someone nearby was working magic, and the sensation was growing stronger and stronger.

"No. Wait, we need to...." She pulled away from Von, her eyes wide open as the beautiful stranger stepped into the room.

"Well, isn't that a touching scene?" the sultry voice taunted just before an intense wind struck them. The tempest drove them off their feet and rolled them across the ground. The unknown woman spoke another spell, the words increasing in volume and pitch until she practically shouted the last command. As the two young lovers struggled to regain their feet, a loud roar and intense heat struck them. The heated airburst forced them off their feet and rolled them across the ground once more. Von could not break out of the wind's force. Desperation drove his actions as he clawed at the pedestal that had held the ruby. Somehow, he caught hold with three fingers but lost his grip when the wind increased in strength. Once more it threw him across the room, his body only slowing once he struck the adjoining wall. The unknown sorceress continued to blast his body with wind and loose sand from the floor of the sanctuary.

He could not make out Mekiva through the wildly blowing debris. As his vision dimmed, Von suspected he was seriously hurt, perhaps even dying. His back had twisted and at least one rib had punctured his lung. One leg would not move and the other was raw and bleeding. Scarlet dribbled freely from his mouth and his nose. Blood loss left him little strength to fight. All he could hope to do was hang on until the spell had run its course... and trust he survived until Gwen could heal his injuries.

Mekiva fared a little better. She managed to half-roll, half-slide her way out of the main torrent until she could escape the wind by crouching behind one of the fallen statues near the ancient altar. There she watched in terror as the winds' surges brutalized Von. She could do nothing to help him escape the woman's attacks. The curve of the statue's arm allowed her to see but she could not identify the mysterious assailant. Whoever she was, she appeared intent on destroying Von. Mekiva was forgotten as the unknown woman directed her rage against the helpless man. Without waiting for the first spell to fully dissipate, she struck again, sending bolts of lightning into the body of the severely wounded man.

Each time a bolt struck Von's battered body, Mekiva jerked as though she, too, was being tortured by the electrical discharge. It seemed hours, but she knew only seconds had passed since attack began. She had to help him! The simple spells they had taught her at school seemed insignificant against the superior skills she faced. *Von is dying! I've got to try something, I... I love him!*

Then she remembered the scrolls she'd found in the secret chamber. Several of them were offensive spells. Maybe one of them would help. Frantically, she untied the leather case, dumping its contents on the ground. She dug through the spells, scattering the various sheets as she searched for anything that might help. *Yes! This one could work!* Using the statue to brace herself against the wind, she stood and, after taking a deep breath, read the words aloud.

Time slowed... then everything happened at once. The words on the scroll twisted, blurred and ran together as the magic welled up inside her and exploded forth in a burst of flame. Fire coursed thru her body, leaving her feeling as if the heat was flowing through her, engulfing her body and all her senses. She held her hands before her and directed the flames toward the black-garbed mage.

The woman had stopped her assault and was now poking at Von's body with her foot. She threw back her head, laughing when he didn't react. As the first flame stuck the invisible shield she had placed around her body, she turned to see who dared to interrupt her.

Izabal stared into Mekiva's eyes, and at that moment, she came face to face with madness brought about by the indescribable loss. Mekiva's emotions fed the spell, and it overwhelmed the shielding. Izabal struggled to counter the spell and failed. In desperation, she tried once again, and then fell screaming as Mekiva's flaming whip left blistering lines of blue fire across her skin, searing deep swaths that cracked and flaked into gray ash as the mage writhed within the growing conflagration. The fiery inferno grew in intensity as the distraught young girl willed it to lash out, striking the sorceress repeatedly. Her entire body seemed lit from inside as the love conjured whip burned away Izabal's flesh, leaving nothing but bone. Her voice failed as flames erupted from the countless bloody tattoos lacerating her body, her strident cries fading, then stopping, as the searing flames engulfed and immolated her form. Time seemed to slow, then raced ahead. The room lit up with a blinding blue-white light, so bright it blurred her vision through closed eyes. Once Mekiva's eyesight returned, all that remained of the sorceress was a pile of ashes and a few scattered fragments of blackened bone.

She stumbled across the room to the pile of tumbled stone and sand and began pushing the broken stone away from Von's body. Mekiva refused to believe he had not survived the unexpected attack. The woman had struck him so many times he had to be dead. She cried aloud when she saw his chest rise and fall. He was alive, but his appalling injuries left little doubt of his chances of surviving much longer. The sand had flayed his body. Multiple bones had snapped, the flail had stripped his hands down to bare bone. He had to be in intense pain. No one could endure that amount of damage and remain conscious.

For a breath or two, she felt sick. Her body trembled, bringing with it waves of cold and cramps. It was hard to concentrate on anything except helping him. She struggled to pull Von's head into her lap and allowed tears to flow as a low moan escaped blackened, heat-cracked lips. Those beautiful lips... Tears streamed down her face as she cradled him. A puddle of blood slowly seeped around her fingers, staining her flesh red. She felt weak, no powerless, and mad... very, very mad. She'd killed animals and fought assailants from a distance, but it had not affected her. Those days were gone. She wanted to hurt someone, anyone, just to let go of the pain. Not even the memory of that raven haired witch writhing in agony could cool the flames of anger growing inside her soul. She finally understood her mother's grief after a boar killed her brother. She pulled at her hair... but it didn't help. She wanted to hurt someone... anyone... just to let go of the pain. She screamed.

CHAPTER 32

Startled awake from a deep sleep, at first Jaxx's mind didn't register the significance of the wailing cries resonating throughout the room. Seconds later, she was out of her bedroll and running toward the temple, axe in hand. *Something was seriously wrong with Mekiva! Where was Von*? Twist was no longer curled up atop Von's bedroll, where he'd been when she laid down earlier that afternoon. Mekiva's bedroll appeared unused.

Brinn pulled on his boots, preparing to follow her. He hadn't realized he'd dozed off. Gwen was standing by the door, unsure about whether she should follow Jaxx of remain in the room. By now, Raffi was most likely running in that direction. He would follow the girl's cries, the same as Jaxx.

He stopped, surprised when he noticed the floor was moving.

"Get back! I don't know what it is, but I saw what it can do. You don't want it to touch you. That slick stuff is like acid. It dissolves any flesh it touches." The creature had no eyes, but it seemed to know where everyone was standing. It chose Gwen and began slithering toward her. She screamed again and again as the mass of writhing tentacles slid slowly across the room.

Jaxx and Brinn stomped and yelled, hoping to distract it. It gave no appearance of slowing or detouring from its course, a path that led straight to Gwen.

Jaxx knew she had to act fast. She pulled a torch from the wall bracket, wielding it like a sword before her. "Gwen, run. Head back to the main room! I will try to slow it down." Jaxx swung her torch at what she thought was the head of the creature. The flames licked at the surface of its body, but the fire did not slow its advance. Jaxx hit it again and again, but other than a few red and black welts, it did not appear to hurt the gelatinous beast. The jelly extinguished the flame almost as soon as it caught fire. Stepping back, her foot landed on the bleached white remains of a dead rat. And she wavered, lost her balance, and fell, dropping the torch.

Brinn ran toward the creature, snatched up the torch and thrust it at the extended pseudopod, giving her time to scramble to her feet. Jaxx backed slowly away from the viscous cytoplasm, trying her best to avoid the gummy slime that ate at her boots like acid. She tried unsuccessfully to use her ax as a shield from its writhing tentacles. One searching appendage grasped her arm, tightening its grip until she could no longer grasp the handle. Her skin blistered, turning red and purple. She screamed as the ax fell from her grasp.

Before the giant crypt crawler could move closer, Raffi was at her side, swinging her torch at the writhing appendage that held her. The heat made it pull away.

"My ax," she shouted as Brinn pulled her toward the solid double doors.

"Leave it. We can get it later, "he replied as Moth slammed them shut behind them. Within seconds, a thin film of jelly began seeping under the door.

"It's flowing underneath. We need something to slow it down. I don't think we can stop it." He used hot wax from a candle to discourage a searching pseudopod. Three more replaced it.

"You wouldn't know a freeze spell, would you?" Raffi and Brinn strained to hold the immense steel door shut. They could stop an occasional finger of slime, but if the door gave out, they would have to leave everything and run through the secret panel. The creature would follow and without the fire there was no way to hold it back. The pounding pressure coming from the other side continued until the entire room trembled. Both knew it was hopeless. there was no way they could continue bracing the enormous steel doors for long. Already, the stresses being exerted by the creature were more than their overstrained muscles could contain.

Moth was reading thru his spell book, looking for anything that might stop the creature with little luck. Everything that might help needed spell components he did not have with him.

Raffi shouted over his shoulder at Jaxx and Gwen, standing just behind him. "Quick, look around and see if there is anything we can use to wedge it shut. That will slow it down. But hurry; we can't hold it for much longer. My arm is already going numb." His eyes darted over to Brinn. The older man's body was tense and the muscles in his arms bulged as he strained to keep his side of the door from opening. Raffi knew he would never give up while the women were in danger. Thinking of women reminded Raffi that Von and Mekiva had not arrived at the rendezvous point. They should have joined them by now. Raffi scowled. He liked Von but sometimes he had the worse sense of timing. Knowing the randy young man, he'd probably stopped along the way to talk, using the opportunity to be alone with Kiva. He would not consider the possibility that the crypt crawler might have trapped them... or worse.

Jaxx and Gwen hastened to do what Raffi had asked, searching around the edges of the temple for anything that might be useful. The room was barren except for the Statue of Ligarza, the stone altar, and the two enormous sconces holding the black candles. Jaxx tried to move one of the ornate metal candle sconces. Someone solidly attached it to the floor, making it too heavy for her to move alone.

Her eyes went to the candles. *After we wedge it shut, maybe they could melt the wax to seal the bottom of the door?* "Come here, Gwen," demanded Jaxx, "I need you to help me rock these back and forth, and maybe between the two of us we can break one loose." Jaxx put her back up against the tall sconce, pushing urgently while Gwen continued to pull. The heavy sconce was tightly secured. The two could not loosen it without help.

We need something to use for leverage.

"Gwen, go get the axe from Raffi. We can use the handle like a lever and break the drassted thing loose from the floor."

Once she had the ax, Gwen wedged the handle under the thin legs. She strained upwards while Jaxx continued to push. Jaxx strained against the pain. Her tunic showed streaks of pale red moisture as the warm blood from the raw skin mixed with her sweat and the ooze from where the snail thing had burnt her arm.

Gwen was torn between the need to block the door and her urge to heal Jaxx before she lost the use of her arm from the damage. Jaxx was right. They needed to stop the creature from getting inside before anything else. "I think it's working," Gwen exclaimed. "Keep on pushing, it's bending."

"Any time would be all right with us." Raffi called out, between panting breaths. "I don't know how much longer I can keep this up. And Brinn looks like he might pass out."

There was plenty of warning when the bolts gave way; the strangled shriek from the weakened metal joints tearing reverberating around the enormous room. Jaxx fell backwards as the supporting metal dropped out from behind her, landing in an undignified plop upon her buttocks. Unconcerned with Jaxx's loss of dignity, Gwen continued to pull forward on the sconce, dragging it behind her toward the door. Jaxx hastened to join her.

"Take the end and put it through the handles," Ras gasped between heaves, "use it to wedge the door shut."

Gwen guided the heavy metal pole between the stout metal handles while Jaxx pushed as hard as she could, praying the two would be strong enough to hold it closed. As soon as the pole had secured the door, first Brinn then Raffi joined them in pushing; ramming the shaft in as far as it would go. The heavy metal bar held for a moment, then the strain was too much, and it bent. The slight weakening made it clear the pole would not be enough to hold it at bay for long. What was worse, whatever this creature was, it was intelligent enough to adapt its manner of attack. The glow around the edges of the door frame brightened more and more with each passing moment, and they could see tiny strings of gelatinous goo along the cracks where the door and walls met up. Since it could not break through all at once, it was squeezing through the gaps.

"We've got to block the door some way." Gwen said, looking wildly around the empty room. But how, other than wax, there is nothing to seal the gap around the frame."

"Get away from the door." Mekiva's voice came from the atrium behind the creature. "Everyone needs to get back, head for the treasure room. Run! I'm going to kill it. Go now!"

"Where's Von?" Raffi asked, but Mekiva did not answer. Her hands shook as shock set in. She was having trouble taking a full breath, taking small rapid pants instead. Raffi could hear her chant, but he was too far away to hear the words. She stopped shaking and started taking slow deep inhalations then pointed at the crawler. She only knew one spell that had a chance of stopping it. Somehow, she had to do this; she would not lose anyone else.

Her hand held a pinch of salt and a drop of her blood. She pointed at the creature and blew a puff of air. Waves of cold flowed toward it. It screamed as ice formed. Then it flowed away, slithering back toward the front of the temple. Mekiva followed it, puffing bursts of icy air in its direction. The creature could move faster than she expected. She steeled herself for a final burst of ice. The creature surprised her by slipping into a crack in the wall she had never noticed. Before she could move into range, the crypt crawler had vanished down the hole. Mekiva screamed and ice formed, filling the crack and most of the area behind it. It took longer than she expected. Finally, she was certain it would not return.

She approached the vestibule door and announced, "It's safe to come out. She turned and trudged back toward the main part of the temple.

Gwen hesitated for a few seconds, unsure if she should try and stop her. Brinn and Raffi were already walking that direction. Mekiva was acting strange, so she decided she better follow the others. She wished she had brought medical supplies, but no one had thought that far ahead.

As Mekiva's second mournful keen echoed through the silent sanctuary, her heart leapt. This was serious. Then she heard Jaxx screaming her name. Heart hammering, she ran toward the front of the temple. Brinn was right behind her.

At first, Gwen didn't recognize Von's charred and broken body lying on the floor of the chapel. The fire had burned his face beyond recognition. Only Mekiva's keening and Jaxx's pallid visage convinced her it was really him. Only bits of bone remained on one hand and the other was missing fingers. His clothes were in shreds and much of his flesh had burned away. What little flesh remained was blackened and oozing. He bled from several lacerations caused by a broken bone tearing through flesh. But he was still alive... at least for now. She fought back a wave of fear without succeeding. The damage was more than she'd ever attempted to heal. It was too severe for an experienced Shii-Lakka healer. For Gwen, it was suicide. Even if she somehow survived the healing, she'd be permanently disfigured... or worse. But she had to try.

Taking a deep breath to settle her nerves, she placed her hand against his chest and prayed, beseeching Rheaaz for her help, vowing unquestioning service, promising her body and soul, if Rheaaz would only heal her friend. At first, nothing happened. Then her hands glowed. She bit her lip against the first wave of pain as a warm flush swept over Von's ravaged body. The old burnt skin fell off as the glow grew in intensity, leaving patches of healthy pink flesh behind. Gwen steeled herself against impending agony as she moved next to his shattered leg. She used her own weight to draw the shattered bone back into place, then cried out as her leg broke while Rheaaz knitted the cracked and splintered tissue into solid bone. The goddess required her clerics experience the same pain the patient was feeling. Her body could not handle it. Tears streaming down her face, the young shii lakka' healer set back on her heels, exhausted and unable to continue. It wasn't enough. Despite everything she'd done, Von was still dying.

"No! You can't stop now. Gwen, you need to continue. Von will die if you don't." Mekiva's face was white. Her hands shook as she tried to drag Gwen back to his side.

"I'm sorry Mekiva. I have no more left to give." She held out her hand, showing Mekiva her cracked and blistered skin. "Rheaaz won't allow me to absorb more than my body can handle."

"Then I invoke Dy'shalla! I invoke the right of

sacrifice."

Brinn and Jaxx watched all the color drain out of the young girl's face. They did not know what Mekiva had asked, but it was obvious Gwen did not want to listen to her pleas.

"No! Mekiva please--- it's too much. You don't understand what you're asking me to do. Let him go!"

"I do. I love him! You are Shii-Lakka. Accept what I offer freely."

Gwen studied Mekiva, noting the firm set of her mouth and flash of fire in her eyes. Once freely offered, The Right of Sacrifice was sacrosanct, and as Mekiva stated, an offer she couldn't deny. But the cost! Using your own life force to heal another, that could be fatal even to one anointed by the goddess. Mekiva had no such protection. What her friend was asking of her was wrong. Mekiva was only fifteen! *Rheaaz, I beg you. She's thinking with her heart, not her head. Have mercy!*

The Goddess wasn't listening. Gwen saw her hands begin to glow and knew the Goddess had accepted Mekiva's request for Dy'shalla.

Crying openly, Gwen placed her hand on Von's chest. The other hand grasped Mekiva's outstretched palm. Once again, the glow began moving across Von's body, but this time it continued to grow until it encompassed Mekiva, too. Slowly, a rosy flush appeared on the new skin, and his breathing strengthened. Then his wounds closed once more. Gwen could hear Mekiva's breathing grow strangled and slow. His heart began beating erratically, then a sharp pain struck. Von gasped one last time, and Mekiva collapsed. Gwen swayed and then she fell to the ground beside her.

CHAPTER 33

Mekiva was awake. Outwardly, she was displaying no ill effects from the previous night's events, but mentally she was barely hanging on. Jaxx was doing a little better. She had not spoken a word since she went with Moth and Raffi to recover Von's body.

Breakfast was a somber meal. No one was hungry. No one wanted to talk about Von. Instead, they spent the morning discussing the strange gelatinous snail like creature.

"Well, it was interesting." Raffi said as he nibbled halfheartedly on a chunk of Gwen's fresh hoecake. "Does anyone know what that thing was?"

"I saw something similar back home in a cave, but much smaller. And like the cave one, this thing was almost colorless, the creepy white of a fish's belly that never saw the light of the sun."

"It could be related to a crypt crawler. They look similar. I have never seen one so big."

"The size could be a mutation from the mage storm. Or it could be like that jellyfish thing that's made of thousands of little jellyfishes."

"No way to know. It explains why the bones

we see everywhere are so clean. We stumbled up on it just as it was finishing the demon Moth shot yesterday. I did not see any eyes, so it must hunt by smell. We were running too fast for it to follow us by sound."

"I'm glad it doesn't have eyes. It was fast for something without legs. Did you see how fast it glided across the floor?"

"Somehow it survived the bane, living off the dead bodies. It may have never left the temple." Brinn said. "That's why we were not bothered by rats or lizards."

"Well, I for one hope there are not two of them.," Gwen gave a brief shiver. "First that giant worm in the cave and now a slimy snail thing that eats the dead."

Jaxx actually laughed at Raffi. "We could make a fortune with one of them back home."

Gwen wasn't in the mood to cut up. Von was dead.

Mekiva had run off the crypt crawler before collapsing.

After she'd collapsed, Jaxx took Mekiva's unconscious body into her arms and carried her back to the makeshift campsite in the former kitchen. Gently she laid her upon her bedding and covered her with Von's cloak, hoping the familiar scent might comfort her as she slept. Behind him, he could hear the sibilant words of some type of prayer, but he couldn't make out the words Gwen whispered. Soon Mekiva stopped shaking and started taking slow deep inhalations as she drifted into a soporific slumber.

Gwen stood silently, watching as Jaxx made her as comfortable as possible under the circumstances.

Her friend would never be the same. Rheaaz had accepted her sacrifice. The goddess had allowed Gwen to heal his burns and broken bones, all the damage wrought by the unknown wizard. But there was always a catch. His outward injuries healed, but Mekiva had collapsed... and Von's overworked heart had failed.

She tenderly brushed a lock of pale-gray hair away from Mekiva's face. The cost of Rheaaz's help was clear. She had aged about forty years, now appearing to be about the same age as Gwen's own mother. The damage to her sister's mind worried her. Hopefully, that damage could be reversed if they could get her safely back to Cabrell before it became permanent. There was nothing she could do. Mekiva was physically healthy, just older.

"It's likely that Mekiva is beyond caring anymore," she whispered as Jaxx blew out the lantern next to her bed and made her way back to the hearth. Gwen offered her a steaming mug of kava. "Only true love would have allowed her to give so much of herself."

Now she was sitting in the corner, staring into space, stroking Twist. The Mir-cat was not making things better by his erratic behavior. He knew Mekiva was alive, but something was wrong. Raffi had three deep slashes on his arm from the flying cat lizard's claws and preferred not to receive anymore. It was easier to leave him there.

Brinn listened but added nothing to the conversation. Raffi had returned to guard the top of the ramp and he wished he had an excuse to join him. Mekiva looked old enough to be his mother, and that had shaken him to the core. No one had expected this expedition to be easy, but they had lost Sayed and Von, Mekiva was in terrible shape, and they did not know what was going on with Keeyun. Jaxx was maintaining remarkably well, considering she had been a man when they started the trip. It was pastime they got back on the road and headed for home. He stood up. "I want to leave as soon Moth arrives with the pack animals."

Jaxx was sitting by herself, her back against the wall. At Brinn's words, she nodded, unable to speak. *No one could understand how much I was suffering. Von is gone. I loved him like a brother. Every time I looked at Mekiva I think about her sacrifice, and for what? Von had died anyway.* Her frozen expression hid more than her tears.

Gwen sensed her need for quiet and left her alone. She slipped down onto her bedroll and closed her eyes. Then she let the tears flow.

"Uhhh.... Jaxx?"

Jaxx raised her head, curious about the hesitation in Gwen's voice. She was standing just inside the doorway to the kitchen. Next to her stood Keeyun, one arm grasping her around the waist, the other holding a knife blade pressed against her neck.

Jaxx jumped to her feet, moving toward the pair in the doorway.

"I'd think about that again before you make a big mistake," Keeyun warned. He pressed the dagger against the Shii girl's throat, allowing a bead of blood to dribble down her neck. "Just drop that axe and she will be fine."

Jaxx dropped it, but she didn't back away. *All I need is one opening. My hands will do the rest.*

Keeyun laughed as if he heard the Duaars' thoughts. Moving faster than Jaxx thought possible, his blade lashed out again, an indifferent stroke that sliced deep into Jaxx's arm before exiting the muscle near her shoulder. Her left arm hung limp by her side. Even injured, she fought to protect Gwen, stepping closer to the Keeyun's body to limit the length of his swing. The older man spun, his serrated blade whistling as it slipped into the space between them. Somehow Jaxx blocked the knife, but she knew it was only a matter of time before he landed a killing blow.

She didn't realize Raffi was behind her until he suddenly jerked her down to the ground beside him. Keeyun's swing would have taken her head from her shoulders. Jaxx fell forward onto her face, busting her lip. But otherwise, she was unhurt.

Raffi pivoted, drawing his sword as he turned. He raised it in time to deflect Keeyun's next blow. The blade caught the side of his arm as it passed, slicing into the muscle above his wrist. The cut was not deep, but it had nicked a vein, sending a steady stream of blood down his wrist. He shook his hand to remove as much blood as possible; wincing at the pain as he moved his wrist. His fingers turned red and slick from the blood oozing from the ragged cut. The warm blood made it difficult to securely grip the pommel of his sword. Once more, he moved to protect Jaxx from injury. With his wrist injured, it was all he could do to keep Keeyun's blade away. Raffiel spun, his serrated blade whistling as it cut across the space between them. Keeyun caught the blade on his cross guard. The quillons preventing the blow from landing. Raffi stepped back and set himself before Kee could take advantage.

Keeyun frowned. He might be younger, but Raffiel was a more experienced swordsman. He needed to wrap this up and leave. All it would take is one solid blow in the right spot. Even an accident could cause his death, or at least a serious injury.

Raffi knew time was working in his favor. Moth could return at any moment. Gwen was waking up, and she would take care of Jaxx's cut. He had to keep Jaxx alive until help arrived. He slashed out at Keeyun's leg, nicking him on the calf before he jumped aside. His sword flared momentarily, a flickering blue flame raced up and down its length as it tasted the shape changers blood, a sure sign that magic was present. It startled Raffi but seemed to have no effect on his drive to remove Keeyun's head.

Dancing to the right, Raffi landed a second blow, catching Keeyun on his right forearm. The sword flared again.

Keeyun raised his sword to finish him but hesitated and addressed Jazz instead. "Just give me the jewel, and you can go free."

"Not until you tell me why you have been trying to kill Jaxx."

"Because it pays more than killing any of the others." There was a brief blurring of his vison and Raffi realized the man he was fighting no longer looked like his former partner. "Kee?" he asked, unsure of what he'd seen.

"Well, not exactly." His voice had changed to match his new appearance.

Kee increased the speed of his strikes, pushing the Duaar to make a mistake. He faked a blow to Raffi's head, then changed the direction of his swing, striking him low on his left side with the flat side of his blade. Raffi gasped and doubled over from the pain as his kidney spasmed, sending throbbing pangs radiating across his back and up and down his spine. Kee did not give him a chance to recover. He brought the back of sword down hard against his head. Raffi's legs buckled, and he dropped unconscious to the ground.

Recognizing the voice, Gwen jerked her head around and gasped. "Castillo!"

Castillo laughed at her expression. "Not exactly Castillo either, though that is a name I have used in the past. It works for now."

"What happened to Keeyun?"

"He doesn't need your help, Raffi does. Where is the jewel? You might have defeated Izabal, but that doesn't change my orders. I never answered to the witch, anyway."

"Let the girl go and you can have it." Jaxx said. She kept one eye on his sword. There was no way she could prevent him from stabbing Raffi.

"It doesn't work that way. First the ruby, then the girl."

"Jaxx, give it to him. Its cost us enough already." Brinn said. He was trying to get to his feet, but he was still too weak to stand.

"Here, take the stupid thing and go." Jaxx said vehemently. She thrust the leather pouch holding the ruby into his hands.

Keeyun practically snatched it from her hand and smugly allowed himself a triumphant smile. He finally had his hands on the stone. Izabal had trusted him to bring it back, and he had never failed her, no matter what endeavor set before him. This would be no different.

No treasure was worth another life. Ignoring Keeyun or Castillo or whoever he was, she crawled to Raffi, cradling his head in her lap. Tears ran down her face as she realized he still breathed easily. Gwen could heal him once Keeyun left. Raffi would live to help her avenge Von like he had promised.

"I did not want to hurt you, but I was not going back to Cabrell without it."

"And you are not going back with it." Moth declared as he released the bowstring. The arrow flew straight, striking Castillo just to the left of his breast and driving the metal arrowhead deep into his heart. There was a whirring sound, and then his body was struck by a second one that passed through his back and lodged in his chest.

Castillo looked down at the arrow tip breaking through his chest. "Good shot. Too bad, I don't keep my heart there." His body melted and flowed, shifting first to a brown and white goat, then to a featureless white creature, then to Keeyun, before reforming into Castillo once again. Both arrows lay on the ground at its feet. He tossed the arrows to Brinn, winked at Gwen, and ignored Raffi. He'd made a serious miscalculation by assuming that his superior intelligence was a match for their raw animal cunning; not to mention the rabid fury building in each of their souls. He locked eyes with Moth as he slowly backed from the room. One day, he might have to kill him, but not today. The jewel was what was important. There would be other opportunities to settle the minor matter of his new scars with Moth. They were certain to meet again in the future. Leaving was the smart thing to do. He grinned once again and bowed to Gwen, then left.

"Stop," Gwen urged as Moth made to follow. "Just let him go."

Moth hesitated; then he just stood watching the thing wearing his cousin's form until the darkness swallowed him up.

"What happened? Keeyun hi..." Raffi sat up, wincing as the blood rushed to her head.

"Thank your ancestors for thick bones. You have a hard head. The creature surprised me, too. I thought he'd kill you, but at the last moment, he turned the blade, striking you in the temple with the hilt instead. He took the ruby."

"Then let's go after him."

"You've been out for a while. Tomorrow you'll have a horrible headache--- but you'll live."

Raffi didn't need to feel the fist-sized lump on his temple to know he was lucky to have survived the fight. He rubbed at the swelling above his right ear. He flinched when his hand brushed against the swelling, but there was no blood. Then his hand traced the cut he'd taken in the side. "My side? That was a killing blow. I should be dead." His back was sore like he'd been sleeping on too soft a feather mattress, but his kidney didn't hurt. In fact, he felt little pain at all.

"Rheaaz must like you." Jaxx sighed, wanting to comfort him, but afraid of his reaction.

Once Gwen found out Raffi would live, she'd ignored him, choosing to sit beside Mekiva's bed. Hours had passed and Mekiva showed little sign of improvement.

"Where's Brinn?"

"He's helping Moth pack the animals. He wanted to leave this morning. After it hurt you, Brinn said to let you sleep." Jaxx looked tired. She continued to berate herself over everything that happened. *I failed. It was all for nothing, Von, Mekiva, everything.*

Raffi understood. No one could have known what was going to happen. No one was to blame. But that changed nothing. "Stop blaming yourself, it will not bring him back."

Tears welled in Jaxx's eyes. "No, you don't understand. It was my responsibility! I was supposed to keep them safe. Now my brother's dead, and Mekiva's little more than a walking vegetable."

"Stop." Gwen shouted, surprising them both. "Neither of you is to blame. It like a nightmare and you can't wake up. Mekiva was my rock, the sister I always wanted. Now she's older than my mother. You want to hear the sad part, at least you get to bury Von and walk away. I have to take my nightmare home with me."

Jaxx stood. "You are right. I'm going to the crypt to tell him goodbye." She snatched up her pack and headed toward the hidden chamber below the main chapel. They had decided it was the best place to leave Vons' body. By the time they returned, his body would have deteriorated, making it impossible to be in the same room.

Raffi arrived shortly after Jaxx had stormed out. "The animals are all packed and everyone was waiting. Do you need me to help you with anything?"

"No. My things are already on the camel. Maybe you can help Gwen with Mekiva."

"She's awake, but still in shock. Gwen was leading her to the entrance when I left her." He paused, unsure how to say what he wanted to say. "Do you think someone at the Rosemont can reverse the spell once we get her back to Cabrell.?"

"No, you don't get it. It wasn't a spell. Gwen said it can't be reversed. Mekiva literally gave up her life force to save Von. And it still wasn't enough. Von's heart gave out."

"My father always said, 'Yesterday was the last good day.' I never really understood what it meant until now." His look was cold and sharp, like the blade of a knife. "You need to say good-bye so we can close this room."

"Drasst!" she screamed. She threw his axe, slinging it across the room and into one of the marble statues. It landed with a clink, chipping the corner off the base.

Stomping over, she bent down to pick up her axe again, then paused. There on the base of the statue, directly beside the chipped section, some-one had carved the godforsaken wyvern! "Yaaga, carry me away! There's a wyvern on the statue. The base is hollow. My axe knocked a hole in the corner."

"Why would they put a sigil there?"

"I knew it was too easy. We followed the wyverns all the way, and then the ruby was just sitting there on the pedestal in plain sight. I bet it was just another ruse to throw us off the trail of the real treasure. Castillo stole the decoy heart." She began chipping away at the edge of the opening, enlarging it until she could see inside. Sure enough, there was a bundle hidden in the hollow base.

"Let me check, it could have a trap." Raffi kneeled by the stature and poked the package with his knife. When nothing happened, he reached for the cloth wrapping. His fingers touched the bundle, but he could not grab it.

"Move out of the way. I think I can reach it," Jaxx stated. "My hand is smaller than yours."

"No," Raffi replied, "I'll make the hole bigger. It's probably dipped in poison. I'll need you safe, so you can drag me to Gwen if anything else goes wrong." He widened the opening, then cautiously reached inside, removing a small, linen wrapped bundle. He laid the bundle on the pedestal next to Von's body. Inside the faded wrapping was a shiny black stone etched with unknown runes.

"This is it? This is the great treasure everyone has been looking for. Von died for this... a rock. No, it must be the ruby. Greed, I can understand. Love, I can understand. Why would anyone steal and torture for this?" Jaxx was baffled. There was nothing about the rock that made it different from a million other rocks lying on the ground. The glyphs, and any good scribe, could have carved them. "I'm done with it," Jaxx shouted. "Rock or not, Von died for it, so he going to be buried with it. After we seal the door, I'm going to make sure this room can never be opened again." She dropped the stone on Von's chest and walked away.

Raffi ignored her outburst and wrapped the

stone again. Then he dropped it in the pouch he wore around his neck.

He caught up to her at the switch to the hidden room.

"Don't break it. I shut the door to the room. We need to get back inside for the rest of the treasure. "

Jaxx glared at him as he closed the secret entrance. He decided he'd had enuugh. He grabbed her and kissed her.

When they finally broke apart, she didnt say a word. Raffi decided to stay quiet, too. Together, they walked up the ramp to the exit.

———

Brinn stood beside Moth, one hand on his shoulder. Raffi had never seen Moth upset. The stoic druid preferred to keep his emotions under check. They had helped Mekiva onto her horse and tied the reins to Gwen's saddle.

Raffi reached into his tunic and pulled out a leather pouch. "Keep this safe. It's more important than it looks." He tossed it to Brinn, then swung his leg over the big bay gelding. After adjusting his pack, he debated kicking one of the oryx's. Instead, he winked at Jaxx. This hunt, successful or not, was now finished. The treasure had been located. It was time to go.

"Lets go home."

LET'S STAY IN TOUCH!

Click the +Follow button on my Amazon author page.

For more information about upcoming releases, please join my email list at www.bellbookandclaw.com

You have my word you will not be inundated with emails. I do plan to send out emails periodically to keep my readers informed.

Follow me at:

Facebook: https://www.facebook.com/VCSanford/

Instagram   https://www.instagram.com/vcsanford-books/

Web: https://bellbookandclaw.com/

One Last thing...

If you enjoyed the story, I really would appreciate it if you could leave a review.

I realize its a hassle, but it helps authors more than I can explain. It would take another book to list all the ways.
So Thank You in advance!

VC Sanford

CPSIA information can be obtained
at www.ICGtesting.com
Printed in the USA
BVHW081353081121
621076BV00005B/75

9 781737 068839